JENNIFER HARLOW

A
F.R.E.A.K.S.
SQUAD
INVESTIGATION

DEATH TAKES A HOLIDAY

MIDNI...
WOODBURY, M...

FIRST EDITION
First Printing, 2013

Book format by Bob Gaul
Cover design by Kevin R. Brown
Cover illustration by Carlos Lara Lopez
Editing by Nicole Nugent

Midnight Ink, an imprint of Llewellyn Worldwide Ltd.

This is a work of fiction. Names, characters, places, and incidents are either the product of the author's imagination or are used fictitiously, and any resemblance to actual persons living or dead, business establishments, events, or locales is entirely coincidental.

Library of Congress Cataloging-in-Publication Data
Harlow, Jennifer, 1983–
 Death takes a holiday: a F.R.E.A.K.S. squad investigation/Jennifer Harlow.—First Edition.
     pages cm.—(A F.R.E.A.K.S. Squad Investigation; #3)
  ISBN 978-0-7387-2712-7
1. Women psychics—Fiction. 2. Paranormal fiction. I. Title.
PS3608.A7443D34 2013
813'.6—dc23
                          2013007518

Midnight Ink
Llewellyn Worldwide Ltd.
2143 Wooddale Drive
Woodbury, MN 55125-2989
www.midnightinkbooks.com

Printed in the United States of America

For Ryan, Liam, and Trevor:
Thanks for helping to make me
the tough broad I am today.

Home is a name, a word, it is a strong one; stronger than magician ever spoke, or spirit ever answered…
—Charles Dickens

He's obviously had Nana's baked ziti.
—Beatrice Alexander

ONE

IN LOVE AND WAR

I SO HATE RUNNING. Especially when I have to do it or die.

People who run for fun are mental. There are very few times humans should run, like when they're being chased through the Everglades by a basilisk. Only reason I am right now. And the longer I run, the more I begin to think death is preferable.

Panting harder than a geek at the Playboy mansion, my legs pump through the wooded area surrounding the swamp. The thick, wet mud covering my jeans and sneakers adds unneeded resistance, and I am no Flo-Jo to begin with. That huge snake is gaining. I probably shouldn't have shot at it. It might have ignored me while it feasted on that alligator, but what was I supposed to do when I happened across a forty-foot snake with horned fangs and it flicked its tongue at me? Fire and run. Exactly.

I race through a thicket of ferns before jumping across a small ravine. I land in more mud, my hands and feet enveloped. Without missing a beat, I leap up and continue my sprint. The thick trees I just passed rumble and shake as the basilisk charges through. She's gaining. And mad. I hope she doesn't know I was the one who smashed her eggs yesterday. I see an orange marker, the first one I put up. Almost there. Legs and lungs, don't fail me now.

My legs don't listen. My foot catches on a stray root, and I tumble to the ground. A shooting pain vibrates through my left arm as I brace my fall. My knees hit at the same time, and hard fabric rips against my skin, stinging worse than a dozen bees. Acknowledging the pain wastes a second I don't have. As I stand and turn, I see the basilisk clear the ravine about fifty yards away, gliding. Jesus, she's like an anaconda on steroids. She moves upright, locomotion provided by her hindquarters. If a person meets a basilisk's eyes, their brain hemorrhages within seconds and they drop dead—that is, if the venomous bite doesn't get them first. This one has a white marking on its head but is otherwise brown. It's one of those mythical creatures that are sadly not a myth. Like vampires. And werewolves. And people like me.

I fill my mind with the image of the skinny, dying tree the snake is about to pass, yanking on it with all my might. It's heavy. Heavier than I'd normally attempt. My temples throb as the trunk cracks louder than lightning, falling right on the snake. *Timber.* The snake hisses in pain but recovers within a second, bucking side to side to unpin herself. Her tail smacks the nearby trees, splitting one in half. Fascinating to watch, but it's time to recommence the running. I vault over other fallen trees and smack branches out of my way, really wishing I had my machete, Bette, with me. The rumbling and quaking start again far too soon, but I don't dare look back.

"Bea?" Carl says over my earpiece. "Give me your status."

"Running. For. Life," I pant. "Almost there."

I finally see the grassy clearing through the trees. I pump my legs for all they're worth, trying to ignore not only my throbbing head but the hissing behind me. The trees part. I keep running. I don't stop until I'm behind the two FBI agents toting flamethrowers. Agents Rushmore and Chandler, both in their thirties with brown and black crew cuts, respectively, don't even acknowledge me as I pass. Their eyes, along with those of the other two men strategically waiting around the meadow, stay on the tree line. Carl, all five-six of him, holds a tranquilizer gun as big as he is off to the right. On the other side Agent Wolfe, another FBI agent, holds the same gun. No sign of Will.

No sooner than I take my second much needed lungful of air does the basilisk slither out of the trees, fangs as tall as a man exposed. Cue the fireworks. Carl and Agent Wolfe shoot the darts into the belly of the beast. The snake whips toward Carl as his dart hits, then changes direction as Agent Wolfe's makes contact. As those gunners reload, the fire brigade pulls their triggers. Two jets of fire blast from the guns, engulfing the snake. It shrieks in pain so loud that I have to cover my ears, its brown scales popping with blisters while other parts char black. Carl and Agent Wolfe shoot again as the fountain of fire continues. The basilisk hisses, turning to retreat.

"Alexander!" Agent Chandler shouts.

I know. I grip the snake's head with my mind and keep hold. The throbbing intensifies as the ton of snake attempts to wrestle out of my invisible grasp. Psychokinesis, mind over matter, I'm told ya gotta love it. I only have to grasp her for a few seconds as two more darts finally knock the behemoth out. Her body slumps half in, half out of the forest and the ground shakes as I allow her head to fall with the rest of her. I wipe the blood streaming from my nose.

The four men, guns still at the ready, slowly approach the slumbering giant. Smoke from the burns rises in patches. Strangely the smell isn't too bad; not pleasant but not nauseating. Carl lightly kicks it.

"Don't kick the poisonous snake!" I admonish.

"Sorry," he says with a shrug.

I walk—well, more like limp—toward the group. "I think it's out."

"Are you okay?" Agent Wolfe asks as he scans me up and down. I must look like a mud monster, but these guys have seen me a lot worse. The mosquito bites don't help. I seem to attract bloodsuckers by the droves.

"Peachy," I say.

"What do we do with it now?" Agent Chandler asks me.

"How should I know?"

"This was your plan," he responds a little harsher than I care for. Not that I don't expect it from him. We haven't exactly seen eye to eye on anything in months.

The men stare at me, waiting for me to speak. My head hurts. I'm covered in Florida swampland. I've run close to a mile. And half my co-workers hate me. Now I have to dispose of a giant snake. *How is this my life?*

But it is.

Rolling my eyes, I move toward the van parked near the dirt access road. My girl is right where I left her, between the shotguns and Kevlar vests. She's covered in silver with yellow flowers and her name, Bette, painted on her long blade. My machete shines in the sun like Excalibur. The team just stands there as I stalk back toward them. They part as I raise my girl over my head, bringing her down like an executioner's axe, blood spewing as Bette slices. Red drops rain over me as I continue chopping through the five feet of flesh. For some reason the guttural shouting that accompanies each swipe makes me feel much better. It's weird how much this doesn't bother me. Four lops and the head severs. The river of blood almost reaches my ankles. These shoes are toast. The men leap away. I take a few deep breaths, quelling the anger and fear coursing through me before I look at them. "Burn it."

Agents Chandler and Rushmore nod. The rest of us step away as the flames begin, Carl and Agent Wolfe smartly moving the opposite direction from me. I make it a few feet before a not so friendly face springs out of the tree line holding a machine gun. His green eyes glance at the snake, then my blood-soaked form. A scowl forms on his face, a smirk on mine.

"So glad you could join us, Will," I say as my smile grows. "We finished without you."

The look he gives me is deadlier than any basilisk's.

I should be happy. Team Bea won this battle, but as Will walks away and I feel that ever-present anger wafting from him, instead I want to cry. War is hell.

Especially when it's not one you want to be fighting.

———

Like most wars, the trouble had been brewing for years between the factions, but the shot heard round the world in this case occurred after my fellow F.R.E.A.K.S. member—of Federal Response to Extra-Sensory and Kindred Supernaturals—Oliver and I went undercover to stop a cabal of killer vampires. We did, but an old enemy of Oliver's found out and tortured him almost to death. It was my fault. I let myself get kidnapped, and he had to save me. Will was there too, but he refused to help me rescue Oliver. A lot of bad blood there through the years. Will eventually stepped up at the last minute, but if I wasn't there, he would have let Oliver die. And this was the man I have a raging crush on. My illusions were shattered. This was a man I admired, respected, and who I trusted with my life. My Prince Charming. I had no idea what to feel about Will's tarnished image, so I chose avoidance. Plus there were more pressing matters after Dallas.

Oliver was wrecked—emotionally, physically, and mentally. Because of me. I barely left his side. I spent most nights playing nurse, but not in the fun way. I got him blood, we watched TV, and we talked. Nothing more. Okay, there may have been *one* kiss involved, but that's it. We didn't even use tongues. And I only kissed him because he had saved my life and he was so wonderful to me and … I don't really know why I did it. Seemed like a good idea at the time. The next time I saw him, I pretended it had never happened, and he followed suit. Nothing since. Though nobody, least of all Will, believes us.

When I passed Will in the hallways, it didn't take a psychic to know he was angry. He'd either pretend I wasn't there or give me so much space he hugged the wall. Either way he never looked at me. Never spoke to me unless work related. The cold shoulder reached frostbite proportions when Oliver and I were together. We'd walk into the library or kitchen, and within thirty seconds Will would get up and leave. Knife to my heart every time.

Things came to a head on an investigation in Maine two weeks after Dallas. A boy who could talk to animals was having them create diversions while he robbed convenience stores. It came to our attention when animals escaped from the zoo and began following the boy's crush around. He was seventeen, and Lord knows even I did stupid stuff at seventeen, but Will's plan was to go in guns blazing and arrest the kid. Oliver's tactic was to talk to the boy; put the fear of God in him, but give him a second chance. No one had gotten hurt and the kid promised to give the money he stole back. Heck, the only reason he stole it was to get the girl a plane ticket to France for some band competition. The problem was that Oliver and I did this behind Will's back. I tried to convince him of the road less scary, but he wouldn't have listened even if I told him the world was round. He got a little shouty in front of everyone and half the team stuck up for me, the others not so much. Sides were chosen.

Thus began the war.

Those who believe what Will says is gospel include Agents Rushmore, Chandler, and Nancy, our teleporter. She just sides with him because she has a huge crush on Oliver and can't stand that he and I spend so much together. Teenagers. Really I'm just an easy target for her anger about Irie's death; I can take it. The others, Carl and Agent Wolfe, tend to side with us. Carl just does it because our approach is usually less threatening and dangerous. Agent Wolfe is using Will as his grief target; Irie was his girlfriend. I was there when it happened, and it was in no way Will's fault. I even sat Agent Wolfe down telling him this, but he has to blame someone. The only one who refuses to participate in this idiocy is Andrew, our blind medium. He keeps his mouth shut at meetings, does his work, and leaves. Smart man.

The first full-fledged battle started during a case in Seattle where we were helping a witch clear out a poltergeist. It was supposed to be easy, with us just handling the equipment and me catching the objects the ghost threw. But I went to the bathroom at the wrong time and Agent Rushmore suffered a concussion when the ghost tossed a mirror at him. The others jumped on me for leaving my post while my supporters defended me. The debate went on for ten minutes, scaring even the poltergeist away. The "Beatrice goes to the bathroom" fight ended in a draw, but it was one tense plane ride home.

Things grew worse after that. Little arguments morphed into screaming matches. My favorite pieces of clothing disappeared from my locked room. The men refused to train with me or each other. On ops, people wouldn't listen to each other's opinions about even commonsense issues. Now the two factions can't be in the same room together even though they've worked together for years. Our boss, Dr. George Black, tried to step in. He called Will, Oliver, and me into his office, but the men just sat there like sullen children while I shrunk in my chair from embarrassment. I found myself out of the mansion more and more, Oliver usually accompanying me. We've been to the mall or the movies in the past five months more times than I can count.

Battle seven began yesterday, and I can safely say we won. We usually do. Last week a family out on their fan-boat came across the basilisk and the dad made the mistake of looking into its eyes. He dropped dead on the spot. Three others met the same fate the next day when a posse went after it. We were called in after that.

After two days riding around on fan-boats run by men missing all but one of their teeth, trekking knee deep in mud and muck with alligators and snakes scurrying around, and enough mosquito bites for people to think I have the chicken pox, we still hadn't found the basilisk. I suggested research—going through old newspapers to track all the sightings, not just relying on the eyewitness testimony from the last few weeks. Will vetoed the idea out of hand, saying we should concentrate on the places we knew it struck before. Of course I did the research anyway. I blew off the third day in the Glades for an air conditioned library. I narrowed it down to two spots a mile apart. This time the entire mosquito-ravaged, sunburnt team agreed to my plan. It worked, though I had the misfortune to have the "winning" zone, not Will. My snide comment after the kill didn't help, but I couldn't stop myself. Me and my big mouth. Now I feel like crud.

So right now I sit on a jet divided. Again. On the right, the enemy is spaced out in five rows. Their leader rests in the front staring out the window deep in thought. I'm parked in the back with the nearest person two rows away. Even on the tiny plane I may as well be in Madagascar. This is standard now—my isolation. Oliver usually sits beside me on the night flights, but he's below in the cargo right now. As I gaze at Will I feel an actual, physical pang of sadness. I'm tired. I'm *so* tired of all the drama. Of being the pariah slut of the F.R.E.A.K.S. I swear it's not going to be the zombies or goblins that kill me, it'll be a heart attack from all the stress.

No more.

Will's troops eye me as I move down the aisle to the front of the plane. Nancy glances up from her iPad to sneer at me, but Agents Rushmore and Chandler stay deceptively neutral as I pass. With his super-werewolf hearing, Will probably heard me from the moment I stood up, but he doesn't turn from the window as I lower myself next to him.

My heart pitter-pats, as it always does when I'm near him. He's so handsome that even now, after all this, I want to mash my lips against his, run my fingers through his thick brown hair, and ... I should not be having these thoughts about the enemy. He's a big man, almost a foot taller than me and thick. The two times we've hugged, the man has enveloped me. He's muscled but not grotesquely so. Just sculpted. From behind he's imposing, but his face strips most of the intimidation away. It's rugged yet boyish with thin lips, strong jaw, and largeish crooked nose from a break in childhood. And his eyes. Green as grass and so kind. Well, they used to be.

He displays no reaction as I settle in next to him. I don't say a word for a few moments because, well, I have no idea what to say. *I'm sorry*? I have nothing to apologize for. I didn't start this. *Kiss me*?

"Yes?" he asks, still staring out the window.

"I think we should talk," I say quietly.

"We have nothing to talk about."

"Come on," I scoff.

His head whips toward me. "Fine. I have nothing to say to you."

I smile sweetly. "Oh, I'm sure you can come up with a few choice words, mostly four letter ones, right?"

He doesn't take the bait. "If you don't require something, then please return to your seat. We'll be landing soon." He looks away.

Another pang of sadness hits me so hard this time I stop breathing. I don't know if it's coming from me or him. Clairempathy, feeling strong emotions from others, is almost as bad as psychokinesis. I close my eyes and force the air in and out. "This has to stop, Will," I whisper. "It's affecting our work. This isn't just about us, it's about all the people we're supposed to help. We've been lucky before, but if this feud doesn't end we'll start hating each other. Not trusting each other. I know you don't want to, but we have to talk. We *have* to end this. Us. You and me. Please."

"Will?" Nancy asks. I open my eyes as she steps in front of us, putting her hand on her hip. "Can I ask you about something? In private?"

Will glances at me, then begrudgingly nods at her. Gathering all my pride from the floor I stand up, internally shaking my head. Nancy smiles to herself as I take a step.

"Alexander?" Will says behind me. Everyone's attention, including the two men supposedly sleeping, diverts to Will. "Tonight. Six o'clock in the billiard room. We *will not* be interrupted," he says, voice set in granite.

I nod, and then with my head held high, I return to my seat.

Peace. I think we can all use some of that.

TWO

IN ANOTHER BEDROOM

THE ENEMY'S WAITING FOR me when I arrive at five minutes to six. We've both changed our clothes since arriving home. I'm in my skinny black jeans and tight V-neck powder pink sweater, and he's in khakis with a loose green T-shirt. Dressy casual, perfect for a peace accord. I just wanted to look nice.

The *Jaws* pinball machine lights up in the corner as does the Dance Dance Revolution video game we all pitched in to get Nancy for her birthday in June. She and Irie spent hours getting the steps right. As far as I know Nancy hasn't set foot on it since Irie's death. I offered to be her partner before total war broke out, but she refused. Then, when she caught Oliver and me on it, items started vanishing from my room.

Will stands by the pool table with two cues in one hand and beer in another. Another bottle rests on the side closest to me. Mine, I guess. He's expressionless as I step in. I smile nervously as I shut the door behind myself. I pick up the cool bottle of beer, taking a sudsy sip.

"Thanks," I say.

"I thought we'd play while we talk," he says as he extends the cue across the table to me. "You play, right?"

I take it. "Yeah. Oliver's teaching me." As the words leave my lips, I want to gobble them back up. If this is going to work, the O word must be used sparingly.

Will remains stony as he chugs his beer then sets it down. "Mind if I break?" He takes position and breaks. The balls clatter against each other and one goes in the far side pocket. "Guess I'm solids." I take another drink of the beer as he shoots another one in. "So, Agent Alexander, you called this meeting. Say your piece."

"Okay. I want the tension to cease. It's not healthy for any of us." He shoots another ball into the pocket. "We're supposed to be one team, us against them, not us against us. You and I need to set the example. We need to work through our issues, and everyone else will follow suit." There, I said it. Not so hard when you've spent the last fifteen minutes practicing those words in front of the mirror.

He misses the next shot. "Your turn."

I line up my shot and take it. Ball in the side pocket. I look up at him. "Do you agree?"

Will squares his shoulders. "The only issue I have with you is your reckless disregard for orders. I'm the tactical team leader for a reason, and though you may disagree with my strategy, you must trust I know what I'm doing."

Ugh. I knew it. This is going to be like pulling blood from a stone. Pointless. "Fine." I set the cue down on the table. "I don't want to play this game with you, Will."

"What do you mean?"

"I mean I'm done playing games. We've been doing it for months, and I'm sick of it. Sick of the snide comments, the dirty looks, the complete discount for anything I have to say. I'm tired of you punishing me."

"I'm punishing you?" he scoffs.

"Yes! And we need to talk about it!"

He tosses the cue on the table, sending the balls clattering all over. "*I* am not punishing *you*."

"Okay, good," I say. "Get it out. So tell me, why do you think I'm punishing you?"

"You know."

"Dallas?"

"Of course Dallas!"

"Fine. Then let's talk about Dallas. Are you still mad I didn't tell you I was going? Because we've been over that. It's my job. I did my job."

"You lied to me."

"Because you were having a fun vacation! I didn't want you to worry about me. And you know that."

"It was reckless," he says.

"That's part of the job description, remember?" I sigh and rub my temples as they throb. "You need to dial back the anger, okay? It's giving me a headache, and I just got over the last one. Take deep breaths or something."

Surprisingly, he does. He stands perfectly still and takes deep breaths. The pain ebbs to something more bearable within a few seconds. "Thank you," I say.

"Maybe we shouldn't do this."

"No. We have to." I stop rubbing. "We have to get this all out no matter what. Meteor, Godzilla attack, we're not leaving. Okay?"

With reluctance, he nods.

This is going to take awhile. I grab the nearest chair, lowering my tired body into it. That mile run has caught up to me. He follows suit, sitting across the pool table so all I can see are his shoulders and head.

"Dallas was messed up from the start," I say. "Everything could have been handled differently. There's enough blame to go around."

"Then why do I get the impression that everyone, especially you, blames me for it?"

"We don't," I say. "Will, nobody blames you for Irie."

"I thought we were being honest," he says.

"I am. She was killed by a vampire, not you."

"Wolfe—"

"Wolfe is grieving," I cut in. "He's just trying to act tough. Men deal with anger better than sadness, and being angry at you is just how it's manifesting. Grief is abstract; you're concrete."

Will peers across the table at me, mouth set straight as this sinks in. After a second he looks down at the floor. "She was my responsibility, and I failed her. I couldn't save her."

He looks up, but this time I look down. "But you saved me. Twice."

"I thought you'd forgotten that," he says with a half-hearted scoff.

"Of course not."

"Then why…" He trails off and sighs.

"Why what? Say it."

He folds his arms across his chest. "Then why the hell were you avoiding me? Why were you so cold to me?"

"Honestly? Because no matter how grateful I was for what you did to *me,* I couldn't get over how you acted toward *him*." There. The elephant in the room is no longer ignored. Let the fireworks begin.

"What are you talking about?"

Honesty. Total honesty. I can do this. "You and I, before Dallas, we were really close, right?" He doesn't answer. "Well, from our . . . dealings I'd formed, um," okay, *partial* honesty maybe, "a high regard for you." His breathing slows and his whole body becomes rigid. "I thought you were brave, and just, and . . . well, I thought you were one of those people whose moral compass always pointed due north. That, um, impressed me more than I can say. But when you refused to save Oliver, I guess that image became tarnished. I don't trust a lot of people, but I trusted you to always do the right thing."

"I did show up," he reminds me.

"Yeah, but because *I* was in danger, not him. You would have let him die and that, to me, is unacceptable."

"You think if the roles were reversed he would have acted differently?"

"Yes."

"Then I think you've given us both too much credit," he says with a sneer. "Well, I'm sorry I didn't live up to your expectations, and I promise not to say I told you so when your boyfriend fails to live up to them too." He stands up, stalking toward the door to my right.

"We are so not done here," I say.

He tries to open the door, but it won't budge. He yanks and yanks, but it doesn't move. His werewolf strength is no match for my power gripping the door. "Open this door," he orders.

"No. Sit back down and let's finish this."

He smacks the door and steps toward me, those nostrils expanding again. "We're finished."

"Sit down, Will, or I'll make you." He knows I will. My glare is as serious as his, but I know he'd never do anything to physically harm me; this does not go both ways. He does as I say, resuming his dour, stony body language as he returns to his chair across from me. We're silent for a few uncomfortable moments until I can find the right words. "I was chilly to you after Dallas, and I apologize for that. I was grieving, I was processing the whole op, and I was … tending to a sick friend. And yes, I was mad at you for not being the White Knight I made you out to be." His shoulders and jaw stiffen even more. "But, I still consider you a good, kind, brave man. I know when I need you, you'll be there. Even in spite of all of this." I swallow, buying myself a few moments before I have to say this last bit. "But, I am disappointed in you. Not just for that, but for the past few months. You instigated a lot of it, so it's up to you to end it. The both of you. I'm positive the only way to resolve this whole mess is for you and Oliver to sit down and sort out your differences. I've said the same thing to him a dozen times, and I'm sure he'd be willing if you were."

Will shakes his head. "You're so naive. You've known him for what? Seven months?" He leans in, arms still crossed. "I've known him for seven *years*. Seven years of insubordination, of arguments, of … monstrosity. You think *I* have questionable morals? Let me tell you something about your boyfriend. Five years ago on an op in Des Moines, we were on a vamp hunt. One of our four witnesses was another old pal of his. On sight they got into a knockdown, drag-out fight. I had to pull them apart. A couple days later, this same vamp came to me saying he had information on your Oliver. Never got around to telling me what it was. The next day, we found his head in a field, and it wasn't because of the vamps we were investigating. We'd killed them the night before. I'll spare you the details of the case that brought him to the F.R.E.A.K.S. I'll just say there was a girl in Virginia who grew up an orphan in part because of him."

I attempt to maintain my composure, not letting him know that inside I'm wigging out. I knew Oliver had done bad things, just not so recently. I've never really given much thought to his past. It's hard

16

to reconcile the man I went ice skating with last week with a cold-blooded killer, but this is not the time to sort this out. Harmony is the watchword tonight. "Is that why you hate him? Because he's a killer?"

"Yes."

"Do you hate me? Because I killed my first man at age eight."

"That's different."

"Is it? I've killed in cold blood. Marianna. Freddy."

"But you regret it. You have a soul."

"So does he."

Will tosses his hands up. "Look, I thought this little get together was about you and me. I don't want to discuss him."

"Well, tough! Because we both know this whole thing is about *him*. And my relationship with him."

"I don't give a damn about your relationship with him."

"Bull!"

"My only concern is how it will affect the team when he breaks your heart. I've lived though it before, and it is a pain in my ass. And he *will* break your heart. No question. You're just the last in a long line of idiots who fall into his trap. You want to talk shattered expectations? I expected *you* to be smarter than that."

"You know, I am getting more than a little sick and tired of having to tell you people this!" I meet his eyes. "We are not sleeping together! A man and a woman can be friends without having sex, okay? So once again I say—and pay attention this time—I never have and have no future plans of having sex with Oliver. None. *Nunca*. Did that get through your thick skull this time?"

"You're in his room every night," Will hisses.

"He's a vampire. If I want to see him it has to be at night! I go into Carl's and Andrew's rooms too, you think I'm sleeping with them?"

"That's different."

"No, it's not!"

"I've seen the way you two look at each other," he spits out like acid.

"Will, I swear on my mother's ashes, I have never slept with Oliver Montrose!"

The door opening startles us. His burning ears must have drawn him here. Oliver steps in with Grin Number Three across his face. This one hides the fangs and is reserved for slight amusement. Will is right about one thing: I do look at him a certain way. Most women do. Oliver is six feet even with a medium build. Under the blue jeans and tight black sweater are muscles from his time as a farmer. His thick, wavy brown with strands of gold hair hangs loose tonight, framing his glorious face. Pale skin, full red lips, straight nose, and hypnotic gray eyes all create the most beautiful man I have ever laid eyes on.

Will's anger spikes to headache proportions as it always does when they're in the same room. Oliver just keeps the grin in place as he glances at Will. "I can attest," Oliver says, his usually faint British accent a little more pronounced, "that our fair Trixie has not yet succumbed to my advances."

"Oliver, get out of here," I order.

"No. Your honor has been questioned, I must defend it."

"Get out!"

"No," Will says as he stands. "I'm leaving. We're done here. I have nothing else to say to you. Either of you." He brushes past the still grinning vampire, not acknowledging either of us. He slams the door so hard the balls on the pool table clatter. Great. I hang my head in my hands. That could have gone better.

"Was it something I said?" Oliver asks.

Oh, that is it. I jump up and shove the jerk as hard as I can. "You stupid jackass!" I slap his arm a few times before he shrinks away.

"Stop," he laughs.

I hit him once more. "This is not funny, Oliver. You ruined everything!"

"My dear, from what I heard, the conversation was going in circles."

"You were eavesdropping?"

"It was difficult not to. If one desires privacy, then one should use their indoor voice."

"I was making headway."

The grin finally drops. "You owe that man nothing. He is acting like a spoilt child, lashing out because he cannot have what he desires."

I scoff. "What about you? You're just as bad as him. Flirting with me whenever he's in earshot? Challenging him at every turn? Goading him?"

"Well, I must receive my thrills somehow as you refuse to let me thrill you." Grin Number One surfaces, full fang. This one is usually followed by me glaring at him, and now is no different.

"I am not in the mood."

The grin grows. "You never are."

I don't smile. "Stop it. I mean it," I warn. "You two need to sort yourselves out, or I *swear* I'll never talk to either of you again."

"Idle threat. You cannot keep away from me," he says.

"Watch me."

I push past him out the door. I expect him to follow, but he doesn't. Smart man. With each step up the staircase, my anger rises. I am tired of being used like some pawn on a chessboard. By the time I reach my bedroom, I feel like punching someone. There's a noise in the room across the hallway, which happens to be Will's bedroom. I've been listening for the open and close of that door before leaving my own room to avoid him for the past few months. Like a coward. I shouldn't have to do that in my own home. I'm no coward.

I'll prove it.

I pound on his bedroom door. "Will, open up!" Nothing. I pound again. "We are not done talking! You open this door or I'll blow it to pieces! I swear to God I will. Open the fu—"

The door swings open with a seething werewolf on the other side. "We're done."

"The hell we are," I say as I bump him on my way in.

I've only been in this room a handful of times, but it hasn't changed. Dark blue sheets and comforter on a solid, no frills bed with a wooden headboard. Like every man he has a plasma TV taking up half the far wall. The deep green recliner sits off to the side with clothes strewn across it, almost as if he was trying on clothes for the meeting. My bed looks the same. The boxing dummy in the corner looks as worn as the recliner with bits of the foam gone. Simple yet masculine.

"You don't get to walk out in the middle of a conversation," I say as he shuts the door. "Nothing's been fixed."

"I have nothing more to say to you." He rests against the door, folding his arms.

"You haven't said anything to start with!"

"We don't have to like each other, we just have to work together, okay?"

"No, it's not okay. We live in the same house. Our lives are in each other's hands. And ... " I close my eyes so I don't have to look at him. "We were friends. *Good* friends, and I don't have that many. So losing one ... it kills me. And it's for such a *stupid* reason." I open my eyes and look at him. "I miss you. A lot. I miss the sparring lessons, and the trips to the coffee shop. I miss riding in your truck to Wichita, and your stories about DC. I miss learning to be a better agent from you. And eating dinner with you. And watching you smile at one of my crap jokes. And the way you try to protect me even when I yell at you for it. I miss that you do it anyway because you care about me. I miss you. Don't you miss me?" He doesn't respond, but his arms drop.

I take a step toward him. "I want ... you to teach me how to pick a lock. I want to smile at you. I want us to be friends again. More than *anything*." I take another step. "But ... you have to stop punishing me for something I didn't do." I take another step. "And I'm sorry, but even if I did sleep with him, you're not my father. You're not my boyfriend. You're barely even my friend anymore, and who I choose to spend my time with isn't up to you. Oliver is my friend. That isn't going to change. And it's not in any way, shape, or form right for you to treat me like you have because you're jealous. It's petty and cruel and I know deep in my heart you're neither of those. You can't make me choose between the two of you because I shouldn't have to. And if you keep doing it, you will lose me forever. Is that what you want?"

His face falls. "Of course not," he says in a low voice.

"Then, *please* let go of all this anger."

"I just ... I ... " he sputters, searching for the right words, "guess we both have problems with managing our expectations."

"Well, then, maybe we should be clear about them." I take another step. "I expect you to treat me with respect. To listen to my ideas. To not judge me, especially when you don't have all the facts."

"And I expect you to not question my every order, and to talk to me when you have a problem with me."

"I will. And I'm sorry I was so cold to you when you needed a friend the most."

"And I'm sorry for judging you and letting my issues with your ... *friend* spill over into our relationship."

"I accept your apology." I extend my hand for him to shake. "Friends again?"

He shakes my hand hard. "Friends."

This doesn't seem like enough. I release his hand before bridging the small gap between us. I toss my arms around him, bringing our bodies so close not even a germ could get between us. He's so warm. Solid. Safe. He hesitates for a split second, body tensing until he wraps those large arms around me, resting his cheek on the top of my head. His fingers spread across my side, index fingers lightly touching the base of my breast.

"See? Isn't this better?" I ask.

"Yes," he whispers. "I'm so sorry."

"Me too," I whisper back into his throbbing heart.

He gazes down and I up. Our eyes meet, and I swear I'm hit by lightning. He looks shocked too. Yet happy. So damn happy that those green eyes twinkle as if filled with fairy dust. I'm surrounded by magic all day, but nothing like this. His left arm leaves my body so he can hesitantly trail his thumb down my cheek. I manage to block the shudder of lust sprinting down my spine. Our shallow breaths sync. This is it. Even through the war I've dreamt of this, longed for it since I first opened my door to him all those months ago. He clutches onto my shirt as he slowly lowers his lips to mine. I'm literally vibrating with anticipation. I close my eyes.

Merde.

They fly open when there is a knock across the hall. "Trixie?"

Jesus, Mary, and Joseph. I am going to kill him. Dead. He won't get up from this one, no siree Bob. *Dead.*

"Trixie dear?" Oliver says after another knock.

The magic's gone. We both feel it. We've missed the window. Damn it, damn it, *damn it*! Will's arms leave my body as he pulls

22

away. I can't bear to look at him, so I have no idea what he's thinking as he walks to his door. "She's in here," he says. "Come in."

In the hall Oliver glances at Will, then me, expressionless. Will steps aside to let him pass. "I was actually venturing to speak with you, William."

"Then why were you knocking on *her* door?" Will asks in the tone he reserves for Oliver. Annoyed with an undercurrent of fury.

"To apologize. I should not have interrupted your conversation earlier as I did."

"And yet here you are, doing it again," I point out, my tone coming close to Will's.

"I did not know."

"Bullshit," Will says.

"You question me?"

"Always."

Oliver's lips spread into Grin Number Two, mischievous with half fangs yet somewhat restrained. "William, had I known she was in here, I would have interrupted sooner. With your recent brutish behavior, I would not dare leave an ogre in your presence alone, let alone a dear friend."

The enraged werewolf almost lunges at Oliver. "*You're* calling *me* dangerous, you psychotic lowlife piece of shit?"

"Can you not see, Trixie? There is just no talking to him. I come to soothe the waters, and he verbally assaults me. Why you care what this cretin thinks about you is beyond me."

"And it bothers the shit out of you that she does care, doesn't it? You worried I might be able to get her to see the real you? A cold-blooded leech?"

"Better that than a petty, small dog who ostracized her just because he could not bear the thought of her with another man."

"I know what you're doing," Will says, shoving his finger in Oliver's face. "This is all just an act. You're playing the nice guy so you can suck her and toss her aside like all the others. Lori. Cassie. Rachel. Irie. I'm shocked you haven't made a go at Nancy. You liked them young before."

"You are disgusting," Oliver spits. "Do not presume to know about my relationship with Trixie. You know *nothing*," he literally snarls, showing all of those white, sharp fangs, "about my feelings for her. How could you? What do you know of friendship? Of love between two people? The only person you ever loved you let die in front of you and did *nothing*, like the coward you are."

I anticipate the next move in time. Just as Will lunges at Oliver, I grab them both with my power, tossing each as far from the other as possible. Oliver slams against the wall, as Will lands on his bed. "That. Is. *Enough*!" I shout. "Both of you!" They both gaze at me, eyes wide in shock and anger. "I swear if either of you says another word I'm going to scream! For Christ's"—Oliver flinches—"sake! What the hell is wrong with you two? I feel like I'm back in elementary school and you're fighting over a kickball. Except they're more mature!"

"He—" Oliver says.

"Shut it!" I say. "I am done. I'm done being the kickball! Sort your crap out and neither of you so much as *look* at me until you have."

I storm out, slamming both Will's and my door as hard as I can behind me. I pace around my room, shaking my emotions out through my hands, attempting to calm down. Jesus Christ. Jesus effing Christ. I can't take this anymore. I can't. I'm about to leap out of my skin. It's not like I don't have enough to deal with, risking my life every day. No. I'm done with them. I'm done. I'll avoid them, that's what I'll do. I won't leave my bedroom. I'll—

My cell phone chirps on the dresser. I pull it off the charger and step into my bathroom, shutting the door. Both jerks have superhearing, and I wouldn't put it past them to listen. I sit on the toilet and flip the phone open. "Hello?"

"Hello," Nana says on the other end.

With the sound of her dusky voice, I burst into tears. I love my Nana. Stupid statement, but I'll say it again: I love my Nana. She raised me when Mom put her head in our gas oven after I killed her boyfriend. He was trying to molest me, and I used my mind to squeeze his heart until he keeled over and died on my bedroom floor. I was eight. Mom gave her final swan song a month later. On good days I convince myself she did it for bringing that pervert into our lives. On bad ones it's because her freak daughter killed the man she loved. The bad days outweigh the good.

Nana, who I had only met once in my life before that, flew in and picked me and my brother, Brian, from the police station in Phoenix, whisking us from the desert to the beautiful sea. The following few days were a blur of tears, catatonia, and fear. My strongest memory is of Brian glaring at me through the memorial service. Such hatred. Such pain. To this day our relationship is strained at best. Another way of putting it is Brian hates my guts. It doesn't help that I almost killed him a few months ago. That was the night I joined the F.R.E.A.K.S. I haven't seen Nana since.

"Oh Nana," I sob into the phone, rocking back and forth on the cold porcelain.

"Bea, baby, what's wrong?" she asks, her voice a mix of concern and fear. "Bea?"

I sob and sob, unable to even form words. Within seconds, I can't even breathe. My entire body jerks with each wracking cry. I start hyperventilating, trying to draw air, but the sobs won't let me. I've only cried this hard twice before. Once was the night I killed Leonard, and the other was during my first case. Oliver held me that time, rocking and hugging me until I fell asleep in his arms. The beginning of a beautiful friendship.

"Beatrice?" Nana says forcefully. "Beatrice, listen to my voice. Calm down. Do you hear me? *Calm down.* You are going to pass out. Control your breathing. Breathe in. Breathe out. Do it!"

I attempt to draw breath but can't. So much is out of control, but this is something I can control. I can draw the air in. I can. I will. I try again, this time managing it. Another follows, then another. The tears lessen, and within a few seconds and breaths, I'm out of the danger zone. I can breathe without forcing it.

"Good girl," Nana whispers. "Good, good girl."

"Thank you," I cry. The tears won't stop but at least speech is possible now. I breathe deeply.

"Oh baby," she says with relief. "What happened?"

"I—I … everyone here hates me. I'm scared all the time. They keep yelling. I can't do this anymore. I just can't. I can't."

"Bea, I don't understand."

"Everything is just so … confusing. I have no idea what to do. Everything I try only makes it worse."

"Honey Bea, if you're this miserable then quit."

I've thought about it. No more concussions. No more kidnappings. No more running for my life. But let me say the look on a victim's face when I told them I've stopped the monster is more addictive than heroin. "I can't."

"Then I don't know what to tell you, baby."

I wipe my eyes and my snotty nose. "I—I just don't know what to do anymore."

She's silent for a moment. If my Nana had a power, it would be the gift of wisdom. She never steered me wrong. She's the one who told me to ignore Sarah Cale when she was picking on me. She's the one who told me to keep going to April's house even after she found out about the psychokinesis. She's the one who told me to break up with my ex Steven if I had any doubts when things got serious. We should have her on the team.

"Nana?"

"Christmas is in a week. I think you should come home. You missed Thanksgiving."

I did. Stupid vampires killing prostitutes during the holiday season. Jerks. "I had to work."

"They can do without you for a week or two, can't they? How else can I spoil you rotten?"

"I don't know." And I don't. I'm not exactly clear on the F.R.E.A.K.S. vacation policy. But she put it out there and honestly, how many day-care center emergencies can there be? I've used the excuse with April on her birthday, and with Nana for Thanksgiving. She's right. A vacation is exactly what I need. That and Christmas presents. I love presents.

"Beatrice, if you're working for a company that expects you to miss Thanksgiving and Christmas, then maybe it's not the kind of company you want to work for no matter how much they're paying you. I'm sure you could find another teaching job here."

My loved ones believe I left my beloved career as a teacher to pursue a lucrative one as Director of Childcare Services for Black Industries. They think I fly around the country with my co-workers setting up daycare centers at all the branches. The truth is I joined the F.R.E.A.K.S. to gain control over my psychokinesis. And I have gotten more control in the past ten months, but not enough that I'm comfortable working around small children. Beds and lamps still float when I have a bad dream. I'm not even close to chancing sex. One orgasm and my partner's head could literally explode. I still have a lot to learn, and this is the only place to do it. But Kansas is disgusting in the winter with the sleet and sub-zero windchill; San Diego is in the high fifties. I'd be an idiot not to go. Postponing my troubles. Sounds like a plan. Worked for Scarlett O'Hara.

"You're right. You're totally right. It's Christmas. They can fire me. I'll book a flight tonight."

"Oh Honey Bea, I'm so happy to hear that. I miss you so much."

"I miss you more, you have no idea. I love you so much."

"I love you too, precious baby girl. I'll start cleaning your room right away. Call me with your flight info."

"I will. I love you. Bye." I hang up.

A getaway. No vampires. No dead bodies. No egos the size of China. Just me, Nana, and April shopping, talking, and drinking too many margaritas. And no men. Heaven here I come.

———

I love this bed. I really do. It's lovely. Thousand thread count sheets, padding made of clouds, and enough room to lay wherever I want. I pull the pink comforter up to my chin and sigh. How sad is life when sleeping is the highlight of your day?

My ticket is booked, my suitcases packed, and all that's left is to ask George for the time off. Backwards, I know, but I'm sure he'll say yes. If he doesn't, well, there's always men's Kryptonite: tears. Now I just have to—

Someone knocks lightly on my door. Great. Can't get a moment's peace. There is no way I'm leaving my cloud, so I say, "Come in."

The light from the hallway frames his large body and reflects his shirtless torso. Toned with abundant pectorals and a hint of abs smattered with dark chest hair just the way I like it. How many times have I fantasized about trailing my finger down that straight line starting from the bellybutton down? The thought makes me quiver.

"Will?" I say as he steps in, shutting the door behind himself. The only light now comes from the brilliant, almost ethereal moon radiating through my window.

"I'm sorry," he says desperately as he rushes over to me. "I'm so sorry. Please forgive me."

"What—"

Those rough hands embrace the sides of my face, pulling me toward him. Warm lips meet mine, mashing so hard they hit teeth. At first I'm too stunned to move, but that changes fast. I kiss him back with the same ferocity. Months of longing. Months of fighting when all I wanted to do was this. Passion driving both. His tongue breaks the seal of my lips, finding mine. My body arches into his as we grip each other for dear life. He's hot, like a tropical beach at noon. He tastes just as divine. Of peppermint, beer, and man. My fingers fan out in his soft hair, close to yanking it. Our lips continue to move in unison as if dancing while our tongues explore. I lower him on top of me, his hard body pinning me to the bed. Through his jeans I feel his erection grow. The bulge presses into my thigh. Me. I did that to him. Amazing. All that doubting, of second guessing myself. The proof of what I knew is right against me, and God do I want it inside me.

We break apart as he yanks off my top, exposing my bare breasts, my nipples hardening against the cool air. His mouth lowers as he grips my back, pulling one greedily into his mouth. I haven't had sex in two years. I almost come as he nibbles and kisses that sensitive area. I don't even care that I might explode his brain, I just don't want this ecstasy to end. He moves to the other side, doing the same thing to my left nipple while caressing the spot he just abandoned. I run my fingernails down his back almost hard enough to draw blood. We moan in sync. He stops and gazes up at me, eyes hungry and wild. Like mine.

He's wanted this too. As badly as I have. Probably from the first moment he saw me. This revelation almost drives me over the edge. "I—" he says in a low voice. I kiss him forcefully, rolling us to the center of the bed with me on top, straddling him.

"Shut up," I say before undoing his jeans and yanking them down as he watches in awe. He knew what he wanted and dressed accordingly. No boxers. Only him. Long, wide, and ready for me. I trail my finger down his hard chest to the end of him. He shudders under my touch, and then my tongue as I play with him. I bring him to the brink but pull back at the last moment.

"Don't stop," he groans in equal amounts of pain and pleasure.

"You don't get off that easy," I say, voice husky. I take his hand in mine, sucking on two fingers, caressing them with my tongue. I scoot up so I'm hovering just above his chest, move his hand under my pajama bottoms, then gouge his fingers into my throbbing, burning center. I groan as he explores me. I move against those rough fingers. He toys until he finds that sweet spot most men never do. I cry out again, gripping the comforter. After a few seconds his fingers leave me as he clutches my wrists and flips me below him on my back. His erection presses into me, the only thing separating me from him is my thick flannel pajama bottoms.

He tears them off, and I'm totally naked. For a split second, self-consciousness floods in. I'm aware of my belly, wide thighs, stretch marks. But his lips and tongue moving down my torso, over the worry spots, quickly banish any negative thoughts. "You are so beautiful," he whispers, looking up at me before those fingers find their way inside again and that mouth is toying with me in perfect motion. All the sensations overwhelm me. I toss my head back and my body follows.

"You *are* beautiful," a familiar voice says as a cold hand presses against my feverish breast. My eyes fly open. Oliver lies on his side, head rested on his free arm, as naked as I am. Toiling in the fields from birth to rebirth did wonders for his body. His alabaster skin glows in the moonlight. Another shiver of ecstasy rips though as Will presses his fingers deeper into me. If he knows we have a visitor, he doesn't let on. "So beautiful."

Oliver's mouth presses against mine as his chilled thumb brushes over my nipple. His skin, mouth, everything is icy against my searing skin. It sends another shudder through me. The kiss is gentle, more playful, as is his tongue. As mine thrusts his parries, staying out of reach until he's ready. I run mine over his pointed fangs.

Then it stops.

Both mouths leave my body. My eyes open, passion instantly replaced with terror. A shark-eyed, gnarling vampire hovers over me. Below a grotesque half-man/half-wolf, sharp teeth bared, growls as drool drips from those teeth. I let out a bloodcurdling scream as both sets of teeth plunge into me.

"No!"

I'm still screaming as my real eyes fly open and I battle the thick covers surrounding me. I swat at the imaginary attackers, instead just hitting pillows. My bed, with me on it, thumps up and down like a student in PE class doing jumping jacks. The TV on the wall implodes as my lamp crashes to the floor from its non-existent perch. Crap.

Another girly scream of mine fills the room as my door flies open. Will rushes in fully dressed in an oversized Redskins shirt and blue pajama bottoms. "Bea?" he asks, voice as panicked as I feel. I stop screaming, instead panting like I was just … never mind. He perches on the edge of my bed, gasping a little himself. I look around the bed getting my bearings. I'm fully dressed. No blood. No monsters.

Hard hands grip my upper arms, shaking me. "Bea?"

My eyes whip toward him, then away. I can't look at him. I still throb from the dream. I want him as far from me as possible until I've calmed down. I want him gone. Right now.

Another figure materializes in the door. Oliver's figure. He's in the same clothes as before, and his eyes are the normal gray. Behind him Carl joins the party. I've woken the whole house. "What the hell happened? What did you do to her?" Oliver demands as he charges toward us.

Will releases me and turns to Oliver. "Nothing."

My would-be protector stops a foot from the bed, poised for a fight. "Liar!" he sneers. "She was screaming!"

Will leaps off the bed. "You asshole, I'd never—"

"Shut up!" I screech. The bed levitates and falls again without my meaning it to. "It was a nightmare! Get the hell out of my room! Both of you! *Get out*!"

Neither Alpha male moves until I push them with my mind. They stumble back, getting the message. They glance at me, then begrudgingly start toward the door, first Oliver then Will a few feet behind him. Only Carl remains at the door watching them go. A moment later, I hear a door shut across the hall. Carl turns to me. "Are you okay?" he asks barely hiding his smirk.

I fall into my pillows and shut my eyes. "Nope."

———

"I think it is an excellent idea," my boss George says as he hands me a cup of coffee.

I gulp it down even though it's my third cup in as many hours. After last night's, um, *nightmare* I couldn't get back to sleep. I lay in my bed doing everything I could not to think until the sun rose and I knew I'd be safe from at least one of them.

"I'm sorry I didn't give more notice. It was just sort of an impulse."

George lowers his tall, almost emaciated body in the chair across the desk. He's in his seventies but doesn't look it. He looks much, much older. Dr. George Black, parapsychologist and leader of the F.R.E.A.K.S. for over thirty-five years, who found me ten months ago and convinced me to join. He saved my life. Good guy. "It's Christmas, allowances can be made. We'll miss you."

"I kind of doubt that."

"You're wrong." He sighs. "But I do think your vacation will give everyone some time to reflect."

I play with my coffee cup on the desk, not wanting to look at him as I say something I've been thinking about since before the sun rose. "I was actually thinking... maybe this shouldn't just be a vacation."

He's silent for a moment, taking this in. I remove my hands and the cup continues spinning on the desk. "Beatrice," George says, "these tensions are not your fault. I know that. It's been growing for years."

"I'm not making things any easier though. I don't know what else to do." The cup stops twirling.

George doesn't respond, but his sympathetic face says everything. "I'll arrange for someone to take you to the airport."

"Thank you." I stand up and walk out without another word.

———

The black BMW idles in front of the mansion as I walk down the steps with my two suitcases. Today is much the same as yesterday: gray, freezing, and windy. It's been like this for almost two months, doing nothing to improve my mood. Sunny San Diego is just the remedy. I toss the suitcases in the open trunk and run to the passenger side before I freeze to death.

My heart leaps into my throat when I see my chauffeur. After a moment's hesitation, I get in anyway.

"Put on your seat belt," Will orders as he pulls away from the door. Nary an emotion crosses his face as we maneuver down the driveway and past the electric fence that surrounds the mansion. I gaze out the window, trying to keep my mind a blank slate. I'm about as successful now as I was last night. My cheeks flare as I remember his mouth on my breast. The sensations it brings even now. Sure it wasn't real, but my body didn't seem to realize it. "Want me to turn down the heat?" Will asks.

"It's fine," I mutter. Think of other things. The beach. Playing with the kids. Joking with April. The heat fades from my face.

"This wasn't my idea," he says. "George told me to pick up fuel for the flamethrowers in town and get this car serviced. I didn't know I was dropping you off until the last minute."

"Oh."

"I wasn't trying to trap you, is all."

"I didn't think you were."

One of our dreaded awkward silences follows. I watch the fields of dirt go by, keeping my mind blank. He fiddles with the radio but shuts it off in frustration when he doesn't find anything but Christmas music. The tension is so thick not even Bette could slice through it.

34

"Are you looking forward to seeing your family?" he finally asks.

"Yeah."

"Well, we'll get your room fixed before you come back." He shakes his head. "Sorry. *If* you come back." My stomach drops. Stupid George. Will glances at me to gauge my reaction. He's troubled by my embarrassed face. "He wasn't lying. You're really thinking of quitting."

"Just a thought."

He looks back at the road, face tense as his mind circles. "I don't know what to say. Do you want to quit?"

"I don't know." Tears bubble to the surface of my eyes, and I push them back down. I will not cry over this. I've cried enough. "I just can't take this anymore. I can't. You two... you're driving me crazy. Literally. I can't sleep. My stomach hurts all the time. I can't even breathe when you're both in the room."

He grips the wheel tighter. "And if I said I was sorry? Would that matter?"

"Are you?"

I gaze at this handsome face and see nothing but pain and fear. For once we're on the same page. "Would showing you how to pick a lock convince you?"

A laugh escapes me at the absurdity of that statement. "It wouldn't hurt." He follows suit, a large guffaw coming from his side of the car. The tension lessens enough so it's not suffocating. "Guess I have to come back now," I chuckle. "What kind of girl could resist that offer?"

We chuckle for a few seconds, but they fade away from us both. The smiles stay a little longer. I peer back out the window away from his still sad eyes. His gloved hand slowly moves to mine. I don't pull away.

"I'm sorry," he says quietly. "I'm so sorry."

My fingers entwine with his. "Then prove it."

THREE

AFTER THE CLICKING OF HEELS

HOME WAS A FOREIGN concept when I first flew over the Coronado Bridge eighteen years ago. My previous eight years had been, to call it something nice, nomadic. The longest we ever stayed in one place was ten months. For the most part we moved every six, mostly around the Southwest: New Mexico, Texas, Utah, and finally Arizona. Mom took bartending, waitressing, and even stripping jobs wherever she could find them. Of course she'd then meet a guy, sometimes move us in with him, then when it inevitably ended we'd pick up and move onto the next "adventure." For those eight years I was trailer trash, and now I live in a mansion. Life is so weird sometimes.

After Mom's swan song, Nana brought us back to San Diego with her. The first time I saw that bridge was two days after the gas stove incident. Mom's body was underneath us in the cargo hold on her way back to her hometown. I don't remember much about that week, only snippets like the bridge. I thought the color was so pretty and wondered if the people driving on it were worried they'd sink into the water below. The worry must have shown on my face because Nana kissed my forehead and held my hand until we landed.

"We are beginning our decent into San Diego International Airport. Please fasten your seat belts and turn off all electronic devices. Thank you."

I haven't flown commercial in months, and even though my new job allows me to be able to splurge on first class, it's still not a multi-million dollar private jet. After one of those, everything else is the bus.

We land without incident. I worm my way through the crowded terminal all the way to baggage claim. Nana is nowhere in sight. The woman is the only person in all of America without a cell phone, so I don't know if she's held up in traffic or right beside me. I am so spoiled now. Usually I just walk off the plane with my heavy suitcase, which lately Oliver carries for me. I could pack a brick wall and it'd be like carrying a feather to him. Since I never know how long I'll be in one place now, packing light is not an option. He doesn't mind being a valet and I'm not one of those über-feminists who gets offended when men pull out chairs and carry my heavy things. It's just good manners. Since my friend with the super-strength and the multimillion-dollar jet are both back in Kansas, I'll wait patiently for my bags and heft them to the car myself. I suppose I—

"Oh. My. *God*!" a familiar voice squeals to my right.

A wide grin stretches across my face as I turn.

April Diego, my best friend for almost twenty years, stands a few feet away with a matching smile. If she wasn't the sweetest, sassiest, most accepting person on the planet, I'd have to hate her. People are always mistaking her for Eva Mendes and me for Eva Mendes's assistant. She modeled all through high school until Javier got her pregnant a few months after our high school graduation. Out went the catwalks of New York and in came cosmetology school and spit-up, but being April, if she ever minded, it didn't show. She's a phenomenal mother to Carlos, Manny, and Flora and doting wife to Javi. And she does it all with perfect hair.

Next to her, Nana squints at me. I take after her. We're the same height with squat, sturdy legs and large everything else. Our ancestors were of hardy peasant stock. At sixty-nine she looks good. Thick, wavy gray hair cut to her shoulders. Wrinkles in the proper places over tan skin but not noticeable from far away. Cute, slightly upturned nose and thin lips, both of which I inherited. She's what I'll look like in forty years. I can live with that.

Never the wilting flower, April literally pushes her way through the crowd with a skeptical Nana close behind. Those toned arms wrap around me, hugging me so tight I think she might be part boa constrictor. I inhale the scent of Obsession perfume as I hug back. She releases me only for Nana to take her place.

"Hello, Honey Bea," Nana whispers. I almost puddle in her arms.

"Hi, Nana."

"We almost didn't recognize you!" April says enthusiastically, her eyes almost popping out of their sockets.

"Really? I've only been gone nine months."

"You've lost so much weight! You look so good!" April tends to talk in exclamation points.

"I do?"

"You do," Nana says. "You look fantastic."

I guess I've lost about thirty pounds since March. I'm still by no means skinny but I can pretty much buy whatever I want and look halfway decent in it. I had no intention of losing weight, but the need to run for one's life on a regular basis is a great motivator to work out. Being a size eight is just a happy byproduct.

"Thank you. I found a great gym."

The three of us line up at the belt with me in the middle. April beams and entwines her arm with mine. "I can't believe you didn't call me. If I didn't call Nana Liz for her cornbread recipe I wouldn't have known!"

"I wanted to surprise you."

"You did! And the kids are excited. They're working on a banner right now! Javi's already bought the *carne asada* for the barbecue tomorrow."

"A barbecue in December? I must be back in Southern California."

"Was it terrible in Kansas? I'll bet it's all cold and snowy. I hate cold and snowy!"

"It was both those things when I left," I say. "I never knew it could get so cold. The other day there was a negative windchill."

"Well, you're home now," Nana says.

"And we're having a heat wave. We can go to the beach every day if you want!"

"I have missed the beach," I say as I grab one of my bags. The other is close behind.

April's mouth drops open. "*That's* your bag?" It's just a regular black suitcase, though the pink LVs save it from total boredom. "It's a Louis Vuitton. They're like a thousand dollars each!"

"Really?" Nana asks.

"I can afford it now." I pull out the handles and walk away with my family behind me. "You think I moved to Kansas for my health?"

"How much do you make?"

"April!" Nana says.

"It's okay," I say as we walk toward the exit. "A lot." Yes, the life of a monster hunter is lucrative, and it's all take-home too. I don't have rent, I have half a dozen cars at my disposal, and I pay nothing but credit card bills. So yes, I splurge on ridiculously expensive suitcases.

"Are they insane?" April asks. "You get that for setting up daycare centers?"

"It's not as easy as you think."

We step outside into the perfect weather San Diego is known for. It's in the mid-seventies, sunny, blue skies, with a slight breeze coming from the ocean. April takes my arm again, resting her head on my shoulder. "I can't believe you're here! I have missed you *so* much!"

"We talk on the phone twice a week!"

She raises her head. "It's not the same and you know it. Have you missed me?"

"Horribly. Painfully." I touch Nana's shoulder. "Both of you."

We reach Nana's old white Saab, and I toss my suitcases in the trunk. Nana and I climb into the front and April in the back. She chatters on about the latest gossip as we pull out of the lot. She's made it her duty to keep me informed about everything she learns at the salon. A lot of our old classmates pop in. April knows who has gotten fat, cheated on, married, and divorced. Quite a few meet all of the above categories.

" …and do you remember Caleb? Your crush du jour in high school?"

"How could I forget?" Though I have. There are just too many men as it is to occupy my mind.

"He disappeared! Can you believe it? His parents even called in the FBI. He just vanished. Weird, right?"

Not really. "Totally. I hope he's okay."

"Who knows? What a world we live in, huh?"

"You have no idea."

Nana pulls up to the parking lot booth to pay, but before she can I give the cashier a twenty. "Beatrice, you didn't have to do that," Nana says.

"You're doing me a favor by picking me up," I say, getting my change back. Nana's lips purse in disapproval, but she drives onto Harbor Street which runs along the edge of the city.

"So, Nana Liz was kind of stingy on the details. I thought you couldn't come home for Christmas," April says.

"My schedule cleared. They figured they could survive for two weeks without me."

"Well, good! I was beginning to worry."

"About what?"

"I don't know," April says. "You disappeared in the middle of the night? We haven't laid eyes on you since? You know my overactive imagination. I thought maybe the government abducted you or something."

There's no way she can know, but I tense regardless. "That's ridiculous," I chuckle nervously.

"I know, but still! You vanish and never come home. Not even for Thanksgiving."

"I have to *earn* my salary," I say.

"We're just glad to have you home now, Beatrice," Nana says, ever the peacemaker. "And you're here for two whole weeks, so we'll all have plenty of time to catch up." Her cool, soft hand squeezes mine.

"So, April, how are my godkids doing?" I ask.

For the rest of the ride April gushes about her three kids: their classes, extracurriculars, and the holiday pageant in eight days. Our friendship is perfect. She likes to talk, and I don't. I half listen as she rambles on about the snowflake costumes she has to make as I take in the city.

Like all cities, San Diego has its share of problems like homelessness, gangs, and condemned buildings, but I still love it. We pass the Maritime Museum, an old black-and-white ship like something Orlando Bloom would sail. Soon we're in the heart of the city with the gray Midway aircraft carriers a few blocks from the convention center with its blue glass and white awnings. I am confident enough to admit I have attended the famous Comic-Con held there every year. For those four days every year, it's as if the city has been invaded by aliens, Goths, and the just plain weird. And this from a person who can move things with her mind. The red MTS trolley passes as we wait next to Petco stadium where the Padres play. My ex-boyfriend Steven had a season pass, so I've been in there way more than anyone with ovaries ever should.

A few minutes and red lights later, we leave the skyscrapers and boutiques behind and enter the "community" of Stockton, where Nana has lived for close to fifty years. There was a time when it was a nice community, but in recent years it has turned into a crime-ridden ghetto. When Brian and I arrived it was in transition. The little Mom and Pop stores along Market Street were still in business, still had money to paint their fronts, but about half had bars on the windows. Now the few that are open have bars, gates, and water damage. The signs are in Spanish and there are few clerks who speak English. My Spanish is okay but not enough to ask my dry cleaner to remove wine from a cotton/poly blend skirt.

The homes in the area haven't fared any better. The one-floor, ranch-style homes made of adobe or concrete all have bars on the windows and dying or overgrown grass. Nana held out on the bars as long as she could, but she relented after the second break-in. At least she hasn't gotten the latest neighborhood accessory: chickens. Clucking and crowing can be heard in about a third of the back yards.

Compared to the other homes on the block ours is, well, a mansion in Kansas. The lawn is a lush green and surrounded by bushes to camouflage the chain-link fence. She specifically chose the black bars to match the red clay color of the walls. The only thing we've ever been able to leave outside without it getting stolen is the turquoise dream-catcher hanging from the awning.

Nana pulls into the driveway, and I get out. As I turn to the right, the Holy Cross Cemetery fills my vision. Yes, a large, multi-acre cemetery was my playground growing up. April and I would run around in there hiding behind the gravestones or stone crypts. Sadly, it was also the setting of my first kiss with Tommy Millet. When I first moved here I was convinced that ghosts and ghouls would climb out of those graves and attack me in the middle of the night. Strange how right I was. It seems my life has always been surrounded by death. But in the daylight it's rather pretty, especially during the holiday season. Families bring poinsettias, garland, and even Christmas trees to leave for their loved ones. Even the hearse parked there now has tinsel around the back.

"*Hola, bonita!*" a woman calls to me. Mrs. Ramirez, my next-door neighbor of almost twenty years, waves to me. She barely breaks five feet and is as round as an apple. She's also as sweet as apple pie and was like a second grandmother to me.

"*Hola*, Mrs. Ramirez," I say. "*Como estas?*"

"*Muy bien.* Come home to visit *su abuela*?"

"*Si. Por dos semanas.*"

"Well, don't you forget to visit me, *no*?"

"Never." With a smile her way, I pull out the handles of my suitcases and walk up to the front door, where Nana is on lock three of five. When she opens the door the smell of baked cheese wafts from inside. Yummy.

Nana grew up in New Mexico on a cattle ranch, and when she and my grandfather finally settled down after he retired from the Navy, she decorated her final home like her first. The walls are a bright peach and Native American artifacts, more dream-catchers, paintings of sunsets in the desert, and cacti are scattered around the living room. Even the tablecloth in the dining room is turquoise with red zig-zags.

The only items out of place are the three urns on the mantle above the TV. My grandfather, Aunt Casey, and Mom all sit in a row. Grandpop Ed's is the dark mahogany. He died of cirrhosis the same year Brian was born. The little I've heard about him was not the greatest. He had a temper when drunk, was a stickler for rules, and rarely laughed. Mom left when she was seventeen and never looked back. Apparently life going from man to man, job to job with two small children in tow beat living at home. Nana never brings him up, and I know better than to ask.

Next to him in the pretty pink urn is my Aunt Casey. She was born three years after my mom and three years after that she was dead. Leukemia. I've seen a few pictures but she's another no-no topic. I resemble her a little—the Alexander light brown eyes with gold flecks, wavy hair, and a slightly up-turned nose. I have wondered on occasion how different things would have been had she lived. Would Mom have gone wild child and run away? Would Nana have smiled more? Who knows.

Last but not least, next to her sister, is my mother in the dark green urn, her favorite color. At the clubs she danced at, meaning stripped at, her stage name was Emerald. When the other dancers came over they'd call her that, and I'd get confused. Brian took me aside and explained that when you don't want people to know the real you, you lie, even about your name. Smart guy, my brother. Always knew what to say. Later he'd use this skill to wound me so deeply I'd almost kill him.

Which brings me to my last memory of this house.

My eyes dart to the dining room wall. Nana must have hired someone to spackle the two edges together after I cut through it like a piece of bread. Nana notices me staring at the wall. "I cleaned. Did you notice?"

I look away. "Yeah. The place looks great."

"Your bedroom's all ready for you."

"Thanks," I say with a small smile. I walk quickly past the dining room and into the hallway with the three bedrooms. Mine is the corner one with the green and purple "Beatrice's Room" plaque on the door.

When I open the door I'm transported back in time. I lived in here, dreamed in here, and did my homework in here until I was twenty-four and saved enough for my own apartment in Chula Vista, ten minutes away. Not a lot has changed over the years. A Brad Pitt poster from *Legends of the Fall* that April gave me for my birthday a million years ago hangs over my white plastic desk. A white TV stand with small TV sits across from my double bed. The only other decorations are pictures and paintings of mermaids I bought when I was in the throes of a mermaid obsession fifteen years ago. The carpet is dull beige, but a pink and yellow daisy rug covers most of it. The sheets and quilt on the bed match the rug. This room was obviously decorated by an eight-year-old who never grew up.

I have a lot of happy memories in this room. Nana reading me stories as I fell asleep. April and me lip syncing to Cyndi Lauper with our hairbrushes. Dressing for my high school graduation. This was my sanctuary. This is also where one of my lowest points played out. The last time I was in here, I tried to kill myself. I flip on the light and fan above and look at the rug. No signs of that night remain. No puke and no pills. Nana must have cleaned it up.

"Are you okay?" April asks behind me.

"Huh? Yeah, I'm fine." I step in. "Just jet lagged." I toss my suitcases on the bed as April closes the door. "You'd think I'd be immune by now."

"You always did want to travel."

"Yeah, but I meant to New Orleans and Washington, D.C., not Stone Bridge, Colorado, and Venus, Texas."

"But I thought you saw all those places when you drove cross country," April says as she sits at the desk.

Crud. Forgot that lie. "Yeah, but that doesn't mean I wouldn't like to go back." I start unpacking as April watches.

"But you like your job, right?"

"It's a job. Don't want to do it for the rest of my life or anything." She doesn't respond, which is unprecedented. I turn from the closet and she's biting her lower lip. "What?"

"Nothing."

"Say it."

She shifts in the chair. "If you don't love the job, then why do you stay? I mean, Will's still giving you crap right?"

"It's getting better. He drove me to the airport, and we had a good talk." And we didn't stop holding hands until we reached the airport.

"On a semi-related note, I have something to tell you. But you have to double-dog pinkie swear not to get mad and that you're still coming to your party tomorrow."

"I triple-dog swear."

She takes a deep breath and lets it out. "Javi invited Steven to the party."

Oh joy and bliss. And I came here to escape men.

"Is he bringing Allison?" I ask.

"Nope. Remember? I told you they broke up a month ago!"

"Right. Forgot." Didn't really care.

"With how hot you are now, he's going to totally regret never fighting for you."

"It wouldn't have done any good."

"He should have at least pulled a Lloyd Dobler with Peter Gabriel underneath your window," she says.

"Grand romantic gestures were never his thing. Remember what he got me for Valentine's?"

"Nothing."

"Yes, nothing. Not even stale candy. Not even a 'Happy Valentine's Day,' even after I said it to him. And what did he get me for my birthday the same year? A Padres throw rug."

"So he sucked at gifts."

"And cleaning up after himself, and listening to me, and taking into consideration what I wanted. How many days did I spend at the Del Mar tracks? The gun range? A million? And how many times did we go see a play or movie without an explosion in it? About two?"

"Okay, so he wasn't the best boyfriend. At least he never played games with you."

"That's because it requires creative thought."

"I just meant he was uncomplicated. Normal. I thought that's what you wanted!"

I open my mouth to defend my decisions but have no idea what to say next because once again, she's right. That is what I want. It's what I always wanted. I was never greedy. I don't want a million dollars or fame. All I want is a loving husband, a house, and happy children. That's it. I had that chance with Steven, but it didn't felt right. *He* wasn't right.

"You're still coming, right? I already invited everyone. For me and the kids?"

I roll my eyes. "Fine."

"Girls," Nana calls. "Dinner's ready!" Thank God.

Nana's big on family meals, no eating separately in our rooms or on the couch. It drove Brian nuts, but I kind of liked it. At the mansion I try to take my meals with Carl and Andrew at least a few times a week. Maybe now that a semblance of peace has been achieved, Will and Nancy can join us too. One big weird, dysfunctional family.

"Smells great, Nana Liz," April says, sitting down. "It's wonderful to have a dinner that I didn't cook."

I sit across from April in my old spot. As Nana dishes out the ziti I scan the room. The table is the same, which means I didn't break it and there isn't even a hint of a crack on the wall. Nana sits at the head of the table and smiles at us.

"It's nice to have someone to cook for," she says.

"Doesn't Brian drive down sometimes?" I ask before taking a bite. Yum.

"Every Saturday with Renata and the baby," Nana says, sideways glancing at me to gauge my reaction.

"Oh. They had the baby?" April asks, also glancing at me. What, are they afraid I'm going to burst into tears or something?

"Three weeks ago. A boy. Mark."

"Awesome! They must be so happy," April says.

"He's adorable. Looks exactly like Brian. They'll be here Saturday." Another two glances my way.

"Does he know I'm here?" I ask nonchalantly.

"Yes."

"And he's still coming?"

"Of course. They'll be here for Christmas."

"I thought she was Jewish," I say.

"Which is why they'll be here."

"Well Nana Liz, you must be so excited to have everyone under one roof again! Especially the new baby!" Her cell phone starts playing "Diamonds are a Girl's Best Friend." "Oh crap," she says, opening it. "Hello? Javi?" She listens. "I can't hear you over the screaming! What?" She listens, rolling her eyes. "Carlos did what? He smashed Manny's diorama! We spent two days on that stupid thing! How could you let him do that? No, fine, I'm on my way home. Okay!" She flips the phone closed. "I am so sorry. Javi must have let them have caffeine or something!"

"It's okay," I say.

April stands up. "Dinner looked great, Nana Liz. I'm sorry."

"I can wrap you up some."

"No, it's okay. I'm sure Javi didn't make them anything, so I'll have to cook anyways. Lucky me." She walks over to me, leaning down and kissing my cheek. "Call me tomorrow morning, okay? And don't make plans for tomorrow evening. Either of you. Barbecue, my place. Everyone's coming."

"We'll be there," I say.

"Bye!" she says, rushing out of the house.

"She's such a sweet girl," Nana says after the door shuts. "She comes by once a week and we have coffee."

"Yeah, I really missed her."

"And we really missed you," Nana says, squeezing my hand.

I smile as she pulls her hand away. "It's weird being back."

"Do you want to talk about last night? You really scared me."

"I was just stressed," I say before taking another bite. "I had this huge fight with my boss and then Oliver."

"Well, you just have to work with them. Just be glad you don't have to live with them too."

If only. "It's just that the team spends so much time together. We're so close knit and we have to rely on each other, so when everyone hates each other, things get pretty unbearable." I take another bite. "But Will and I spoke this morning, and things should be better when I get back."

"It's unfair of them to put you in that position. I'm surprised they didn't fire him."

"He's just … been through a lot. His wife died, and he has this incurable disease that he's had to get used to."

"Still. That's not your fault."

We eat in silence for a little bit. "So," I finally say, "how are Brian and Renata adapting to parental life?"

"Very well. They have a nanny, which helps, but I've never seen him so happy."

"He's okay with me being here? If you want I can spend Saturday at April's."

"Nonsense. You should meet your new sister-in-law and nephew."

"I'm just not sure they want to meet me."

She sets her fork down. "That was an accident," Nana says.

"I almost killed him, accident or not. *I* wouldn't want to spend Christmas with me."

"That was a horrible night, but it's time to move on. It's over. It'll never happen again."

She looks down at her plate and starts eating again, ready to put the topic to bed. But I'm not. "I know I said it before but … I'm sorry.

I'm sorry I lost control like that. I'm sorry I left the way I did. I know I scared you. I'm just ... sorry."

She keeps her eyes on her plate for a few moments, then lifts them up to mine. "I know you are, Honey Bea."

"You're not still scared of me, are you?"

"Of course not. I love you. No matter what."

"I love you too," I say, near tears. They just snuck up on me. I shake my head to clear them.

"Are you okay?"

"I'm just tired. It's been a long couple of days."

"Go rest, baby."

I rise and take my plate to the dishwasher before slinking back to my bedroom. I fall face first onto the bed. With all the travel I do one would think I'd have mastered jet lag, but it always gets me. I inhale and exhale slowly. It has been a day. I'll just unpack stuff for the night and save the rest for tomorrow.

When I pull out my cell phone charger I suddenly realize it's been off since I got to the airport. I find it at the bottom of my purse and switch it on. I have four voice messages.

"Hello, Bea, this is George. It seems in your haste you neglected to fill out your incident report. If you could type it up and e-mail it ASAP, I'd greatly appreciate it. Have a safe flight."

Crud. Not even being a government secret saves me from bureaucracy. I wonder if the guys at Area 51 have as much paperwork as we do.

"Um, hi," Will says. My heart skips a beat. *"I just, um, wanted to say, good talk this morning. It was ... good. Enjoy your family. I'll, uh, miss you."*

Darned if my smile isn't from cheek to cheek.

"Hey," April says. *"Where are you? Call me."*

Must have been at the airport.

Last one. "*So, Trixie dear,*" Oliver begins, "*I arose this evening ready to eat an entire murder of crows to regain your good graces, only to find you have fled the state. I do hope it had nothing to do with me.*" He pauses. "*Please call me,*" he says seriously.

Great. A vampire with bruised feelings is a disaster waiting to happen. He's either terrorizing Will or moping around like Hamlet. I do have terrible taste in men, even when it comes to office husbands. I should divorce him and take up with Andrew. Less blood, more laughing at Carole Lombard movies.

I settle into bed before calling. If I'm lucky he'll be out and I can just leave a message. But alas, he answers at the third ring. "Hello, Trixie," he says so I can practically hear the grin on his face. "How was your flight?"

"Uneventful. How are you?"

"Perplexed. Concerned. Despondent."

"And why is that?"

"You departed without saying goodbye."

"You were asleep."

"You could have left a note."

"You are not my keeper, Oliver. I don't have to get your permission to fly home for Christmas."

"*This* is your home."

Neither of us utters a sound for a few seconds. He always does this. He always says things that I have no response to. So I do what I always do: humorous deflection. "What? Are the others there picking on you now that I'm not there to defend you?"

"I am being avoided, per usual."

"Then go hunting. I'm sure the bar girls are waiting with bated breath to succumb to your charms."

He doesn't answer right away. "So I take it you have no desire to discuss what transpired last night? Because the last time I saw you, you were screaming as if under attack and now are fifteen hundred miles away without warning."

"You were worried?"

"Of course. So tell me, Trixie darling, should I serve up William's head on a platter or would you prefer it in a hat box?"

"Neither," I warn.

"You were in his arms bellowing last night," he says harshly. "He is lucky I did not rip his throat out there and then. I—"

"Stop it," I say. "*This!* This is why I came home, okay? I'm sick of you two threatening each other. Did you not listen to a word I said last night?"

"I did."

"Well, apparently not because we're right back where we started. Have you apologized to Will yet?"

He's silent.

"Then I have nothing to say to you until you two sit down and settle things."

"And if we do not?"

"Then ... maybe I'm not coming back in two weeks," I find myself saying. "Goodbye, Oliver. Call me when you've grown up." I shut the phone off.

And now I have a headache. I hate tough love. I'm so not good at it, but it's all he responds to.

That man! Ugh! He drives me up a wall. He knows all my buttons and can't help himself, not a good combination. No wonder I'm his only friend. Enemies he's got in spades but friends ... Heck, I think I'm the first in decades. One would think he'd treat me better. Okay, most of the times he does. Anyplace I want to go, he'll accompany me without complaint. Movies, book readings, even shopping. Metrosexuals take their cues from him. Half the new stuff I've bought he picked out, and boy do I look good. Clothes aren't his only forte. The man's a millionaire, as are most vamps. Something about being alive for so long the trends become predictable. I've almost doubled my investments.

There are some obvious perks to being buddies, but the drawbacks are wearing me down. Besides the ostracization by my fellow agents, there's also the constant flirting, jealousy, conceitedness, and the fact that at least once a day I have the strongest desire to jump his bones. The guy is sex on a stick and *boy* do I want a lick. But he's a walking dead man with serious commitment issues and the relationship would have the longevity of a ruler. No, friends is good. Friends I can handle. *If* he takes what I've said to his barely beating heart. Because as much as I value him, I value my sanity more. But honestly … I can't imagine my life without him.

And that scares the hell out of me.

FOUR

THE BELLE OF THE BARBECUE

"Nana, I'm home!"

I haven't said that in awhile. She and Mrs. Ramirez stand in the kitchen talking and mixing something in a big bowl as "All Alone on Christmas" by Darlene Love plays on the radio. Both women grin as I walk in with my shopping bags. God, I love vacation. I slept until one, had Nana take me to get a rental car, then spent most of the day shopping before visiting April at the salon, gossiping with everyone while being pampered. I feel like a new woman.

"We're making potato salad for the party," Nana says, adding the mayo.

"Your hair looks nice," Mrs. Ramirez says.

"I just got a trim and blow-out for the party," I say, running my hair through it. "Are you coming with us, Mrs. R?"

"Of course she is," Nana says. "She even made guacamole."

"I do love a good party."

"I thought about making gingerbread men, but I didn't know if there was a Christmas theme or not," Nana says.

"I have no idea," I answer, kicking off my espadrilles.

"I love Christmas," Mrs. R says. "What do you want, *bonita*?"

"Peace on earth and goodwill toward men. That or a pony." I smile at them, then start toward my room.

"We'll leave in half an hour!" Nana calls.

I shut my bedroom door. With the ex-boyfriend factor thrown in, a quick costume change is required. Yes, *I* dumped *him,* but it would be against the girl code if, given the chance, I didn't make him rue the day he ever lost me. The five-hundred-dollar Carolina Herrera sleeveless blue and white polka dot halter dress with V back and matching patent leather heels should do it. Still. I am a tad nervous about seeing Steven again.

Officer Steven Weir of the Chula Vista Police Department, my only true-blue boyfriend. (The man I lost my virginity to doesn't count unless therapy sessions constitute dates.) Steven and I met on a double blind date with Javi and April. Steven and Javi met at their gun club and became friends over their mutual love of killing paper men. He'd go over to April's house, drink beer, and hang out. Why she thought these would be selling points when pitching the date is beyond me. But it was Friday night, and as usual, I had nothing better to do. There might also have been the promise of free French fries. I am a weak woman.

My first thought when I saw him was, *Hawaiian shirts are so two decades ago*. It was bright red with tiny martini glasses on it. Besides that he was pretty cute. Short sandy brown hair spiked up, medium height and build, small brown eyes, and rounded baby cheeks he never grew out of. His smile was his best feature. Mischievous. That elevated him a tad in my book. Dinner was pleasant enough. We talked about work, politics, the usual first date stuff. He called the requisite three days later and asked me out again. Couldn't think of a reason to decline, so I went.

For two years we got together three times a week just like clockwork. We'd go to a sporting event, barbecues, or occasionally a movie. And once a week, usually Friday night, we'd have bland sex. It was okay. If we had fun beforehand, it could be a good night, but nothing to write home about. Twenty minutes from start to finish. My fault though. If I felt even the slightest hint of an orgasm, I'd fake one and end it, though this only happened once or twice.

All in all we had a decent relationship. He told cool cop stories, gave good foot massages, and unless he was working, I always had something to do Friday night besides laundry. Then the idiot went and spoiled it all by asking me to move in with him. I said no. He said say yes or we're over. I said goodbye. Thus ended Steven and Beatrice.

April tried to talk me out of it, but I wouldn't relent. No one knew why I had done it. On paper we were a great couple: mature, responsible, friendly. We didn't get on each other's nerves. He'd make a good husband and father. But every time I imagined our lives together, I'd never get past the wedding. We had little chemistry. We had nothing in common. He was … boring. I knew we weren't right together early on but kept going because, heck, no one else was lining up to ask me out. Normal women had boyfriends, and I'd be darned if I wasn't one of them.

He handled the split well, rebounding with another officer on the force within weeks. We were cordial if we ran into each other. He even sent flowers when I was in the hospital. Like I said, nice guy, just not for me.

As I spray my now gorgeous hair with gloss, my cell phone buzzes. It's the mansion. Ugh.

"Beatrice Alexander," I say in my professional voice.

"It is I," Oliver says.

"Have you apologized to Will?" I ask without missing a beat.

"No, but—"

"Then bye." I snap the phone shut and start on my mascara.

"Beatrice!" Nana calls. "We're already late for your party!"

The phone buzzes again, but I ignore it. I could simply turn it off, but this will torture him more. He'll keep calling and calling all night this way. One thing about vamps, they have eternity, so patience and tenacity come naturally.

I fluff my hair again and walk out feeling pretty darn good. I look spectacular and there's a gorgeous man going nuts because I won't pay attention to him. I couldn't ask for more when going to meet my ex. Except if I arrived with Oliver on my arm.

Well, there's always my next high school reunion.

––––––

When I first met April, a week after I moved to San Diego, she lived two streets over until she was kicked out the day her parents discovered she was pregnant. She lived with us for a month until Javi rented a house five minutes away, where they still live today.

The cramped street is bumper to bumper with cars, as usual. I recognize Steven's red Jeep with the NRA bumper sticker on it right in front of the house. We park two blocks away, and I instantly regret the heels. *Price of beauty, Bea.*

April's house is a lot like ours: a one-story ranch with an attached garage, though toys and bikes litter her lawn. All the lights shine inside and music booms in the back yard. Christmas lights hang from the roof with a huge wreath right above the garage. We walk in without knocking, the privilege of a best friend. Various stains from juice, blood, and food are visible on the beige carpet. There are people around, about a dozen in the living room, some I know. Yolanda from the salon smiles at me. April's cousin Luis and a woman sit on the red and black plaid couch with a quilt on the back. He holds up his beer and nods as we come in. Action figures, Matchbox cars, and the odd Barbie doll lie in piles around the room. Just as I remember it. April's never had much patience for cleaning or decorating.

I say hello to those I know before making my way to the kitchen, April's domain. Instead I find April's husband, Javi, with their son Carlos sitting on the counter as his father rolls a Band-Aid on his knee. Javi looks descended from Mayan gods with square jaw, broad nose and forehead, and straight black hair pulled into a ponytail. Carlos is a tiny version of his father, though the boy was lucky to inherit April's lips.

"Aunt Bea!" the boy cries. He leaps off the counter and scurries over to me, squeezing me tight with his tiny arms.

"Hi, big guy," I say hugging him back.

"We made you a poster for you coming home!" he says, releasing me.

"Did you? I can't wait to see it."

Javi hugs me too. "April was right. You do look damn good, *chica*."

"*Gracias. Y tu*. And look at this guy! He's grown so big!"

"Did you miss me?" Carlos asks.

"So much."

"Mommy says I'm a'posed to make you feel bad for going away so you'll move back."

Javi pulls the boy closer by the shoulders. "*Mijo*, you weren't supposed to tell her that."

"Oh. Sorry."

"And where is Her Royal Sneakiness?" I ask Javi.

"In the back yard. She did tell you Steven's here, right?"

"Yeah, don't worry. I'll be on my best behavior." I look down at Carlos. "Can you take me to your mom, please?"

I extend my hand, and Carlos takes it. He all but drags me through the sliding glass doors. About a dozen more people mill around in the back yard, talking and eating as "Make Me Lose Control" by Eric Carmen plays on the stereo. They went all out for my homecoming. White Christmas lights dangle from the awning with Tiki torches flaming every few feet. The picnic table is covered with food, everything from salad to flan. Javi's brother, Edgar, stands behind the grill flipping burgers and chatting with Steven. Both men, along with every single person but Nana, has a Corona in their hands. A huge white banner about eight feet across hangs on the fence with "WE MISS YOU AUNT BEA!" written in multi-colored letters. Mrs. Ramirez stands at it with a marker in her hand, writing on it. There are a lot of scribbles on it and even a few hand prints from the kids. That is so thoughtful I could cry.

"Mommy!" Carlos shouts as we walk out.

All eyes find me as I scan my crowd. Most seem pleased, but Steven's reaction is priceless. His eyes all but bug out of his head. Thank you, Carolina Herrera. He hasn't changed much at all. His hair is still spiky, and he wears an ugly black and white Hawaiian shirt with brown cargo pants and loafers. I tried for two years to get him out of those shirts. If we'd ever gotten married, I'd bet he and all his best men would wear them at the wedding. Reason number eleven I dumped him.

April has Flora, her two-year-old daughter, over by the picnic table. Flora insists on wearing only dresses, the pinker the better. Tonight is no exception. This one even has butterflies on it. She's so easy

60

to shop for. Carlos leads me to them, and Flora's face lights up when she spots me.

"*Tia* Bea!" she says.

"Hello, lovely!" I say as I take the girl from her mother, hugging her tight. "Oh! You've all gotten so big I can hardly believe it!"

"I'm a big girl now," Flora says.

"You really are."

The little girl releases me and wiggles out of my grip.

"Did Daddy fix you up?" April asks Carlos, her attention diverted.

"He gave me a Spiderman," Carlos answers.

"A Spiderman!" she says. "Good. Now go take your sister inside with the other kids and you can play with the Wii. Take turns!"

Carlos takes Flora's hand, and they go back inside. April hands me a beer. "You look fancy."

I pop the top and chug the beer. "Yeah, I'm a regular debutante," I say with a smile.

"Steven hasn't taken his eyes off you," she says in sing-song.

"That was kind of the point of the dress," I reply in sing-song.

"How diabolical of you."

"I've been taking lessons." I take another swig before Kenny saddles up to us, red Solo cup in his hand. Kenny works with April at the salon and is the definition of fabulous, or so he insists. Skinny, tall, nearly black skin, platinum hair. He spent an hour grilling me about Oliver and Will today. The bad thing about gossip is it goes both ways, and I've been the topic *du jour* for months. "If it isn't Cinderella. You look faboo. Is that Chanel?"

"Carolina Herrera."

"Spin for me, girl!" Kenny says.

I set my beer down on the table and twirl, catching a glimpse of a still-staring Steven. "There. I have performed my monkey trick of the night."

"Can you believe this is the same girl who used to think Target was high end?" Kenny asks.

"Hey, don't diss Tar-jay," I warn.

April peeks over my shoulder. "Oops. Looks like Nana Liz cornered Steven."

I turn around and sure enough Nana is chatting with my ex like two old friends. They did always like each other. She'd bake him banana bread, and he'd fix her shower. Yet he never fixed my shower, or toilet, or that picture frame he broke. "That's what landlords are for," he'd say. Ugh. Steven glances at me, and I turn back around.

"I always thought he was kind of cute," Kenny says.

"He is," I say after another swig. "He's also inconsiderate, boorish, and just plain boring."

"He was so in love with you," April says, gazing over at them.

"And yet he never said it or showed it in two years."

"Oh who cares?" Kenny asks. "She's got two hot *tamales* fighting over her now."

"They are not fighting over *me*," I say. "They're fighting between themselves. Not about me."

"Yeah, just keep telling yourself that," April says.

"Can we please stop talking about this already?" I ask. "I came home specifically so I wouldn't have to think about this stuff."

"Right now you're the interesting one," Kenny says. "That's never happened before."

"Gee, thanks," I say.

"You're welcome."

"She was always interesting," says April. "Just in a muted sort of way."

"So why did Steven and Allison break up?" I ask, seriously wanting to steer the conversation away from me.

"He told Javi they ended things because she wanted to get married and he didn't," April says. "Looks like you ruined him for other girls."

"Did not!"

"Well, I heard a different tale," Kenny says. "I heard from Lola over at Misty Salon where Allison gets her hair done that *she* broke up with him."

"Really?" April asks.

"Yeah. She thought he was cheating on her."

"Steven would never do that," I say.

"He's a man," Kenny says.

"He doesn't have the imagination or initiative to juggle two women," I say.

"He's. A. Man," says Kenny. "No, Allison told Lola that he'd say he was going out with friends, but he wouldn't invite her or tell her where. She even tried to follow him but lost him."

"Sounds like a wonderful, trusting girlfriend," I mutter.

"He wasn't cheating on her," April clarifies. "He just joined this bowling team and didn't want her to tag along. That's what he told Javi anyway."

"Told ya," I say to Kenny. "That man loves his bowling." I feel his eyes on my back and on instinct my head swivels around. Sure enough those brown eyes are on me. Caught, he shyly smiles and looks away. I do the same. My ears are burning. I sigh. "I'm gonna have to go over there, aren't I?"

"Eventually," April says. "Let him stew a little bit more."

"Wiggle your ass," suggests Kenny. "Drive him nuts."

"Shut up," April says. "She's not that mean."

Kenny and I look at each other, smirk, and I shake my booty in time to the music. Kenny does the same, but April rolls her eyes. I've gotten in touch with my evil side in the past months. Mind you, torturing my ex doesn't come close to some of the other stuff I've done, but this gives me a sick little thrill those other times didn't. Oliver would be so proud.

"You're going to hell," April says, shaking her head.

"Yes, but she'll be the belle of the ball there," Kenny says. "Lucifer himself will ask her to dance."

I stop dancing. "Enough playing." I take another sip and sigh. "Time to get this over with."

"It won't be that bad," April says.

"I have no idea what to say to him."

"'Ha ha, look what you let get away'?" Kenny suggests.

"Go get it over with, and I'll reward you with a cherry margarita," April says.

"With a sugar rim?"

"Of course. What are we? Heathens?"

"I want two. And flan."

"Done. Now get over there. And be nice."

"But not too nice," Kenny says.

"Well, duh," April says.

I roll my tongue over my teeth for any residual lipstick and smooth my dress. "I look okay?"

"Smashing," Kenny says.

I'll take it. I spin on my heels, toss my hair back like I'm in a shampoo commercial, and sashay myself across the lawn. When I reach Nana and Steven, Heidi Klum has nothing on me. I watch him watching me as I approach. Steven's fake surprised smile takes ten years off his already boyish face. With those chipmunk cheeks, they'll still card him when he's forty.

"You looked like you were having fun," Nana says.

"You know me," I chuckle. "When the music's right, I gotta dance." My smile widens like I'm at the orthodontist. "Hello, Steven."

"Bea," he says, looking down at his beer. "You're looking well."

"Thank you. You too." He does. He's either had plastic surgery or he's been eating his Wheaties. His skin has a glow and the small age lines around his eyes are gone—all in less than a year. Lucky him.

"I hope you don't, you know, mind I'm here."

"Of course not. It's always nice to see you."

Nana glances at Steven, then me. "I was just telling Steven about your new job."

"I can see you're doing well," Steven says, still not looking at me.

"I think I'm going to find Hilda," Nana says. "You two talk."

I shoot her a look. Nana squeezes my arm before walking away. I'll bet after a beer or two she and Mrs. R will be dancing on tables or passed out on the couch, or in the corner scrapbooking. She is the source of my lack of party genes. Before I had to start working nights, I barely left my house after dark. Heck, I would barely ever leave my apartment if not for April. Now I usually wake up at two and spend my evenings at bars or malls or just sitting outside having a glass of wine with Oliver. Weird how I just realized that.

"You really do look good, you know," Steven says.

"My building has a gym," I say, not really lying. "I get bored."

He sips his beer. "So, Kansas, huh?"

"Kansas."

"I was surprised to hear you left. I always pegged you for a lifer."

"Needed a change. Kansas is as good a place as any."

"How's your head doing?"

"Hard as always. I'm completely healed. I don't even get headaches anymore."

"They ever figure out what happened?" he asks.

And here's reason number fifteen I broke up with Steven: I knew if he ever found out what I can do, he'd probably arrest me for possession of a deadly weapon. He's not the most open minded of people. We were together for two years and not *once* did I ever consider telling him about my gift. I took great pains to make sure he never found out. We never spent the whole night together in case I had a nightmare and the bed levitated. If I felt myself get too emotional, I'd walk away. If I ever slipped up and something was banging or floating, I'd distract him, usually with my feminine wiles, which would just lead to more problems. I'm amazed I was able to carry on for as long as I did.

"Blood clot," I lie. "Gave me some medicine and no problems since."

"Good. I was really worried," he says.

"Thank you. The flowers meant a lot. Really." His cheeks flare up a little from embarrassment. Guess my booty shaking did a number on him. We don't say anything for an uncomfortable moment. Really, what do you say to the man whose heart you broke, or at least trampled on a little? "I'm sorry. About you and Allison. I thought you two were good together."

"Yeah," he says, still looking at his beer. "It hadn't been working for a while. Nobody's fault really. What about you? Seeing anyone?"

"Not really," I say with a small smile. "I mean, it's sort of *very* complicated."

"How?"

I shake my head. "There's this guy I like. A lot. But he's … it can't happen."

"Why not?"

"Well, he's sort of my boss, for one. He's a widower. And … it's just not going to work out."

"That's tough. But you're okay out there besides that? Happy?"

"There are moments, I guess. For the most part I like it. I have friends. The job is very fulfilling when I'm not fending off the crazies."

"One of those crazies do that to your neck and arms?" he asks, pointing to the scar on my neck (Oliver) and arms (zombies).

"Kids. There's always a biter in the lot." Time for a new topic. "What about you? How's the job? Still on patrol with Artie?"

Artie being Artie Rupp, Steven's partner of four years and a huge piece of work. Forty-five, divorced thrice, and still a patrolman after twenty years. From what I'm told, he failed the Sergeant's exam five times before giving up; three for the Detective's. I'm stunned he's passed the physical every year with his constant smoking and forty extra pounds. I would not want him responding to an emergency of mine. He pinched my butt twice before I threatened to tell Steven. Never did though. Partly because I was afraid he'd punch Artie and partly because I was afraid he wouldn't. I put it at fifty/fifty. I'd bet old Artie would flip his lid if he found out I was working for the FBI. It's like the difference between high school football and the NFL.

"Yeah," Steven says, "he's good. Talking about getting married again."

"Really? Who to?"

"Remember Wanda? The bartender at the bowling alley?"

"The one who looks like she's been in the sun since the Seventies?"

"That's her," he says. "They've been dating about two months now."

"Well, good for them. Fourth time's the charm, right?"

"I know you two never got along," Steven says, "but he's changed. Lost a lot of weight. You wouldn't recognize him."

"I'll take your word for it," I say, sipping my beer. I have no desire to spend a second with that oaf. Once again Steven and I are locked in an uncomfortable silence. We've pretty much covered everything but the weather in polite conversation. Duty done. Cherry margarita time. "So, I'm gonna ..." I point to the house.

"Right. Yeah," he stammers. "Talk to you ... later."

"Sure. Yeah." With a gracious smile, I walk away toward the house.

"Shit. Wait!" Steven calls before he grabs my arm.

He turns me around. "What?"

He releases my arm. "I—I had this whole speech planned out in the car. Things I wanted to get off my chest, but I forgot all of it," he chuckles. "You just look so great, and it's a little overwhelming, and I'm not so good with words."

"That's okay," I say.

"Really I just want to say I'm glad you're back. If you get bored, maybe we can do something together. Bowling or movies, whatever you want."

"Um, I'd like that," I say politely. Yeah, right.

He wants sex. He's gone without for a few weeks and now he's sex starved. I'm a likely candidate as he has been down my road before. Okay, I have so been hanging out with Oliver too much to have actually thought that last statement.

His face lights up. "I'll call you then."

"You know the number." With another cordial smile, I escape inside before he can say another word. Carlos runs up to me, eyes wide from excitement and too much sugar. "Hi."

"I want—I want to show you my video game!" he says, bouncing up and down like a rabbit. He grabs my hand, leading me into the bedroom he shares with Manny. A group of kids sit on the two beds and floor. Manny and Javi's niece Tina swing their arms back and forth with white controllers as Mario and Princess Toadstool play tennis on the screen. Oliver and I play this game all the time. He kicks my butt with his super-reflexes but we still laugh our butts off. I almost bust a gut when we play *Just Dance*. And—

Crud. A low wave of sadness ripples through my stomach, giving me pause. I miss him. Not even forty-eight hours, and I miss him.

"Aunt Bea," Flora says as she jumps off the bed. "I love you." Those stick arms wrap around my waist, squeezing out the bad feelings. "Manny won't let me play!"

"This game isn't for babies!" Manny says with a sneer. He swings again but not in time. Tina whoops and smiles at her opponent.

"I want to play next!" Carlos whines.

"No way," Manny says.

"I'm gonna tell Papi," Carlos counters.

"Do it and I'll punch you in the arm!"

"Hey!" I say. "Don't threaten your brother."

With her perfect Mom timing, April walks in carrying two cherry margaritas. She is a woman of her word. Flora darts toward her mother.

"Mami, Mami, Manny won't let us play!"

"Manny, I told you everyone had to take turns. Let someone else play."

"But it's mine!" Manny says in a huff.

"No, it's mine. I paid for it and unless you have two hundred dollars to give me, then that's the way it's gonna stay. Give someone else a turn. Now!"

"I hate you!" Manny tosses the controller down and storms out. Without missing a beat, Carlos scoops it up and starts swinging.

69

"Miss Kansas yet?" April asks.

I just smile.

She kisses Flora's hair, hands me a margarita, and looks back at the kids. "You guys behave."

I follow her out into the hallway, then into the master bedroom. She shuts then locks the door. Like the rest of the house nothing matches in here. IKEA and Wal-Mart furniture fill the small space. I sit on the bed, sipping my sweet drink. You can barely taste the tequila, just the way I like it.

"Okay, so what did he say?" April asks as she sits down.

I tell her almost word for word.

"I knew it! He's still totally in love with you." She sighs. "Man, I am so jealous. Now there are three men who want you."

"And now you know how I felt in high school when the tables were turned."

"So if he calls, are you going to go?"

"I don't know."

"Well, just don't lead him on."

"Of course not."

My cell phone buzzes again. I roll my eyes, but April looks at the purse. "You getting that?"

"No. It's just Oliver trying to drive me nuts. I'm not speaking to him right now."

She raises an eyebrow. "Really?" Before I can stop her, she reaches across for my purse.

"Hey!" I shout.

With a wicked grin on her face, she grabs the phone. "Bea Alexander's phone. April Diego speaking."

"Hang up!" I whisper. I attempt to snatch the phone back. April stands up, still grinning.

"Well, hello," she purrs. "It's nice to finally talk to you. I've heard so much."

I mouth, "Hang up," but she shakes her head and starts walking back and forth listening. "No, nothing like that," she assures him then pauses to listen. "Well, I did hear *that*," she says seductively. I glare, but she smiles at me. "Let's just say if I wasn't married..." She throws her head back laughing. "You are a naughty boy."

I mouth, "What the heck is he saying?"

She winks and continues listening. "Well, I could do that, I suppose, but she seems a little mad at you right now." She listens. "No, right now she's outside madly flirting with her ex-boyfriend." She pauses. "That's the one. They look *so* cute together slow dancing out there. I'll tell her you called, I promise. Have a nice night. Bye."

She flips the phone shut and starts cackling like a madwoman. "Oh my God," she continues, "you totally have to have sex with that man!"

I snatch the phone back, scowling. "Jerk!"

Still cackling, she sits next to me on the bed. "You didn't tell me he's British!"

"He hasn't lived there for years." About three hundred to be exact. "Why did you tell him that stuff about Steven?"

"Duh! To make him jealous, brainiac. It so worked. He got all quiet then said, 'the police officer?' like he wanted to punch him or something. He is so hot for your body."

"So everyone tells me, including him."

"Well, I know sex with Steven wasn't so great, and you didn't like it so much, but I'd bet my kids' college funds that man could get you to change your mind."

"Never happening."

She takes a sip of her margarita, looking over the rim, and her eyes can't contain her desire to keep talking. The dam breaks a second later. "But you really, really, *really* could use it. And here's this hot guy like aching for you and you're just like, 'No. Whatever.' That's beyond wrong. You're only young once and a mind-blowing orgasm is a life experience you need. And—"

"April!" I say. "Shut up! I am not sleeping with him. Not now. Not ever."

She calms down a little and pouts. "I just want you to be happy."

"Well, you know what would make me happy?" I stand up. "A hot dog. I'm starving, and you're neglecting your guests. Let's get back out there, okay?"

She sighs. "Fine, but this conversation is not over."

"Yes, it is. Come on." I unlock the door and open it for her. April gets up and we walk out together. She hasn't liked Will since the whole war began. She won't give up until I'm spread eagle on Oliver's bed.

She stops dead at the end of the hallway and spins around. "There's something you're not telling me," she says. "I can feel it, and I don't like it. You've never done that before. You can tell me anything, you know?"

"I know," I say. I pull her into a hug. "I know."

I just don't know how to make her understand. Not without telling her everything. About my first case. About Dallas. About what Oliver really is. About how close we really are. And really, how can I make her understand about us when even I don't?

FIVE

YOU CAN'T GO HOME AGAIN

THE NEXT THREE DAYS roll by with ease. I sleep in, I watch a lot of TV, and I eat. My ideal vacation. I play the good granddaughter, taking Nana out to lunch and a spa one day. I play the good godmother, accompanying the Diego family to Legoland. I play the good best friend, baby-sitting the kids while April and Javi go out for their first date in months. It's amazing how easily I fall back into my old life.

The mansion leaves me alone. I receive no e-mails, no texts, nothing. Radio silence. For all I know they're in Hawaii on a case involving a lava monster or doing exactly what I am, enjoying some downtime. Either way they only invade my thoughts in passing, no more aches or mental deconstructions. Even April has dropped the subject, though I can tell she's just biding her time.

I flip the radio station from Coldplay to Christmas music, getting me in the mood for one of my favorite activities of the year: Christmas shopping. I adore shopping, but as much as I enjoy shopping for myself, I like shopping for others more. I just love the look on their faces when they unwrap the gift and see that you know them. That you love them. It's worth fighting the crowds at the mall.

April invited me shopping with her. Great thing having a friend with a ten-percent discount since her salon is in the mall. I let her share mine when I worked at Hot Dog on a Stick in high school, and she returns the favor now. I park on the top level, lucky to get a spot there. The only gift I have at present is a Mexican cruise for Nana and Mrs. R.: five nights in a two-room suite, option for a full spa day. This will make up for all the towels and picture frames they've gotten over the years.

I have no clue what to get everyone else. Heck, I don't even know who I'm buying for. I mean, do I get the FBI agents something? The only one I sort of know is Agent Wolfe and my extent of knowledge on him is he loves golf and Lynyrd Skynyrd. I should probably get the others something too. Coffee mugs, maybe. They do like their coffee. George, Nancy, and the others I'll just look around. Something will strike me. Shopping is where I shine.

April waits outside Macy's in black trousers and T-shirt, scanning the crowd for me. I've dressed down today with my hair in a ponytail, comfortable black jeans, and black Wonder Woman graphic girl T-shirt. I gave up the rich stuff when Flora puked on my cashmere sweater at Legoland. Two hundred bucks in the trash. Corn dog, ketchup, and milkshake do *not* come out.

"Hey!" April says as I walk up. "This place is nuts, even for a Saturday! I've had back-to-back clients all day."

"Sure you're up for shopping?" I ask.

"The day I'm not is the day I jump off the Coronado."

We stroll into a department store where harried men and women dash back and forth in search of the perfect gift. The lines at the registers are five deep, with every other person bouncing up and down in frustration at the wait. A tall man in a business suit holding lingerie sighs and rolls his eyes as we pass. I'll never understand why this time of year brings out the worst in people.

April leads me to the women's section and starts browsing. "I saw this top I think Gabi would like. Here it is." She holds up an orange and black blouse.

"Looks fine," I say with a shrug.

"I hate Christmas," April says. "I should just get everyone gift cards or something. What do you want this year?"

"A gift card sounds great. To Barnes & Noble."

April stops browsing. "I can't get *you* a gift card," she says, putting her hand on her hip. "That goes against the best friend code! I'm supposed to get you the perfect gift, something that you need! That shows I know you!"

"April, last year you got me sneakers."

"Which you totally needed!" Her jaw sets. "You don't understand, okay? The other day I totally realized that . . . you have this whole new life. New state, new job, new friends, even a new look! You're all confident and secretive. I don't feel like a part of this new you. I want to contribute *something* to this new you, something that when you look at it you can say, 'There's April, she's here with me.' You know?"

"I had no idea you felt this way," I say, "but you're wrong. I haven't changed. I'm still me. Insecure, nerdy, all of it."

She can't meet my eyes. "You're not."

I touch her arm. "April, *you* are my best friend. If I move to the moon, we'll still be best friends. That will never change, no matter what, okay?" I wrap my arms around her and she rests her head on my shoulder, hugging me back.

"God, I'm sorry. I'm PMSing hard core right now." She pulls away. "Javi forgot to put the lid on the trash can this morning, and I screamed at him. I should be quarantined."

"It's okay. I threw an orange at Oliver last month when he made a rude comment about my shoes."

April wipes the moisture from under her eyes. "Ugh. I can't believe I ruined happy shopping time."

"It's okay," I say, taking her arm. "It takes more than hormones to ruin happy shopping time. Unless you have a nuclear weapon."

We browse more, finding nothing before going downstairs to the men's department. It's even busier than the women's. April beelines for a display of flannel shirts, picking out a blue and white one. "Javi will love this."

I walk to a nearby rack and pluck a short-sleeved black and white striped sailor cashmere sweater. It screams Oliver. One down.

"Who's that for?" April asks.

"Oliver."

"Clothes, huh?" she asks with a raised eyebrow.

"I'm not buying him underwear."

I select a tie for George, a light blue and white checkered dress shirt for Carl, for Andrew a new pair of sunglasses, and Will a royal blue fleece sweatshirt. It's soft like I bet his hair is. Hope he likes it. I'm on a roll, but almost gasp when it's totaled. April's discount is a blessing.

Her lunch break is almost up, so we make our way back to the salon. I stop at Hot Topic with its fake stone wall and blaring heavy metal. "Mind if we go in here?"

She shrugs and follows me in. The tiny shop is so packed I barely get in the door. Teenagers with holes in their ears big enough to fit pencils though and rainbow-colored hair are everywhere. I wiggle my way to the girl's side where I search through the piles for an *Edward Scissorhands* shirts. Nancy is madly in love with Johnny Depp, so she should love this.

"I'm sorry, but we've been out of high school how long?" April asks.

"Eight years. Why?"

"How could teenagers have changed so much in that time? When did dressing like a corpse and putting holes everywhere become cool? If someone came to our school dressed like this, they would have had their ass kicked."

"The times they are a'changin,'" I say with a smirk. I locate the shirt and push my way to the jewelry section. A pasty, thin to the point of death girl with a skull nose ring, tight black pants, and tie-dyed shirt gazes at me as I reach the necklaces. Her eyes immediately jut to the scar on my neck.

"Who are you buying for here?" April asks.

"Nancy, our intern."

"The one who hates you?"

"Yeah. Can't hurt, right?" I select a necklace with a set of silver vampire fangs on it. I get three: for me, Nancy, and Oliver. He'll get a kick out of it. The strange girl keeps those eyes on me, so I meet her eyes with a smile.

"I think I know you," she says, voice hazy. The poor gal looks ready to fall over.

"I'm sorry?" I ask.

"Don't you belong to Brady?" She points to my scar. "Did he do that to you?"

Oh nuts. I must have left my powers of observation back in Kansas. I take in the bruises on her wrists nearly concealed by bracelets along with the fading one on her neck. She's a companion, or as I like to think of them, walking Happy Meals for vampires. Messed up individuals who let bloodsuckers feed on them every night.

My heart skips a beat, but I don't let it show. I smile graciously at the girl. "I think you've mistaken me for someone else." April stares at the girl as if she's a Martian. "April, let's go." I tug on her shirt and walk toward the long checkout line.

April keeps glancing at the girl. "That was weird," she says.

"Yeah," I say with a sigh.

"Think she's a junkie?" April says with another glance.

She is, I say to myself, *just not the kind you think.* "Looks like one. See all those bruises? Sad." I pause. "Hey, shouldn't you be getting back?"

April checks her watch. "Shit. Yeah. Call me tonight?"

"Of course." We kiss cheeks, and she runs through the crowd like a linebacker. Good. I return my attention to the girl. She stares at the jewelry almost as if she's in a trance. If I had to guess, I'd put her at eighteen, if that. Vamps like them young and docile. Most companions are runaways or outlaws who hang with vamps for about three months before being either killed or discarded with a memory wipe. For those three months the vamps offer them a safe haven, sex with a gorgeous and powerful creature, and—on extremely rare occasions—a chance at immortality. But if what Oliver tells me is true, seven out of ten end up dead.

This girl is on her last legs, and those legs choose this very moment to give out on her. She crumples to the floor as shoppers look on. The girl shakes her head to clear it, but wobbles even on the ground. Crud. I set my stuff on a nearby shelf and rush over to the girl, pulling her up by the armpits. "Come on," I say when she's upright. "Let's get you something to eat."

The teen doesn't protest as I march her out of the store to the food court. We don't say a word as we wait in line, though she keeps glancing at me as if she wants to. I don't want to talk. I'm too busy playing out the rest of her life in my head. Living in the basement, watching TV or sleeping until night comes when the vamp wakes. He feeds, using her whole body for his needs until one night that body gives out. He'll either bury her, cut her up, or toss her in the ocean. The next night he'll pick up a new girl, and the cycle will continue. If she's lucky, and looking at her I doubt it, someone will find her corpse, and maybe I'll be called in to find her murderer. Tragedy.

We reach the fast-food counter. "We'll have two double cheeseburgers, a hamburger, and fries please."

"I don't eat meat anymore," the girl says. "He wants me to be a vegan like he was."

I roll my eyes and look at the cashier. "We'll have Cokes with those." I pay and slide over to where they'll hand us our order. The girl trails me like a lost puppy.

"I can't eat meat," she whispers fearfully.

"You're dangerously anemic. You need iron, and right now these burgers are the closest thing to red meat available." I pick up our tray of grease. "Come on." She follows me to the only free table in sight and sits across from me but will not look up as I hold a burger out to her. "You almost passed out in the middle of the store," I say, not hiding my annoyance. "If I have to force this down your throat, I will. Eat."

Eyes still downward, she takes the burger. "Moon won't like it."

"Well, you tell *Moon* that Special Agent Beatrice Alexander of the F.R.E.A.K.S. told you to do it. And if he has a problem with you taking care of yourself, he can speak with me. I'll sort him out. *Eat.*"

She unwraps the burger and hesitantly takes a bite. Then another bigger bite as I watch. Her eyes all but roll back in ecstasy. Smiling to myself, I start on my burger. I might have just saved this girl's life with the power of fast food. Now this Moon will know he's on my radar and behave himself. A swell of pride washes over me. Having the ability to stop bad guys with a cheeseburger and a few choice words is quite a high.

"Your friend's staring at us," the girl says, bringing me back down to reality.

I spin around in my chair. April stands across the courtyard, her face scrunched in confusion before shaking her head and walking away. Great, another thing I have to explain. Having lunch with a junkie. I shut my eyes and sigh. She was right. I have changed. Old Bea would ignore this girl and her problems. She'd look down on her, not feed her. Shame on her.

"Thank you," the girl says quietly.

I open my eyes and smile at her. "You're welcome."

———

An unfamiliar silver Mercedes rests in my parking spot in the drive-way. It takes me all of a second to figure out who it belongs to. My shopping and good deed high crashes down to the core of the earth where Morlocks will feast on it. I was really hoping he'd find some excuse to skip his weekly trip down, but I'm never that lucky. I park at the curb, shut off the car, and thunk my head on the steering wheel. The last time I saw Brian was five months ago. We managed civility for about three minutes and then got into a screaming match on the sidewalks of Wichita. Time for Round Two.

"Let's get this over with," I say to myself.

After collecting all my bags from the trunk, I walk into the house, scanning the living room for possible bogies, like angry older brothers, and step in. Nobody in sight. My high anxiety lowers from threat level red to orange as I shut the door. Maybe they went for a walk. Or aliens abducted them to save me. Nope. The toilet flushes down the hall. I suppose I could make a dash to the front door and just drive around for a few hours. Or I can—

Brian saunters into the living room before I can implement my plan. My brother is a handsome man. Medium build in his white Polo shirt and pressed chinos. His dark brown hair is parted to the left with nary a stray strand sticking up. We look nothing alike. We both have Mom's light brown eyes, but he got more of her with his height and nose. I take after Nana and my sperm donor, whoever that was.

Brian seems calm when he sets eyes on me. No anger, no nervousness, but also no cheer, as if I'm a useless stranger. Sadly, I'll take it. Better than the usual rancor.

"Hi," I say.

"Hello," he responds in a reserved tone.

So far, so good. He hasn't leapt across the room and tried to strangle me. "Did you have a nice drive down?" I ask for lack of something better.

"Fine," Brian says. "Mark slept the whole time."

"Good."

And then we stare at each other for a few seconds, not sure where to go from here. His eyes dart toward the back door, obviously wanting to escape. Ten seconds, that's his limit. Longer than I anticipated. "I'm going to ... " he nods toward the door.

"Okay, I'm going to ... " I hold up my bags.

He makes a break for the door, and me for my bedroom. I shut my door, but the sound of laughter glides through the open window. "Who were you talking to?" Nana asks through her laughs.

"Bea's back," Brian answers in the vocal equivalent of a poker face.

"She's here?" a woman who I assume is my newish sister-in-law, Renata, asks.

They've been together for close to five years, and I've met her three times. Each conversation lasted about two minutes with the usual stranger chitchat: weather, jobs, and traffic. She was perfectly pleasant but distant. God knows what he's told her about me.

As I set the bags on my bed, Nana steps up to my window, looking in through the screen. "Come outside and meet your nephew."

"I just got home," I say, "give me a minute."

I need to find my emotional suit of armor and slap it on. I also need to lock away my sarcastic side in a lead box so as not to peeve off Brian in front of his new family. He'll be on his best behavior, so I will return the favor. Though I may mention that time when he was seven and made a doody in the pool. It *is* my God-given right as his sister to embarrass him. It's the normal thing to do.

I brush my hair, re-apply lipstick and deodorant, and join the family. The three and a half of them sit around the circular green plastic table and chairs underneath the metal awning. Nana's back yard is tiny with a square piece of concrete and grass everywhere else. It's perfect for a dog and Brian asked for one every day for a month when we first moved here, but animals don't like me. I come within two feet of one and they go nuts. Either barking, hissing, running away, or the occasional alpha male will try to attack me. It never bothered me until I fell for a werewolf. The fact I literally make his skin prickle and crawl does not bode well for our future. We were doomed from the start.

Renata is one of those perfect people who are destined for the good life before they're even born. Her father is an Oscar-winning movie producer, so she grew up with the best of everything. Her good looks come from her actress mother. Glossy brown hair, flawless olive skin, wide doe eyes, and even though she just gave birth, she's skinnier than me. I really wish I dressed up today. Women like her always make me feel like a white trash hag with warts.

Nana holds the newest Alexander in her arms, feeding him a bottle. He has his mother's complexion and a thick head of black hair. Another looker. Nana gazes down at him with such love and adoration a huge smile surfaces on my face. I've never seen her so happy.

"Who's a good boy? Who's a good boy?" Nana says in a high pitch sing-song reserved for deranged preschool teachers. The baby seems to like it though. He wiggles and waves his arms as if he's dancing.

"Hi … all," I say.

Renata glimpses up from her progeny to me, her smile never wavering. Brian glances at me, expressionless. "There you are," Nana says. "Did you have fun?"

"Yeah."

"You look really good," Renata says.

"Thank you. So do you."

"God no! I'm a fat slob," she chuckles. I guess zooming up from size zero to a size four means it's lipo time.

"You're beautiful," Brian says to her. He reaches over to her and kisses her hand. Their eyes meet and you can practically see the love and adoration pouring out of them like Superman's lasers. An invisible someone by the name of envy punches me in the gut, though my smile doesn't waver. I don't think I can do this right now, looking on as my perfect brother lives his perfect life. I save people, and he finds loopholes to earn millionaires more millions. He makes my life hell for years and gets a beautiful wife and baby. I'm stuck lusting after two mythical creatures. I don't know, maybe a person like me who can do what I can isn't meant for this. Maybe I'm just meant to stand on the sidelines protecting those who can have it all. Karma is such a lie.

"Yeah, I never would have guessed you'd just had a baby," I say.

"Beatrice, come sit down," Nana says, shifting the baby to her left arm. "You look like you're about to flee."

"Actually I have—"

"*Beatrice*," Nana says with an undercurrent of anger, "sit down."

Ugh. I take the seat between Nana and Brian. Noticeable to only me, because I'm looking for it, Brian shifts in his chair as far from me as possible.

"So, do you like your new job?" Renata asks.

"It's okay. Lotta travel and paperwork, but it's fulfilling."

"Well, I'm so sorry you couldn't make it to the wedding. I know it was short notice and all, but we would have loved to have had you there."

"Huh?" I ask.

Brian smiles. "You were in Atlanta then, right?" He meets my eyes, not exactly pleading, more like threatening me to keep up his lie.

No, I wasn't invited to my only brother's wedding. I didn't even know about it until weeks after the fact. Heck, if I hadn't flown home, the first time I'd ever get to meet my nephew would probably be at his high school graduation. Now, I could totally blow him out of the water, and *boy* would it feel good, but then we'd get into a fight. He'd storm out and Nana wouldn't get quality baby time. Being good totally sucks sometimes.

"No, I think it was Seattle," I say. "I am really sorry I missed it."

"It's perfectly alright," Brian says. "We understood."

I want to roll my eyes but stop myself.

"He is such a good baby," Nana tells them. "How often does he wake up in the night?"

"Twice," Renata says. Then all of a sudden she entwines her fingers and presses her hands to her chest, tearing up. "We are so blessed."

This time I don't suppress the eye roll.

"We really are," Brian says.

Two flawless teardrops roll down Renata's cheeks. She stands up, embarrassed by this outpouring of emotion. "Excuse me," she says before disappearing into the house.

"Is she okay?" I ask.

"Hormones," Brian says.

"Give it a few weeks," Nana says. "She'll be fine."

Without the need to act as if we're a normal functioning family for Renata, the three of us sit in uncomfortable silence. I'm starting to think *comfortable* silences are a myth. Brian's foot shakes, Nana glances back and forth at us, and I pretend to find the concrete fascinating. The last time the three of us were together, Brian wound up in the hospital and I fled the state. We have now entered Awkward City.

Brian takes it upon himself to fix the situation. "Is Kansas cold this time of year?"

"It *is* winter," I say with a fake smile. "Though it's not as bad as Atlanta, or was it Seattle, in the summer?" First blood is mine.

His jaw sets. "I had to tell her something."

"Or you could have, I don't know, invited me?"

"And risk you killing one of the guests because they ate the last shrimp? I don't think so."

"Stop it!" Nana says. "Both of you. You'll upset the baby."

He looks fine sucking on the bottle with his eyes closed.

"*You* could have told me," I say to Nana.

"Brian wanted to be the one to do it," she says. "And I am done being in the middle of you two. You were both wrong, but it's over. It's time to move on."

"She tried to kill me!"

"It was an accident!"

"It is time to move on," Nana hisses in a low whisper. "We are a family. We are all we have! I want us to act like it, for God's sake!" Now she's on the verge of tears. Brian and I actually unite in our shock and empathy with both our mouths opening and eyes growing wide. Great, we've made Nana sad at Christmas. We suck.

"I'm sorry," I say.

"Don't apologize to me," she says, fighting back tears. "Apologize to each other."

I gaze at Brian, and he at me. We exchange a look that says, "I'm game if you are," though he'll fake the sincerity. "I'm sorry I almost killed you," I say. "Accidently." And I am. It's haunted me for months.

"And I'm sorry I called you all those horrible names."

I want to say "what about the wedding and all those years of acting like a jerk," but restrain myself.

"Okay, then," Nana says. "Brian, I'm going to hand Mark to your sister. Is that alright?"

The flash of panic I feel from him doesn't show. "It's fine."

"Don't worry," I say, "I've held more babies than you."

Nana passes the tiny infant into my cradling arms. God, I love babies. He smells like baby powder with a hint of flowers. He's so light and fragile in my arms. His eyes open and I see my own staring up at me. His face hasn't unsmooched from his journey into life, but he's still cute. A lightness fills me as I run my finger down his soft cheek. I smile. "Hello, Mark. I'm your Aunt Bea."

"He really likes you," Nana says with pride.

"Good taste in women already, huh?" I say to him. "What's his full name?"

"Marcus Stellan Alexander," Brian says.

"I like it. A strong name, like a Roman emperor or something."

"He looks so much like your mother as a baby," Nana says.

"Yeah," Brian says quietly. He runs his hand over Mark's hair.

The baby opens his balled fist and grips my index finger like a champ. I lean down and kiss his forehead. "You are really lucky, Brian."

"I know."

"No. You don't," I say sadly. I look over at my brother. "You really don't."

And for an instant, one instant, my brother's eyes brim with sympathy and even a little love for me. But only an instant. Renata walks back out with a bottle in hand. "Sorry about that. I had to pump."

"TMI, sister-in-law," I say. "TMI."

Renata stops beside me, gazing down at us. "Oh! He likes you!"

"No accounting for taste, huh?" I ask with a smile.

She grins and takes her seat next to her husband. "So what about you, Bea? Caught the baby bug yet?"

What a loaded question. Ever since I was a kid I knew only one thing: I wanted a family. I'd pretend my dolls were my children: feeding them, changing them, telling them stories as I put them in their cradles. I drove April nuts. She wanted to play space warrior princess, and I just wanted to play house. She and I got married about a hundred times with me acting as the mother as she went out to punch aliens and save the world. Odd how real life turns out.

"My biological clock was wound up in my teens," I tell Renata. "I want babies more than anything."

"Any potential fathers in your orbit?" she asks with a huge grin.

I hate the blissful. It's like they're in a cult or something and want you to join no matter what. They won't leave you alone until you're the same as them. As if it's so easy. "No, I'm not seeing anyone."

"No possibles even?" she asks.

"Maybe one or two."

I have on more than several occasions imagined the life of Mr. and Mrs. Will and Beatrice Price, complete with children. They'd have his eyes, hair, and strength but my sense of humor and patience. Two boys and a girl I think. We'd live near here, maybe Chula Vista, so I can be close to April and Nana. The kids would play together in our back yard as April and I gossiped. Will would call from work every day just to tell us how much he loves us all. Then he'd return home and help with the kid's homework while I made dinner and watched my family. He'd never get frustrated with them no matter how many times they asked the same question. We'd go to their events like baseball and ballet, watching proudly in the audience as we held hands. At night we'd take turns singing and reading them to sleep, then retire to our bedroom exhausted but blissful. I'd fall asleep in his strong arms with a smile on my face. A simple life. Not too much to ask for, right?

And when he's not being an annoying jerk, I have found myself wondering what Oliver would be like as a father and husband. Fun for sure. But also loving and protective. I could see him holding the children for hours as they cry. I know this because he's done this for me on more than one occasion. Our children would want for nothing, not attention or security or love. He'd tuck them in and tell them tales of all his adventures, though he'd make them G rated. Of course in this fantasy he has a pulse, so I know it's never to be.

He'd make a fantastic father though, and it saddens me to the core that he can never be one again. He loves children. When we go out, if there are any there, he'll wave and smile, even make silly faces. One night when we were watching a father and daughter skate around the roller rink he mentioned—in passing, as if it was nothing—that he had children before he was turned. A boy and girl. I was floored, had a billion questions, but he changed the subject before I could ask even one. I didn't press, and he hasn't brought it up since. I'll get the story out of him someday.

"Then go for it," Renata says. "It's the most fulfilling thing in the world."

"Someday," I say. Please God, someday. The telephone rings inside, and I all but jump up. I have to get out of here before I tear up. "I'll get it."

I hand Mark to Brian, rushing inside. Thank God, I can breathe again. Talking about that stuff always makes me near suicidal. I think there's a huge part of me that believes it'll never happen. I can and have killed people with a thought. If I can even find a well-adjusted male who can accept that, do I want to pass this trait onto some innocent person? I'm not normal, so what makes me think I can have a normal life? Especially now. My life is steeped in violence and death, and my only potential mates are a living dead guy who can't have children and a werewolf. Even if a miracle happened and Will and I found a way to be together, our children would be psychokinetic werewolves. How would we even begin to deal with that? Their teenage years would be unbearable. Even more so than normal.

I pick up the phone. "Hello?" I ask.

"Bea? It's Steven."

Steven. Nice, boring, reliable Steven, who provided me with the closest thing to an ordinary relationship I've ever and probably will ever have. If I hadn't broken up with him we could have been married by now, maybe with a baby of our own on the way. I think for the first time ever, I regret breaking up with him. Didn't think that would ever happen.

"Hi, Steven. How are you?"

"Fine. Great," he says, sounding surprised for some reason. "You?"

"Brian's here with his new wife and son."

"How's that going?" Steven knows about the strain but not the cause.

"Better than expected."

"Oh," he says, the cheer draining from his voice. "Then I guess you don't want to go bowling."

"Bowling?"

"Yeah, some of us are getting together and meeting down at the lanes. I thought you might like to come. Maybe get dinner after."

If I didn't know better I'd swear I was just asked out on a date. That hasn't happened in months. The last guy who asked me out I met on a case. Joe West, former quarterback with a great smile and even better mother who helped me on the Dallas case. If all heck hadn't broken loose I would have accepted, but things like that never work out for me. At least I got an e-mail buddy in Anna West.

As for Steven's proposal, it's not as if I have anything better to do. God knows I don't want to stick around here much longer. It's only a matter of time before the truce is broken and we're attacking each other like pit bulls. And I doubt Steven would make a move on me, that is unless I gave him permission. Of course that opens up a whole other can of worms.

A nice, boring, normal date with a nice, boring, normal man. "You know what? I would love to."

"Really?"

"Absolutely. But just so you know, I've gotten a lot better since we last played together. I might just beat you for once."

"Bea, if you can break a hundred, I'll buy all your drinks for the night," he chuckles.

"Then bring *lots* of cash."

"We're meeting at six. Remember the place?"

"Considering a quarter of all our dates were there, yeah, I remember where it is."

"Can't wait to see you," he says casually.

"Bye." I hang up. Huh. For the first time in over a year, I have a date. Kind of. Sort of. Sure, it's with my ex at a bowling alley with other people, but my ego will take it.

I meander back outside, plastering a huge grin on my face. I have to sell this if I want out of here with minimal guilt and fuss. Nana holds the baby with the adoring parents watching in awe as the baby suckles his pacifier. You'd think he was splitting the atom or something.

"Who was on the phone?" Nana asks.

"Guys, I am *so* sorry, but I forgot I was supposed to meet Steven in half an hour."

"Your ex-boyfriend?" Brian asks.

"Yeah. We made plans a few days ago, and it completely slipped my mind. This is the only day he has off all this week."

Brian and Renata exchange a look that screams, "What a flake," but I don't care. If I have to spend another minute with The Blissfuls I'll either cry, scream, or puke. Nana doesn't hide her disappointment, her brow furrowing. "Bea, you knew Brian was coming over this evening."

"I know but … " I smile to myself and look down like a demure virgin faced with a naked man, "I really want to see him again."

Okay, I know I'm laying it on a bit thick, but lying is the only way to get out of here without a huge lecture or looks of disapproval for the next few days. She loves Steven, and I'm gambling on the fact she'd like to see us together again.

I believe I'm right because the folds in her forehead disappear. "Fine."

My smile widens. "Thanks." I glance at Brian, raising an eyebrow to let him in on what's really happening. Hope he realizes this is his Christmas present. "You don't mind, right?"

"Of course not," he says. "It was good to see you again, however briefly."

"Lovely to see you again, Renata. See you guys at Christmas!" I say, practically leaping through the open door back inside. My smile doesn't fade until I shut my bedroom door and a wave of desolation rolls through me strong enough I ball my hands into fists.

I don't belong out there. That's my family, my people, and I'm an interloper. A stranger. I should stay. I should *want* to stay, and they should want me to. That's my nephew and sister-in-law, both of whom I barely know. New family to learn about and share stories with. But they don't care, and I guess I shouldn't either. And it's not even that I moved away, that I've missed months of inside jokes and stories. Even if I had stayed, things wouldn't have been different. Brian still wouldn't want me around, Nana would still be worried about me. Little more than an annoyance, me. They're a puzzle, and I'm just a stray piece that ended up in the wrong box. I'll either be thrown out or left alone. Incomplete.

April was right. I have changed. I don't fit anymore, if I ever did.

Don't fit in here, don't really fit in there. Where do I?

SIX

THE NOT-A-DATE DATE

THE PREMIERE LANES IN Chula Vista is not the sort of place you expect to be packed all the time, what with the dingy walls, cracked Day-Glo benches, computers from the dark ages, and smoky odor that will never leave even after years of anti-smoking laws in California, but it is. The shoes are revolting, the lanes scuffed, and the food so greasy you can barely hold onto it. This is where I spent countless hours watching my boyfriend toss a ball down a wooden plank. What can I say? I was quite desperate to get out of the house tonight.

The first familiar face I spot is Leslie Erdman, all six feet of her. The woman is huge in every way: height, weight, face, even laugh. She's not fat, just thick. Her brown hair barely reaches her shoulders and per usual she wears no makeup. She doesn't notice me as she walks out of the bar with two Bud Lites. I follow a short distance behind her toward the group.

All the regulars are there already decked out in their bowling shoes. Jawan Epps, former front tackle at USC, current Narcotics detective at Chula Vista PD, takes up two chairs. He has more muscles than I remember bulging out of his white shirt. He makes room as Leslie takes a seat. She hands him a beer, and he kisses her cheek. Guess they're together now. Mel Daly sits next to Steven across from the couple. He's about thirty with a shiny bald head and nondescript face. Though he's Leslie's partner, they never seem to talk at these gatherings. Sick of each other, I suppose. Steven's dressed up tonight, at least for him, with a white Izod golf shirt that I'm pretty sure I bought him and blue jeans. He says something to Mel after taking a long sip of his Corona.

Leaning over the top of the chairs on the other side, Kristen Winger eavesdrops on their conversation. I was kind of hoping she wouldn't be here tonight. She has never liked me, not one whit. I hooked up with Steven a week after he went on one date with her. He chose me, and she's never forgiven me for it. Why he picked me over her is a mystery. She's far prettier with a slender body, lustrous long brown hair, and big blue eyes. He said something about no chemistry. She's on patrol too, but sometimes works for Vice if they need a decoy hooker. That's how Detective Nick McEwan of Vice joined the group. Skinny, handsome with black Irish looks and cocky smile. The only remnant of his Navy days is the military haircut. Him I know the least. I had a tiny crush on him, so I barely spoke to him.

Finally, rounding out the crew, is Artie Rupp, who stands at the ball rack polishing his custom black ball with swirling flames. He looks—in fact, they all look—fantastic. He's lost his spare tire and some change and even his usually yellowish pallor is vibrant with life. Nick too. The flecks of gray in his hair have vanished. Kristen appears as if she's had work done in the face and boob area. That or they're pumping water from the Fountain of Youth into the Chula Vista water supply.

Artie is the first to notice me. "Holy fucking shit! Look what the cat dragged in. A hot piece of ass if there ever was one!"

All eyes swivel to me. Thank goodness I changed clothes before I came. I went trendy with skinny black jeans, off the shoulder green and black striped shirt, matching sneakers, green headband, high ponytail, and vest leather jacket. The men, especially Nick, drink me in while the women can't believe what they see. Kristen's eyes actually narrow. Yes, you are no longer the pretty one. Ha ha.

"Nice to see you too, Artie," I say graciously.

Steven walks over to me. "I wasn't sure you were coming."

"I know. I'm sorry I'm late. I lost track of time at the bookstore." I wave at my audience. "Hello, everyone."

"Bea," Leslie says with a nod.

"Let's get you some shoes and a beer," Steven offers. Lightly, he touches my back to herd me away. I don't shrink away. "Be right back."

He lowers his hand as we stroll to the shoe counter where we're third in line between two groups of teenagers. "I am sorry I'm late," I say. "You know me and bookstores."

"Did you get anything good?"

"No. I pretty much have everything I want. I just needed someplace to go. I couldn't stay in that house with Brian around."

"What happened?"

"Nothing. He was just there with the new wife and baby. I didn't want to ruin things for Nana."

"I never got why he was such an asshole to you," he says, sipping his beer. "I wanted to kick his ass that one time at Nana Liz's birthday party. All those little digs at you."

"Well, there were no problems today. I don't know, maybe fatherhood is mellowing him."

The first batch of teens walks off with their shoes so we move up. "You look nice tonight," Steven says. "Not that you didn't always before."

"Thanks. I have a friend who's big into fashion. He's made me into something of a project."

"Good. I'm glad you have friends there."

Now comes an awkward silence lasting three seconds as I stare at the kids in front of us and he drinks.

"Speaking of friends," I finally say, "do yours mind that I'm here?"

"No, not really. Surprised maybe."

"Well, thank you for inviting me. Otherwise I'd be suffering though Brian and Renata making goo-goo eyes at each other and the baby."

"Glad to be of help."

We step up to the counter, and I order my shoes. Just as I swing my purse to retrieve my wallet, Steven hands the cashier a twenty. "Steven, you don't have to—"

"I invited you," he says. "My treat."

"Then I'm buying the next round of drinks."

"I doubt anyone will object to that."

Jawan lines up his next shot when we return. Mel scoots to the end of the cracked bench so Steven and I can sit beside one other. Steven drapes his arm across the back of my seat, and once again I don't object. The others pretend not to notice.

"So, you're living in Kansas, huh?" Nick asks.

"Wichita," I say.

"Must be a magical place," Artie says. "You look hot. And rich."

"Artie," Steven warns.

I finish tying my shoe and sit up. "Thank you."

"How rich are you?" Kristen asks with a quick sneer.

"Rich enough."

"Shit, Steve, don't let her get away again," Artie says with a swig of his beer. "Try knocking her up this time."

"Jesus fucking Christ, Artie!" Steven shouts. In all the years I've known him he's never raised his voice like that. "Shut the fuck up! My God!"

Artie holds up his hands. "Hey, chill partner. I was just kidding. Bea got the joke, didn't ya babe?"

"I'm laughing on the inside, Artie," I say, glaring.

"See man? Stop being so damn sensitive." He glances at the scoreboard. "Besides, it's your turn."

Steven, still scowling, hands me his beer before stepping toward Artie, almost looming over him. "Watch what you say tonight, man. I am getting fed up with your shit." Steven walks toward the ball rack, shaking his head. All eyes once again fall on me, none too friendly.

"So much for a fun night of bowling," Kristen mutters.

I seem to have gained a new gift. I can make people hate me in a minute flat. I left Kansas to avoid exactly this, yet here I am dividing a cohesive unit by simply existing. I should just go live in a cave. No, can't do that. No Turner Classic Movies. Only one thing to do.

A waitress walks by, and I wave her over. "Hi, can I get three Coronas, three Bud Lites, a Dos Equis, and what do you like Kristen? I forgot."

Kristen is taken aback by my grand gesture. "Um, Corona."

"Corona, of course. So four Coronas, and you got the rest." I whip out my Platinum card. "Thank you."

"Thank *you*," Mel says.

"No prob."

"Yeah, you keep buying us drinks we *might* just forgive you for dumping Steven," says Artie.

I gulp Steven's beer. "I live for the day, Artie."

On his second shot Steven makes a 7-10 split. "Yes!" he shouts. We all applaud at this feat. "Good job!" I call as he struts back over.

"Lucky shot," Jawan says.

Steven falls back into his seat and once again stretches his arm over my seat. "Talent man. Pure talent."

I hand him back the beer. "I think you cheated," I say, mock smugly.

"Oh do you?" Steven asks in amusement. "And how exactly did I accomplish that?"

"Why, magic of course. It's the only explanation."

A sharp stab of someone's nervousness hits me, but I'm not sure whose it is. It's gone as fast as lightning. Steven smiles. "You got me."

Kristen's eye roll can be seen to Los Angeles. "Excuse me, I have to bowl now." She stands, rolls those blue eyes again, and picks up her ball.

"We each have a frame left then we'll add you," Steven tells me.

"Okay."

"Babe!" Artie shouts out of nowhere.

All eyes follow his to a middle-aged woman with teased platinum hair, skin the color of a deer's from too much sun, and hot pink tank top over jeans carrying a full tray of beers. I remember her from many a night here. Wanda, who always called me Cutie.

"I saw all these beers and knew they were yours," she says in a dusky smoker's voice. She smiles at me as she passes. "And I thought I recognized the name on the card. Hi, Cutie." She hands everyone their beers, which just goes to show they come here way too often.

"Hi, Wanda," I say taking my beer.

She sets the now empty tray on the table and whips out my card and bill, which I sign. "Almost didn't recognize you. Been a long time."

"Come on, babe," Artie says, pulling her into his lap. At first he kisses her chastely, then again. The third time they give each other a full oral exam. Some look away, Nick chuckles, but Steven and I glance at each other, both discomforted.

Nobody notices as Kristen strolls back over. "Oh for fuck's sake!" she says. "If this is turning into couple's night, I'm gone."

Artie and Wanda break apart, not at all shamed by their PDA. Nick reaches up to Kristen. "Hey, you can be with Mel and me. We can take turns. Or go all at once."

Kristen scoffs. "I'm not doing *that* again," she says in a way that I can't tell if she's joking or not. Nobody's expression gives away the answer either. "Leslie, it's your turn."

Leslie retrieves her ball and bowls.

"So, whatcha been up to, Cutie?" Wanda asks me.

"I moved to Kansas and now set up daycare centers across the country." I've been saying this so much *I* almost believe it.

"Nice. So you're just here for a visit?"

I sip my beer. "Maybe. I haven't really decided yet."

"You're thinking about moving back?" Steven asks in surprise.

"Maybe. Things are complicated there. It might be for the best, I don't know."

"Why?" Steven asks.

"The job. The people. Being away from my family. It's just been ... harder than I thought it would be." And I make everything exponentially worse.

"So you're just giving up?" Kristen asks.

I look her square in the eye. "I haven't decided yet."

"Well, it must be so hard buying plastic balls for kids to play in. Poor you."

"Kristen," Steven warns.

99

"What? Here she is complaining about her cushy job to a group of people who spend all day risking their lives for people like *her*."

"You know nothing about my life."

Her eyes narrow. "Then enlighten us, Countess. What is so horrible about your life? Do *you* wake up every morning not knowing if this is the day some asshole shoots you? Have you had to wait with a decomposing corpse for the paramedics to arrive? Have you had to dress up like a whore and troll the streets for johns? Have you?"

The answer is yes on all fronts, and it takes all my willpower not to add, "Well, have you hacked up an army of zombies with a machete? Have you killed fifteen vampires in one day? Have you slayed a forty-foot snake? No? Then shut up and choke on your beer." But I can't. And that is so freaking unfair I want to scream.

Instead I push her bottle of beer into her lap with my mind. She breaks eye contact as she jumps up. "What the fuck?"

Everyone seems confused and watches as Kristen wipes her jeans with her hands. I take this opportunity to collect my purse and walk away with a little dignity. If I wanted to be abused, I would have stayed home with Brian. At least there I could have played with the baby.

"Shit! Bea, wait!" Steven calls after me, but I don't stop. As I walk, I take off my shoes and toss them on the counter before slipping my own back on. I'm out the door when Steven touches my shoulder. "Hey, stop."

"What?"

"Don't go. Please."

"Well, it's pretty darn obvious that I'm not welcome here, so I'm going home."

"I'm sorry, okay? She just broke up with some asshole and is taking it out on everyone. It's not personal."

"Uh, *yeah*, it is. None of them want me there, and I have no desire to be around them either. This was a stupid idea."

I take a step to leave, but he grabs my arm. "No. Please. Don't go." His eyes plead as strongly as his voice. "Look, let me make this up to you. Let's just skip bowling and go straight to dinner. Just the two of us. We can go to that place on the Wharf you like. My treat. Please?"

I really don't feel like going home yet. And they do have the best ahi in California. "Okay."

"Good. Great. Thanks," he says, almost breathless from excitement. "Let me just tell them I'm leaving."

"Okay."

With a huge grin that makes him appear even more boyish, he rushes back inside to make his excuses. A flutter of apprehension rides into my stomach. We have officially crossed into date territory. I am on a real date now. What if he wants to kiss me? Or have sex? Should I let him? What about Wil—

Steven comes back outside, pulling on his jacket. "Ready?"

"As I'll ever be."

———

We take his car, and to avoid any questions on my part, I barrage him with mine. He always loved talking about himself, so it doesn't take much. Work's going well. He was the first responder on a meth lab fire. He pulled a woman out and received a commendation. That story alone ate up half the ride. The Allison-the-ex story took more prodding. Everything was going well until he formed an actual bowling league with Artie and spent a lot of nights with the team. She accused him of cheating and he broke up with her. Low drama ensued.

"I'm sorry," I say as we pull into the parking spot we're paying ten dollars to inhabit.

He shuts off the Jeep. "It was a sucker punch, you know? The not trusting me thing."

I take off my seat belt and get out. "Well, why didn't you invite her along to the matches?"

"She hated bowling. And Kristen. They had this big blowout a while ago."

We walk almost shoulder to shoulder toward the restaurant. "Why are you even friends with her? She's always so hostile and rude."

"We went to the academy together. Most of the time she's fine. It's just with—"

"You really just need to put her out of her misery," I butt in. "Ask her out or sit her down and tell her you'll never be interested in her. Go on from there. It'll be better for both of you. I know of what I speak."

"Yeah, maybe," he says as if he's actually considering it. I know he's not. When it comes to personal confrontation, he's a scaredy cat. We can recognize our own kind.

He opens the restaurant door for me, and we step in. The hostess seats us in the only available table out on the patio, not that I mind with the crashing waves to my left and paper lanterns above. I'm a little cold but after enduring frostbite when running to my car in Kansas, I can survive it. With the waves, the lanterns, and the flickering candles on the tables this place is very romantic for a not-date. The waitress takes our drink order immediately, beer for him and double rum and Coke for me.

"I haven't been here since your birthday," Steven says, scanning the menu.

"Really?" I keep my eyes on the menu.

"I bet I know what you'll order. Ahi with broccoli," he says.

"Yep," I say, putting the menu down.

"Knew it," he says with pride. "And I'll get the crab."

The waitress returns with our libations and leaves with our order. Alone again. I gaze out at the black ocean and breathe in the sea air. "I've really missed the ocean."

"What, wheat and corn not doing it for you?" I glance at the smirking Steven. "I seriously cannot picture you in Kansas."

"I was given an opportunity I couldn't refuse," I say. "It just happened to be in Kansas."

"But you said you might quit."

I sigh. "Things are just very, very, *very* complicated, and I am sick to death of talking about it." I gulp my drink. "I'm boring. Let's talk about you."

"No, no way," he says, shaking his head. "I think we've covered me. Same job, same apartment, same bad luck with the ladies. Your turn in the hot seat."

Ugh. "Fine. What do you want to know, Officer?" I ask with a smile.

"Tell me about the complicated guy."

I gulp again. "Which one?"

"'Which one'?" he asks with a chuckle. "Huh."

"What?"

"Nothing," he says, falling back in his chair. "I just always assumed you were a one-man woman."

"I am. Or at least I was when we were together, if that's what you're thinking."

"I hope so," he says, sipping his beer.

"And I'm not with either of them. They're just crushes."

103

"Tell me about them."

"Well, Oliver is my best friend there. He's a player but a good guy. We hang out a lot." Kissed once. Saved each other's lives a few times. "Just the usual friend stuff. But he's not boyfriend material." Seeing as how he's dead and has slept with half the world, both male and female.

"And the other one hates him?"

"Yeah. Will." As I say his name an involuntary smile flashes on my face. Steven's eyebrow rises. "They're always butting heads."

"Well, it sounds like a no-win situation," Steven offers, sipping his beer. "I think you have no other option but to move back."

"Though you're not biased or anything," I say mock seriously. My flirting skills have advanced levels by hanging around Oliver. I am now a master at the lip pout/sideways glance I give Steven.

The corners of his mouth perk up. "I'm your ex-boyfriend. If the man whose heart you broke wants you back in the state, that should mean something."

"Oh please. I hardly broke your heart. You were dating Allison within weeks."

"Maybe I hide things well."

"Come on," I scoff.

His expression loses its air of playfulness, growing serious as the smile falters. "I loved you, Bea."

His sadness hits me in the gut. "You never said it."

"Didn't think I had to," he says, looking away. "If I had, would it have mattered?"

I try to think of some way to be delicate but draw a blank. "No."

"So what ... why ... " He shakes his head.

"Why did I break up with you?" I finish for him.

"Yeah." He sits up in his chair and stares at me. "Yeah. What did I do? I thought we had a pretty decent thing going for us. I treated you good. We got along. Just...why?"

I could lie, tell him I got scared about commitment or my feelings for him, but I owe him the truth. I'm lying enough as it is. "There were a million little reasons. You never wanted to do what I did. We had no interests in common. You never defended me to your friends. I mean, take your pick."

"And that's it? I didn't want to sit through a poetry reading or whatever so you dumped me?" he asks, sneering. "You could have, I don't know, said something if it meant so much to you."

"I know," I say, "but then I'd get a guilt trip. Like when *Mamma Mia!* came to town. I got tickets but they were for the same day as the Chargers playoffs. I had already sat through four games, and you refused to do that one thing for me."

"You did *not* break up with me because of that. That was a year before."

"But that's what always happened! And if we moved in together, and later got married, I would have gone nuts." I sigh. "But the real problem was...we weren't friends."

"What? We were dating."

"It's not the same thing. For two years, about three times a week, we'd spend a few hours together, but we never really knew each other. We never talked. *Really* talked."

"How can you say that?" he asks, taking offense.

"What is my favorite book? My first crush? Where did my Mom die? Did you ever ask? Did you even care?"

"You never asked me those things either."

"Because if you didn't care, then why should I?" I shrug. "We had an okay thing going, but I just couldn't envision us spending the rest of our lives together. I just couldn't. And I couldn't be myself around you. There are things about me that if you knew, you'd judge me for them. I have certain... quirks that you just couldn't handle. And I'm not blaming you. Most people can't, but... the man I end up with will. And I *knew* he wasn't you. I'm sorry."

We sit in silence with only the crashing waves and happy clatter of the other couples around us. I don't dare look at him for fear of his reaction. He asked though. Instead, I watch as the black water crashes onto the sand. A duo strolls down the beach with their dog, arms wrapped around each other. If they notice the restaurant patrons just feet away they don't let on. I hate them in this moment.

"You weren't exactly the model girlfriend, you know," Steven says.

"Okay."

"We'd go out, and you'd just sit there. Silent. I could tell you didn't like it. Or my friends. They all thought you were cold. You never talked to them, and for some reason I felt like I had to watch what I said or did around you. Like you *were* judging me. And I'm not a mind reader. How could I have known these things?"

"You could have asked."

"Or, if it was such a big deal, you could have told me."

"It was both our faults," I say.

"So let's start over," he says. "Let's be friends."

"Friends?"

"Yeah." He extends his hand across the table, and I shake it. "Hi. My name is Steven Weir. My favorite movie is *Die Hard*, my favorite food is cheese pizza, and when I was twelve my father left my mother for an ex-Playboy playmate. I haven't spoken to him in years or met my half-sister Sharon. His favorite song was 'Hotel California' so every time I hear it I want to punch someone. I became a police officer because I wanted to help people and be a hero. What about you?"

"Um," I chuckle. "I'm Beatrice Alexander. My favorite movie is *Gone with the Wind*, my favorite food is chocolate cake, and my mother killed herself when we were living in Arizona. My brother blames me for her death and hates me. I was a teacher because I love kids and now set up daycare centers."

"And what's your favorite book?"

"*Jane Eyre*. It's the greatest love story I've ever read."

"Well, I will have to check it out. I'm not much of a reader but if you like it, I will make an effort."

"It's a girl book."

"But if you love it, it must be good."

His smile grows so far across his face the edges could fall off. Mine almost has his beat. This is turning out to be a pretty good not-date.

———

"I can't believe you thought our song was 'I'd Do Anything for Love' by Meatloaf," I say, shaking my head.

"What? It was playing the first time we slept together."

We're back in his car driving to pick up my car at the bowling alley after a delightful dinner. It was by far the best one we've ever had. All it took was a break-up. I know more about him in two hours than the two years before. Like I had no idea the reason he wears those Hawaiian shirts is because his stepfather Keith does. He wants to emulate the man so much he even joined the police force because Keith thought it would be good for him. Two years of dating and I never asked, and he never told me. How sad.

"Reason number fifty-seven we broke up. Your horrible taste in music!" I laugh.

"Like ABBA is any better," he says.

"It's peppy!"

"It's crap!"

"But it's peppy crap," I point out.

Still smiling, he shakes his head. I've never seen him grinning so much without a bowling ball in his hand. We ride in silence for a minute, the longest we've gone without talking all night. I gaze out the side window at the lit-up stores and cars passing, but know he's glancing at me. I'm actually a little sad the night's over. We—

Instead of turning left toward the alley, Steven makes a sharp right toward the park, then a quick left into the empty parking lot, his breath heavy for someone not running a marathon.

I have no idea what to expect as he shuts off the engine. "Steven, what—"

He grabs my neck and at the same time leans in, pressing his lips to mine. The kiss lasts only a second before he releases me. He studies my face for a reaction, but all I can muster is shock. I'm breathing as heavily as he is but his face is almost bestial with lust. I've never had a man gaze at me like that in real life. It's amazing. And catching. The shock disappears as the words, "What the hell" ticker-tape through my brain.

I kiss him this time. There's no tenderness on either end, just carnal coupling. Awesome. Our tongues explore as hands rove though each other's hair. It's familiar and not at the same time. Lord, I forgot how much I missed kissing. The skin on skin, the devouring of another person like chocolate. The passion of connecting with a man you want. It's yummy.

To say I'm sexually frustrated is like saying Hurricane Katrina was just a rain shower. All day, every day, I'm surrounded by handsome, sexy men who I dash into life-or-death situations with. Nothing breeds lust like almost dying. Your adrenaline is rushing, you're thankful to be alive, and you want to express it in some way. One time I almost succumbed, all but throwing myself at Oliver and potentially ruining our relationship for a few minutes of ecstasy. It makes me cringe just thinking about it. He put on the brakes, and we never spoke about it again. That was the closest I've come to having sex in two years. I need this, damn it.

I pull off my jacket as he takes off his. We kiss again as I attempt to straddle him, but I bump into the steering wheel. "Ow."

He chuckles then moves the wheel up and seat back so I have more room. "There."

Our mouths connect again, and this time I make it onto his lap. My shirt lifts off followed by his. I'm not the only one who's gone through a physical transformation. He's ripped: six pack, rock hard pecs, and biceps. He must have been visiting the gym twenty-four seven to get these results. Pleasant surprise. I hug his neck and pull him closer, kissing him like the horny teenager I never got the chance to be. His arms wrap around my bare back. I can feel the bulge in his pants grow against my jeans and without realizing it my crotch rubs up against him. He moans a little and I move up and down against him, tingling with each tiny movement. His hands move to my front, first over my bra but quickly reaching under it, his palms massaging my sensitive nipples. I break the kiss as a tiny moan escapes me. His mouth moves to my neck, nibbling and sucking just above my scar.

Involuntarily, I tense up at the first nibble. For an instant I'm back on that grass in Colorado pinned by an insane vamp as his fangs rip into my body. He held me down as he lapped up blood, his tongue toying with my raw wounds and his erection growing just like now. I pull my neck away, but it's not Oliver's confused expression below me. "What?" Steven asks.

"Can you just … not do that?"

"Okay." He kisses me again, but all the passion has drained on my part. I meet his kisses, but my heart and libido aren't in it anymore. Nothing like a PTSD flashback to spoil the mood. We continue kissing, and there is only a small part of me that wants to continue, to have strong arms around me, to have someone inside filling me. But as he unbuttons my jeans and I open my eyes, I realize I don't want *this* person to do these things. Sure we had fun tonight, but he's still Steven. I've been here before and didn't like where it went. And as he unzips my jeans, a flash of Will's face the other night as he gazed into my eyes with such pain and longing, connecting to those same parts of me, fills my vision as if it's occurring now.

"Stop," I hear someone with my voice saying.

"What?" Steven asks.

"I can't do this," I say. "I can't do this. Sorry."

I climb off him and fall back into the passenger seat, just needing to sit still. I don't look at him and actually block that half of the car from my mind. I wish I could just teleport out of here. At this moment it would be great if I was the only person on the planet. I'm a tramp. A hussy. Here I am leading one man on while desiring another. I disgust myself.

Steven doesn't utter a word, but confusion and anger radiate from him enough to prickle my already sensitive skin. I close my eyes and breathe deep to calm myself down. After a few seconds I whisper, "I'm sorry."

He pauses with his short breaths, the only response before he says, "What's the matter?"

"I don't know," I say as I zip up my pants.

"Is it that guy?" he asks in a low voice that almost hides his anger.

I put on my shirt. "I don't know."

We're silent again, both of us just staring out into the dark, desolate park. I have the strongest urge to jump out of this truck and run all the way home. Before I can implement this plan, my cell phone vibrates inside my purse. I've never been so happy to hear that sound. "I have to get it," I say quietly. "It might be Nana." Right now, I'd take Freddy Krueger's call. My purse is on the floor and continues vibrating until I locate the phone. It's a local number I don't recognize. "Hello? Beatrice Alexander."

"Oh God! Please help me!" a girl implores as someone pounds on a door.

"Who is this?" I ask, my eyes growing wide. Steven's expression morphs from anger to confusion.

"Mariah!"

"Let me in!" a man says on the other end through the continuing thumps.

"Mariah?" I ask, having no clue who this girl is.

"M, come on!" the man shouts.

"What's going on?" Steven asks.

"You gave me your card today!" Mariah says. Then as if the phone is far from her mouth she shouts, "Moon, go away! I've called the F.R.E.A.K.S. people!"

"Who?" the man, I guess Moon, shouts back.

"Mariah, are you still there?" I ask.

"Yeah," she says. "He went postal over the hamburger. I think he might, like, kill me."

"I would never kill you," Moon pleads through the door.

Steven, who has been listening to my every word but I pray not to the other end of the conversation, continues staring at me. This is bad. He's a cop. If I let on something is wrong, he'll insist on going with me. Against an angry vampire. With the fangs, and the mind control, and super-strength. So instead of the fear actually coursing through my veins right now, I roll my eyes and shake my head. I press my finger against the receiver and whisper, "She's at a bar. Drunk." I remove my finger. "Mariah, I'm so sorry to hear that. I'm on my way over. Just stay *exactly* where you are. What's the address?" In between Moon's constant banging and pleads, she rambles the address. It's about ten minutes away. "Just stay put. I'm on my way."

"Thank you," she almost cries before hanging up.

I shut my phone. "Sorry about that."

"Everything okay?" Steven asks.

"Yeah. Just the usual break-up depression."

"Do you want me to drive you over there?"

"No," I say too forcefully. "It's okay. Just take me back to my car. I can handle it alone."

I'm pretty sure he doesn't buy this story, but he puts his shirt back on and starts the car. "Fine."

We don't talk in the two minutes it takes to return to the bowling alley. My leg keeps jittering, and Steven occasionally peeks over at me, but we say nothing. I barely wait for him to stop the car before jumping out. "I *promise* I'll call you tomorrow, okay?" I shut the door before he can answer.

My trembling hand finds my keys and opens the car door. As I pull out, narrowly missing an oncoming car that rightly honks at me, I put the address in my GPS and zoom out of the lot. A block later I locate my cell and press redial. She picks up on the first ring.

"Hello?" Mariah asks.

"It's Agent Alexander. Are you okay?"

"Yeah. I locked myself in the bathroom."

"Are you safe there? Can he get in?"

"I think so, but he hasn't yet," she says breathlessly. "He stopped knocking a minute ago. I don't know where he went. I'm really scared."

"I know, but I'll be there in seven minutes. Stay on the phone until I do."

"Okay."

"Um, tell me how you met him, okay?"

She starts talking, but I don't really listen. I just saw in this movie that you're supposed to keep them on the phone and talking to keep them calm. I throw in a few, "Oh really?" and "Tell me more" just so she knows I'm here with her. My low-level panic rises with each mile. I have no weapon or anything that can be used as a weapon except a pen. Then there's the fact I have no backup. The last time I attempted to take on a vamp alone, I almost died. I have no idea what I'm going to say or do. I don't have a plan. I *hate* not having a plan.

Speeding like a NASCAR driver on uppers, I reach the house in five minutes. I'm always amazed that nightmare creatures like vamps, werewolves, and witches live in the suburbs too. Looking at this one-story, stucco ranch house with a dead lawn and chain-link fence, I'd assume I'd find a meth lab not a bloodsucker.

"I'm outside," I say into the phone. "Can you come out?"

"I'm scared," she says. "Can you come in and get me?"

The smart part of my brain screams, "Possible trap, you idiot," but the compassionate part says, "Help her." For the second time tonight I ignore the smart part. She needs help and that's what I'm duty bound to do. Even on holiday. "Alright, where are you?"

"In the bathroom in the master bedroom. The patio door should be unlocked."

"Where's Moon?"

"I don't know."

Great. Wonderful. Perfect. "Okay, I'm hanging up now. Stay where you are." I flip the phone shut and take a deep breath before getting out. Not being a total idiot, on my way around to the back I dial the mansion. No one picks up so I have to leave a friggin' message. "Hi, it's Bea," I whisper. "It's 9:39 pm in San Diego, and if you do not receive a call by ten, please send backup to 4562 Vida Avenue in Chula Vista, California. I am responding to an emergency call regarding a vamp named Moon by his companion Mariah. I really hope you get this."

I keep the phone out and my finger on redial as I open the dirty sliding glass door and step in. The living room just has the bare essentials like secondhand couch, old TV, and heavy drapes on all the windows. It smells stale and musty as if those windows have never been open. The only decorations are a Grateful Dead poster on the wall and black and white Native American blanket on the couch. Cautiously, I walk through the living room, eyes jutting to every possible hiding spot.

"Mariah," I call, "it's Special Agent Beatrice Alexander. I'm here. Come out."

A door squeaks open down the hall, and a moment later the girl walks out. The first thing I notice is the blood on the collar of her tie-dyed shirt. She's paler than before too if that's possible. The black eye and bruise on her cheek really show on her skin. There are more bruises on her arms and legs but they're older, some already yellowing. "Thank you," she almost cries.

I eye the two closed doors down the hall. I wave her toward me. "Come on."

"I need to get some of my stuff," she says before disappearing back into the bedroom.

"Leave it!" Damn! Drawers open and close down the hall. Nobody ever listens to me. Shaking my head, I fall onto the couch and sigh. At least it wasn't a trap. He would have attacked by now. More drawers and hangers clatter. "We need to go!" I shout.

"Almost done!"

Not quick enough. The front door opens, and I leap off the couch just as an extra from *Hair* walks in. His stringy brown hair falls below his shoulders with a bushy beard covering his face. Most of the vamps I've encountered wore skintight designer clothes or nothing, but this guy is decked out in a loose peasant top, camouflage green pants, and sandals. In December. The last living (well, sort of) hippie. And he does not look happy to see The Man, or in this case The Woman, in his living room. I toss my shoulders back and hold up my chin, which improves my threatening quotient about ten percent.

"You the pig?" Fuzzy McJerkface asks as he shuts the door.

"I am Special Agent Beatrice Alexander of the F.R.E.A.K.S.," I say in a hard tone.

"Where's Mariah?"

"In the bedroom packing. We don't want any trouble."

He scoffs. "You have no right to take her. I've broken no laws."

It's my turn to scoff. "You beat her for eating a cheeseburger. You are literally draining the life out of her."

"I'm not keeping her prisoner. According to vampiric law, I've done nothing wrong."

"That's why I'm not taking you in. I'm just here for Mariah. I don't want any trouble."

The girl of the hour walks out of the bedroom now in jeans and flip flops carrying a duffel bag. When she spots Moon, she stops dead. A burst of fear radiates from her as her eyes widen. She glances from him to me and back again. What little menace the undead hippie had melts away when he sees her. "Mariah," he says breathlessly.

She gazes down at her toes like a scolded child. Not taking my eyes off the lovelorn vamp, I edge toward the girl. "Are you ready to go?"

"Do you really want to leave me, Sunshine?" Moon says. "Cause you know I love you."

"You threw me against a wall," she says, still not looking at him. "You swore you'd never hit me."

He takes a step toward us, but I push her behind me. "Don't take another step."

He seethes but doesn't move. "Sorry. I'm so sorry. It was just a surprise, tasting that dead meat in you."

"She made me! Said I needed vitamins or something. And it tasted so good."

"We'll get you more vitamins! And I'll just feed from you once or twice a week. I promise."

"I don't know," she whines.

"Sunshine," he says, taking another step.

"Not another step!" I shout.

He bares his fangs. "Shut up, you fucking pig!"

And he takes another step. Adrenaline and fear take the wheel. Moon flies back into the far wall, shattering the framed poster. Both he and it crumple to the floor. Sorry, Jerry. The dazed vamp remains there, trying to figure out what just occurred. I can practically see the stars and Tweety birds dancing around his head.

"Oh no!" Mariah cries behind me. "Moon!" She drops her bags and rushes over to him. She cups his jaw in her hands examining him. "What the fuck did you do to him?" she shouts at me.

Before I can answer, there's a pounding on the front door which startles us all. A familiar voice shouts, "Chula Vista PD! Please open the door!"

Oh fudge.

The idiot must have followed me from the bowling alley. White hot panic grips me, even more than the kind I felt a few seconds ago. He pounds again. "Police! Open this door or I'll be forced to break it down!"

"You called the police?" Mariah asks near hysterics. Wish I had that luxury.

"No," I say as I find myself walking to the door. "Get him up, follow my lead, and act normal!"

Mariah helps the near cognizant Moon to his feet as I open the door. Sure enough a fuming Steven stands on the porch, his hand resting beside the gun on his belt. "Steven, what are you doing here?"

He pushes past me into the house but stops when he sees the happy couple and shattered glass. "What's going on here?" he asks me.

"Nothing," Moon says, putting his arm over Mariah's shoulder. "Absolutely nothing."

"He bumped up against the poster," I say, "and it fell. Right?"

"Right," Moon and Mariah mumble.

Of course, not being a total idiot, Steven doesn't buy this. "Has this man been hitting you, ma'am?"

"What? No," she says with an awkward smile. "I was in a car accident today."

My turn in the hot seat. "Is this true?" Steven asks me.

I don't answer. I gaze down at my feet to escape his intense gaze. Now, almost panting in anger, he turns back to Mariah. "Ma'am, do you want to press charges against this man for battery?"

"No!"

"I didn't hit her. There's been no crime. And I want both of you out of my house," Moon says. "Otherwise I'll call my lawyer," he looks right into my eyes, "*Connor Lord* to settle this."

I get the message. "We'll leave," I say. "Do you want to come with us, Mariah? I think it would be a good idea."

The poor girl hangs her head. "I want to stay here."

"Ma'am if he—" Steven says.

"He didn't do anything. I swear."

"Leave," Moon orders.

Steven glares at the vamp but turns around and throws open the front door. "Bea? We're leaving."

I take one last look at Mariah. "Are you sure about this?"

Moon pulls her in close. "Yeah."

I meet his angry eyes with mine. "If anything happens … "

"Get the fuck out of our house."

Crap. I sigh. "You have my number," I say as I reluctantly walk out of the house, slamming the door shut. A seething Steven and I walk side by side down the concrete path and through the chain gate. When it clinks shut, he grabs my arm hard enough to bruise, dragging me down the sidewalk to the corner. I yank my arm away. "Let go!"

"Are you out of your fucking mind?" he shouts.

"Don't yell at me!" I yell at him.

"You could have been killed! What the fuck were you thinking?"

"I had everything under control until you showed up! What, are you stalking me or something now?"

He wags his finger right in my face. "Don't turn this around on me! What the hell just happened?"

I bat his hand away. "Get your finger out of my face!"

He grabs my wrists instead, squeezing tight. "What the hell were you thinking?" he screams in my face. "Do you have any idea how many of those situations end in a homicide? Do you?"

"Let me go, and I'll explain."

He tosses my arms down. "Talk."

"I used to baby-sit her, okay?" No idea where that lie came from but they keep spewing out. "And we had lunch today, and I told her to call me if she ever needed anything. He was supposed to be out all night."

"Did he hurt you?"

"We didn't even touch each other. I almost had her out of there when you showed up!"

"I heard a crash! I thought you—"

"He bumped against the poster to let us pass."

"I'm a fucking cop, Bea! I was right there when she called you! Why the hell did you go in there alone?"

"*Because* you are a cop. You'd want to arrest him, and my only priority was getting her out of there, okay? Is the interrogation over? Can I go now?" I try to walk away but he blocks me. "Move, Steven."

"You think I'm buying a word of this?"

"I don't care. Believe what you want." This time he lets me pass but follows me to my car. "You gonna stalk me some more?" I open the car door, but he slaps it shut.

"You're different," he says. "Something about you is different."

I look up into his eyes, my face as hard as his. "And you're not. *That's* the problem." I open my car door, climb in, and drive away with my ex in the rearview.

Where he belongs.

SEVEN

TATTLE TALES

I SIT AT THE computer in the living room with *The Day of the Jackal* playing on the TV behind me. I bet the Jackal would know how to write a report that didn't make him sound like a jackass. Of course how can one sugarcoat the fact that I didn't save the victim, violated a trillion procedures, and almost outed the vamp world to a civilian? That's what I've been attempting to figure out for the past half hour.

For the third time in half an hour I take out my ponytail and put it back. There's this one strand of hair that just won't stay put, and it's driving me nuts. How can I type when this one strand keeps brushing against my cheek? Ugh, I can't stand this a moment longer. I'm just going to have to send the report as is. With a sigh, I hit send. No more. I'm done jumping into the fray until I leave San Diego. If I see someone being murdered, I'll just walk on by. The hero business is hereby closed for repairs.

I fall onto the couch next to Nana, stealing one of her chips. "Was this based on a true story? Did someone try to kill de Gaulle?" I ask.

"I don't think so." We each take another chip. "Finish your work?"

"Yep." We watch in silence as the Jackal assembles his sniper rifle.

"And did you call your boss and April back yet?" Nana asks.

Double ugh. After I phoned Kansas and left another message telling them I was alive and well, I shut off my phone, wanting nothing more than to fall off the grid for the rest of my life. I forgot they have Nana's number too, so that plan went down the crapper. George called only once, but April has tried three times, which either means she's pregnant again and can't wait to tell me, or Steven called and blabbed about last night. Notice that I'm not rushing to the telephone.

"I'll call later," I say, taking another chip.

"Is everything okay?"

The phone starts ringing again, and I groan. "Super-de-duper."

With an annoyed sigh, Nana hands me the bowl and gets the phone. "Hello? Oh, hello April." I wave my hands like a football coach while shaking my head no. "No, she's still shopping and hasn't come back to pick up her cell phone. I promise I'll tell her the moment she gets home. Bye, dear." Nana hangs up. "That makes four."

"I just want to spend one day away from people. Is that so hard to understand?"

"Did you two have a fight?"

"No! I'm just feeling antisocial today. We've hung out every day since I got back. She can survive one day without me."

"And nothing happened last night?"

I put the bowl on the couch and stand up. "For the millionth time, no! I went bowling, end of story." I storm off toward my room. "Stop with the friggin' inquisition! God!" I slam the door shut and fall onto my bed face first. Okay, so last night seems to have knocked ten years off my maturity level. Makes sense considering I made out in a car like a horny teenager with a guy I'm not even sure I like followed by

121

reckless behavior. Next I'll be crawling out my back window and sneaking alcohol. God, I just want a big hole in the middle of nowhere to swallow me up so I can get some peace.

I flip on my back and stare at the ceiling. I can't remember the last time I felt like such an idiot. I mean, what the hell was I thinking making out with Steven? Yes, I was turned on, and he is sort of cute, but that's no excuse. I totally led him on and then yelled at him when he tried to help me. I know better. And then going into a vampire's house without support? I so left my brain back in Kansas.

Speaking of. I can get one humiliation over with so I can attempt to enjoy the rest of the day. I turn on my cell phone and check my messages. All eight of them. Kill me now.

"*Hi, it's April. Who was that girl you had lunch with? Call me.*" I delete it.

"*Hey, it's Steven. It's about 6:15. Are you still coming? If not, that's okay. Later.*" Delete.

"*Listen Bea,*" an enraged Steven starts, "*I don't know what the fuck tonight was about or what the hell is going on with you, but…*" He groans in frustration. "*You're out of your fucking mind, you know that? I should have listened to them.*" Okay, I'd delete that one twice if I could.

"*Bea, it's George. I just received both your messages. I'm so sorry I wasn't available when you called. You're alright, I gather. Please call me as soon as you receive this. Bye.*" Delete.

"*Bea, it's April. What the hell happened last night? Steven called me this morning asking all sorts of weird questions, and he was pissed! Call me.*" Delete.

"*Bea, where the hell are you?*" April asks. "*Call me.*" Delete.

"*I swear if you're avoiding me, I'll kill you,*" April says. "*I'll try the house.*" Delete.

Last one, thank God. At first there's just heavy breathing for a second or two, but then: "*Um, hi, Bea.*" My heart thumps double time. "*It's Will. I was just calling to … see how your Op went last night. Sorry we weren't there to get your message. The team's been in West Virginia taking care of a Green Man. He kidnapped some campers. We could have used you there.*" He pauses. "*Um, anyway, please call m—the mansion so we can go over specifics. Have a great rest of your vacation. Bye.*" I didn't think it was possible, but I'm smiling. I save that last one. For, like, ever.

I call the mansion and this time someone picks up. "Hello?" It's George.

"It's Bea."

He draws a deep breath and releases it. "How are you?"

"Fine. Tired. I just, um, sent my report a few minutes ago. Check your inbox."

"Give me the broad strokes of what happened." I do. "And you're sure your police friend doesn't suspect anything?"

"That I lied, yes. That vamps were involved, no."

"And the girl?"

I sigh. "As far as I know, she's fine. She has my card."

"Very well. I'll review your report and if I have follow-up questions, I'll call. I'm transferring you to Will now."

"Why?"

"He wanted to discuss your solo mission as well. Go over the technical aspects. I'm transferring you now."

The line goes silent, and I find myself pulling my hair out of the rubber band and smoothing it as if he can see me. Yes, I have officially lost my mind.

"Hello?" Will asks, out of breath.

"Um, hi. It's Bea. George said you wanted to speak to me?"

"Oh, um, hi," he says, still out of breath.

"Are you okay? You sound—"

"No, I was just on the rowing machine."

Hot. Dripping with sweat. My overtaxed libido pants. "Oh. Fun."

"Not really."

One of our infamous awkward silences follows. "So, um," I finally say, "George said you wanted to talk to me?"

"Yeah. Yes. I just wanted to make sure you followed proper procedure last night."

"I just sent my report. Everything is in there."

"Good. Good." Another pause. "And you're okay? The vamp didn't…"

"The only thing bruised is my ego," I say with a chuckle. "But what about you? You went to West Virginia?"

"Yes. Just got back a few hours ago."

"And everyone's okay?"

"Few cuts and bruises."

"Well, I'd love to say I wished I went with you, but I'd be lying."

"It was cold, wet, and muddy, so I don't blame you. Unless things out there are … you know. Bad. Or something."

"No," I lie, "everything's fantastic here. Watching old movies, wrapping presents."

"Sounds like fun. We're just … doing the usual."

And awkward silence two is right on schedule. This one lasts ten seconds before I can't stand it anymore. "So, is there anything else?"

"I, uh, guess not. For now. I'll review your report and see if I have any comments."

"Okay. Good. So I'm gonna…"

"Yeah, it sounds like you're busy. I'll let you go."

"Okay. Glad you're okay."

"You too. Um, Merry Christmas."

"You too. Bye." I flip the phone shut, pinch my closed eyes, and groan in abject embarrassment. What the heck is it about that man that turns me into a gawky fourteen-year-old with a five word vocabulary? I should have asked more about West Virginia. About his Christmas plans. If he'd mind naming our first child Elizabeth. Anything.

I don't know how it's possible, but I feel worse than before. The embarrassment, okay the *yearning,* is overwhelming to the point where I can't breathe. I have to leave this house. I have to get away. Somewhere with some freaking air.

My daisy tote bag is still in my closet with the matching towel. I toss in my iPod, the latest Sophie Kinsella book, sunglasses, wallet, car keys, and turned-off cell phone in it. I'm going where I always have when my life is falling apart. It's beach time.

———

Today is one of those gray days where the sky bleeds into the earth, making everything dismal. The sky has infected the sea and my mood with its depressing nothingness. The sun should be setting by now but it's nowhere in sight, hidden by those pointless clouds. Yeah, my temperament has improved leaps and bounds since I arrived here.

I gave up trying to read about ten minutes after I got here and my iPod was discarded shortly after. Instead, I've just been watching the waves crash and the people stroll by. Couples mostly from the Hotel Del Coronado or surfers in their wet suits. April and I used to spend all day here watching those surfers stroll out in their skintight suits, which they would then shed, revealing taut wet muscles. And yet I haven't received a single thrill today. Okay, maybe one.

This beach. When I wasn't boy watching, this is where I'd come to be alone and think. I came here when I realized my high school crush Caleb didn't like me back. I came here when Nana had a cancer scare. And I came here to decide what to do about the Steven situation the first time around. I think the constancy of the waves settles me. No matter what, a new one will crest and crash until the earth ends. And just up the beach is the Hotel Del Coronado where they filmed one of my favorite movies, *Some Like it Hot*. It's totally possible that Marilyn Monroe sat in this exact spot and thought about her problems. She had a rough life too.

I hug my knees closer to my chest and rest my chin on them as another wave lands. Too bad it's too cold to swim. I curl my toes in the soft sand as a surfer leaps up on his board and rides a wave to his idling friends. It's so quiet with only the waves keeping the world from feeling like a total void.

That ends. "There you are!" April shouts behind me. She moves around to face me, stopping with one hand on her hip. "I have been calling you all day! You've been avoiding me!"

"Did Nana tell you where to find me?" I ask with a sigh.

"I will not reveal my sources."

"I want to be alone."

"You know, that line didn't work for Garbo either." She sits down across from me Indian style. "Steven called me this morning."

"Did he? And why would he do that?"

"He's worried about you. He said you went to some strange guy's house. Alone. That the guy beat up his girlfriend or something."

"He has no idea what he's talking about," I say.

"So he lied? You didn't go over to some strange dude's house after the guy beat up his girlfriend?"

I don't want to lie. I just don't have the energy. "It's complicated."

Her mouth opens in surprise. "Are you out of your damn mind?"

"I can take care of myself, okay? I had the whole situation under control."

"Are you on crack?" she shouts. "You could have been killed!"

I can't deal with this right now. Shaking my head at the ridiculousness of my life, I stand up. "I don't want to talk about this." I roll up my towel.

"You're leaving?" she asks incredulously. She leaps up, snatching the towel from my hands. "I am your best friend! I used to know you better than anyone and now ... " She shakes her head. "You leave the state without telling me. You're beyond secretive. You have lunch with weird people. You rush into strange homes with dangerous people inside. And if you think for a second I believe your stories about all those scars, that kids bit you and you were in a car accident, you're nuts! Or about your job! I did some research. Black Industries doesn't exist! So, what the hell is going on?"

I'm speechless. No lies come to me. But instead of panic, I feel relief. I'm like a guilt-ridden criminal who was just caught. It's over, the Sword of Damocles has fallen. So my mouth opens and I say, "I work for a clandestine branch of the FBI called the F.R.E.A.K.S. where I fly all over the country investigating crimes committed by monsters and psychics. I was recruited after I saved a student from an out-of-control car. The scars on my arm came from a zombie. A necromancer raised an entire cemetery, and they attacked a whole town, but I killed him. The scar on my neck is a vampire bite. Oliver's bite. He attacked me, but it wasn't his fault. And Will's a werewolf." I take a breath. "The girl you saw me with yesterday, her boyfriend's a vampire. He hit her, and she called me. That's it. Oh, and I almost had sex with Steven last night. I think that's everything."

The color has drained out of her confused face. I know it's a lot to take in, but she doesn't have to look at me as if I've grown a third eye. "Well?" I ask.

"WHAT?" she shouts.

"You asked."

"You're a ... monster hunter? Like you kill Bigfoot and gremlins and witches? And vampires? They're, like, real, and you're hot for one?"

"Yeah. Not what you expected, huh?"

"I thought you were a drug dealer or something! I need to sit down," my bewildered best friend says after her butt hits the sand.

"I would never deal drugs," I say as I sit across from her.

"You're lying to me, right?"

"Not anymore."

She's quiet for once as she lets this sink in. Then she looks into my eyes. "Holy fucking shit, Bea! Are you out of your damn mind?"

"I ask myself the same question every day," I say.

"And you've, like, killed things? People?"

"Yeah, but they were all bad."

She takes another few seconds to process this. "And your other ... co-workers, they're vampires and werewolves? Like suck your blood, undead, howl at the moon?"

"We also have a medium, a teleporter, and a guy who touches things to know what happened to them. Plus three real FBI agents to help us."

"Holy shit, Bea! You could die!"

"I know."

She scoffs. "*And* you almost had sex with Steven!"

"I know."

We sit in silence as she stares at the sand shaking her head.

"Does Nana Liz know?" April asks.

"No. Just you."

"She should know! Seriously, Bea, what the hell are you thinking? I've known you most of your life. You're a teacher, not a killer."

"I had training. And I have my … ability. I can control it now."

"And that's why you joined," she says more to herself. "They took you in the night you almost killed Brian. And you've been lying ever since! You never drove cross country! Everything you've told us has been lies!"

"I had to. People have been killed for knowing this stuff. I'm only telling you now because I can't hold it in anymore. If word got out about vamps and people like me, it'd be a disaster."

"So you didn't trust me, is that it?" she spits out.

"I was trying to protect you!"

"Bullshit!"

April leaps up and storms away, but I follow. "April, I've wanted to tell you a million times! I just, I don't know, didn't want you to think less of me."

She stops walking and spins around. "What the hell are you talking about? Why the hell would I think less of you?"

"Because! Being a freak of nature is one thing—"

She points her finger right between my eyes. "I never judged you for that! It's *you* who's had problems dealing with it!"

"I know! And they're helping me come to terms with it a little, but it's a big leap from levitating a bed to snapping necks and squeezing hearts for a living!"

Anger is slowly replaced with shock. "You do that?"

"Yeah. And a week ago I chopped the head off a forty-foot snake with a machete. April, I'm a trained killer. I've lost count of how many things I've slaughtered. How the hell can you not be freaked out? I sure as hell am, and I live with it every day."

April looks down at the sand. "Bea…" she looks up and smiles, "you're a moron!"

"What?"

"You say I don't know you, but you obviously don't know me! And that kind of pisses me off!"

"Huh?" This was not the reaction I was expecting.

"I love you! You could tell me you've decided to become a man, or that you want to move to Iraq, or that you've become a monster hunter, and no matter what, I will love you and support you. It's kind of my job! Just like it was your job to listen to me for days when I was deciding to marry Javi. We're best friends! We don't judge, we support as best as we can even when our friend is being an idiotic douche bag." She lightly pushes my arm and shakes her head. "And for the record, I think you're awesome. You save people's lives. You have a machete. That is beyond cool. I may think different of you, but not in a bad way. Though you do owe me a car for not trusting me. Red. With satellite radio."

I grab her and give my best friend the biggest bear hug possible. "I love you."

"Well, I am the best friend *ever*," she says mock serious. "And I love you too." She pulls away and smiles. "Okay, now onto the important stuff. You almost had sex with Steven last night! Oh my God!"

I grimace. "I know. Not my finest move."

"Well, why didn't you round home?"

"I don't know," I say. "We were having fun talking and joking around, and it just sort of happened. And it felt good cause, you know, it's been *forever*, but then Steven kissed my neck and I thought

130

of Oliver and then all of a sudden Will's face popped into my mind, and I freaked. I don't know why, really, but—"

"Um, because you're totally in love with them," she says as if I'm an idiot.

"I am *not* in love with them. Oliver is a dead man, and Will's too in touch with his jerk side."

"And yet they pop into your head when you're about to do the nasty and stop you. Maybe it's not love, but it's something."

"It's horrible is what it is! Oliver is my best friend there, but he's a corpse! A five-hundred-year-old corpse! I mean, eww. How do you get past that? I don't think I could no matter how much he makes me laugh or how safe I feel with him. And Will ... I don't know what's going on there. When I can have an actual conversation with him without shouting or drooling, he's so hot and cold I want to attach a faucet to him."

"Could it be a werewolf thing?" She shakes her head. "I cannot believe that sentence actually came out of my mouth."

"No, it's because his wife was killed by a werewolf, he became one, he hates Oliver, he likes me—but maybe just as a friend when he doesn't hate me for not loathing Oliver—and I'm so powerful I make his skin physically prickle." I sigh. "You know, hearing myself say this stuff maybe I should just apologize to Steven, marry him, and lead a nice boring life where I resent and hate him more and more as the years go by and die with a million regrets. You know, a *normal* existence."

"*Or*," April draws the word out, "you can pick up your cell phone, call Will, tell him how you feel, and spend a whole week in bed screwing like rabbits!"

"No!"

April theatrically scoffs and puts her hands on her hips. "You just got done telling me you took down a huge snake with a machete all by yourself, but asking out a guy who is obviously totally nuts about you is too much for you? Give me a break!"

"Well, for the record, it was a basilisk not a snake. *Much* more dangerous. But I didn't do it alone. The team helped me. And the flamethrowers, they helped too."

"Oh shut up!" She starts walking toward my tote, and I follow. "If you won't call him, I will!" She reaches my bag before I can and turns on my phone. Panic grips me because I know she'll do it. She did in middle school with Joey Pollitt, and what a success that was. I believe the words *eww, gross* were uttered.

I try to snatch the phone but she wiggles away from my hands. "April! Seriously!"

"Stop it or I'll tell Nana Liz your secret!"

I stop. "You wouldn't."

"I would. It's ringing. Keep it on speaker!"

She thrusts the phone into my hands. Someone picks up. "Hello?" I ask.

"Bea?" Will asks.

A wide-eyed April mouths the words, "He sounds cute!"

"Yeah, it's me" I say.

"You got my message?"

Smiling, April mouths the words, "He left you a message!"

"Um yeah," I say. "Of course I did. Why else would I be calling?" I shrug and April smiles.

"And you agree with my assessment?" He sounds so serious the thrill I feel tapers.

"Um, I guess."

"Good. I thought, perhaps, I was being too harsh, but if you agree then—"

"Well, you were a little harsh," I say looking at an equally confused April, "seeing as I did what had to be done."

April gives me a thumbs-up.

"I disagree. There were multiple options available besides running alone into the home of a known violent vampire, assaulting him, and then bringing the civilian police into the mix, especially one you have sexual knowledge of!"

"Hey, there was very little sexual knowledge last night, okay?" As the words spew out I instantly want to push them back in. I grimace as April's mouth drops open.

The other side of the line is dead silent, and that hole I fantasized about earlier is looking mighty appealing.

"I mean, we had a relationship before, but not now. I mean, I didn't invite him to help me. He just followed."

"And now he's suspicious," Will says, voice hard. "There have been searches in multiple databases regarding you today, all originating in Chula Vista and San Diego."

"Look, I'll talk to him. I'll fix this."

"And the inciting incident? What's your justification there? You broke at least three procedural rules just by driving to the house."

"She called me! She needed help! What was I supposed to do? Wait for your guys to fly in while he was killing her? It was one vamp. And a hippie one at that."

"You never go in without backup! Never! You're lucky I don't put a disciplinary letter in your file. There can be far-reaching consequences we don't even know about."

"I did my job!"

"Poorly!"

"Oh … go take a flea bath!" I slap the phone shut.

April brings her hands up to her smiling mouth. "Okay, I totally changed my mind. What a prick! You *like* him?"

"Well, not at this moment." Though he did make some good points, ones I knew would come up. He just didn't have to be such a jerk about it.

"Is he always like that?" April asks.

"No. Just when he's worried about me. Or when I challenge him. Or when Oliver gets within fifty feet of him. Or of me."

"Another emotionally stunted male banging his chest and howling instead of telling you how he feels. Why are they all like that?"

"They're idiots?"

"I'll go with that." She smiles again. "Well, I will say one thing. If what you've said is true, Little Miss I've Lied About Everything for Months, then that boy has it bad for you. Nobody goes off like that unless they care about you."

"He could just buy me flowers," I mutter.

"What did his message say?"

I punch in my voicemail code. I have three new messages.

"*Bea, it's Steven. I need you to call me when you get this. I have a few questions for you.*" Delete.

"He sounded pissed," April says.

"Do you blame him?"

Next message. "*Alexander, this is Will,*" he says, all official. "*I reviewed your report and I must say … there are quite a few things we must discuss regarding your conduct last night. Not only your reckless disregard for procedure, but also for your lack of basic common sense. Being tailed without your knowledge, entering a known dangerous situation without proper weapons or backup? I had hoped the months of*

134

training we have provided would have sunk in by now. Call me so we can discuss this further." Delete.

"Wow," April says.

"And I'm sure the next one is from Brian calling to tell me he wants to burn me at the stake."

Final message. "*Hello, Special Agent Beatrice Alexander,*" an unfamiliar male says. "*I am calling on behalf of Lord Connor McInnis who requests a meeting with you and Officer Steven Weir this evening at Gaslight at seven o'clock to discuss the events that occurred in his territory last night and today. If you wish we can have a car pick you up at 16726 24th Street, which, according to our records, is the home of Elizabeth Alexander, your grandmother. We look forward to seeing you both.*"

Oh fudge. Oh double fudge sundae with ball bearings on top.

"Who the hell was that?" April asks. "Who's Lord Connor? Why did he know your address?"

There isn't time to answer her. Emergency mode has been engaged. I punch in Nana's telephone number with my shaking hand. With each unanswered ring my tension level skyrockets. "Come on."

After the forth ring she picks up. "Hello?"

"Nana! Are you okay?"

"Of course, I was just in the other room. Where are you? I was getting worried."

"I'm fine. I'm with April at the beach." I start collecting my things from the sand. "I'm on my way home right now." With bag in tow, I start speed walking down the beach with April right behind me.

"You missed dinner," Nana says. "There's a plate in the microwave for you."

"Hey, Nana, can you do me a favor? Can you go around the house and make sure all the doors and windows are locked?"

"What? Why? Is something wrong?"

"Not really," I say, my calm façade cracking. "I just, um, have a bad feeling is all. There was something on the radio about an escaped convict. Better safe than sorry and all. I'll be home soon. Don't open the door for anyone and don't go outside, okay? I love you."

"Beatrice, what—"

"I have to go. Be home soon." I shut the phone.

We reach the lot with our cars, and I fumble around my bag for my keys but can't find them in the mess. The sun is setting—or has set for all I know because of those ... stupid clouds! The vamps can come out to play now, not that it really matters. He could have humans working for him. They could grab Nana for collateral. I just—

Hands grip my shoulders, and spin me around. April looks as panicked as I feel. "What the hell is going on? Why was that guy on the phone?"

"Bad news." I find my keys and unlock the door. "I need to swing by your place. Javi still have that Beretta?"

Her eyes pop out of her head. "A gun? You need a gun?"

"I don't have one with me. All I have is silver pepper spray. No, wait, I shouldn't bring a gun. It might be seen as a sign of aggression. Crap."

"Silver—" She does a double take. "You're going to that meeting? Alone?"

"You heard him. He all but threatened Nana. And apparently I won't be alone because he wants Steven there!" Okay, I was relatively calm a second ago, but now my stomach jerks. Lords and Ladies are the baddest mothers in the vampire world. They hold control over all the vamps in their territory, and they do it with power and ruthlessness. Mostly ruthlessness. The last time I faced off with one, Oliver and I almost died. That bastard Moon must have tattled.

"You can't go alone," April says. "Call your people and have them go with you!"

"I have to be there in less than an hour! They can't get here on time! Look, I don't have time to debate this. I need you to drive straight home, lock up your house, and don't let anyone in or out until you hear from me, okay?"

"Bea—"

"Please listen to me for once." I kiss her cheek. "I'll be fine. I love you. Bye." I leap into my car and drive away. She'll listen. She's not a moron like her best friend.

Okay brain, help me out here. Don't panic. This Connor guy can't hurt you without a reason. This is probably just a friendly chat to discuss Moon. Nothing else. Unless he was Freddy of Dallas's BFF and he wants to decapitate me. Then why have me bring Steven? Should I bring Steven? The vamp threatened Nana. If he told me to bring the Hope Diamond I would. No, Steven will be safe. He wouldn't risk harming a human, especially a cop human.

As I speed toward the bridge, I punch in Steven's number. It goes straight to voicemail. "Hi, Steven," I say with an undercurrent of fear, "it's Bea. I really, really, *really* need to see you. It's about last night. Can you meet me at the club Gaslight downtown about seven? It's, um, kind of important. I just need you there, okay? Bye." I shut the phone and take a deep breath. Half of me hopes he won't get the message in time.

I dial another person I have no desire to contact but now have no choice. "Is this who I think it is, or are my phone and mind playing tricks on me?" Oliver asks. "Because I seem to remember—"

"Shut up," I interject. "I need information."

"On what?" he asks, all humor gone from his voice.

"Lord Connor of San Diego. I've been summoned."

The other end is quiet for a moment. "For what reason?"

"My guess, the fiasco last night, which I'm sure you've heard about by now. And no lectures. Will's already given me an earful."

"And you reciprocated, judging from the multitude of slammed doors in the past few minutes." He pauses. "You should not go by yourself."

"Why? How bad is this guy?"

"He has controlled his territory nearly unchallenged for a hundred and fifty years."

Which either means he's God-powerful or Stalin-ruthless. "And do you know him? I mean, is he another pissed-off ex of yours or something?"

"I never had the pleasure, no. He is merely an acquaintance I have come across a handful of times over the centuries. We did spend a summer in Venice together with Alain three hundred years ago. It was rather uneventful as I recall. He is neither friend nor foe."

"So this probably isn't about revenge?"

"You *should not go alone*, Beatrice." Oh crud. He used my full name. Never a good thing. "I can be there in two hours."

"I don't have two hours. The meeting's set for seven."

"You need to wait," he orders.

"I can't do that! He knows where Nana lives, maybe even Brian and April. I don't show, who knows what happens."

"He threatened them?"

"Indirectly, yes. I'm on my way home to check on Nana, but maybe you can have George call the police or FBI to get a patrol around the house just in case. I—"

"Listen to me," he snaps, "you *cannot* do this. The situation is far more dangerous than you can comprehend. You were responsible for the death of a Lord and fourteen of his subjects and now another one demands a meeting. Do you not see the relation?"

"Then shouldn't he be more scared of me than me of him?" I point out. This revelation lowers my fear to a point where I can't hear my own heartbeat. "Look, you can't talk me out of this. It's probably nothing. I've given him no reason to hurt me, right? I was just doing my job. I'll be fine."

"Trixie—"

"If you don't hear from me by eight my time, *then* come, okay? Make sure my family's okay."

"I will be there in two hours," he says with finality.

"No," I warn.

"But—"

"*It's nothing.* I will be fine. Don't. Come."

"You are being ridiculous and idiotic. You require assistance."

"No. I don't, okay? I don't want you here. Promise you won't come unless you don't hear from me. *Promise.*"

He's silent for a moment then says, "I promise."

"And don't tell Will. That's the last thing I need."

"I promise."

"Okay. Good. Thank you. I'll call you before eight."

I'm about to hang up when he says, "Trixie?"

"Yes?"

He's quiet again. "Nothing. Be safe."

"I will. Bye." I shut the phone.

I turn the car onto my street. The only car I don't recognize is a black sedan a few houses down. I glance in as I pass it, but it has tinted windows. I pull into my driveway and sprint into the house. Nobody attacks me before I get inside.

Nana sits on the couch in her pajamas watching the news as I come in, locking everything behind me. I go around shutting all the blinds as a concerned Nana watches.

"What on earth?" she asks.

I start shutting off the lights too. "You need to keep these closed, okay? And keep the lights off too."

"Beatrice, there is nothing on the news about an escaped convict. What—?"

"Look, I can't explain right now. I will, I *promise*, but right now I just need you to trust me, okay?"

Before she can answer I rush into my room, turning on the lights and reaching under my bed for my suitcase. In a tiny pouch is a small can of silver nitrate spray. That's all I brought with me, and it was un-intentional. Then I open my drawers until I find the next weapon in my arsenal. Black shirt, black jeans, black tennis shoes, and black leather half jacket. My big, bad monster-killer outfit. Bravado will be my biggest asset. I helped kill fifteen vampires in one day, including a Lord. I can show no fear. *That* is what will save me tonight.

Though I closed my door, Nana walks in without knocking as I get dressed. "Beatrice Suzanne, you need to tell me what is going on *right now*. Are you in trouble? Is it drugs?"

"Why does everyone think I'm a drug dealer?" I ask.

"Are you? Are drug people coming for you?"

"No!" I pull on my jacket and then put the canister down my cleavage. They never think to look there. "Look, I helped this girl last night, and it got kind of out of hand. I just have to go meet someone and explain everything. It'll be fine. Steven's going with me, okay?" I pick up my purse. "I have to go now. I'll be late."

I quickly wipe some powder on my face and apply red lipstick. I've found that vamps love the color; if scaring him doesn't work, I can always switch to flirting. Every vamp thinks he or she is God's gift, might as well use the fact to my advantage.

Nana folds her arms, watching me as I throw my wallet and cell phone in my purse from last night. I doubt a trained killer would show up with a daisy tote. "You're lying to me," Nana says.

I look at her. "I'm not. I swear I'm not. I just need you to trust me. When I get home, we'll sit down and I'll tell you everything. But I can't now, okay? I love you." I kiss her cheek. "Keep everything locked. Don't answer the door for *anyone*. And don't let anyone in, and if you don't know someone *don't* look in their eyes. No matter what."

"Their eyes?"

"Yeah. I gotta go. I love you."

I wait outside on the porch until I hear all the locks click then pull out my keys and start toward my car, keeping my eyes on the black sedan. But instead of getting in my car, I walk past it, my head back and a hard scowl on my face. Let the games begin.

I tap on the tinted window. After a second it rolls down revealing two huge bald men with matching scowls. "Hello. Just wanted to let you know I'm on my way to my meeting with your boss now. I'm thinking that you two need to follow me away from my grandmother's house, otherwise I will turn back around and crush this car like a tin can with both of you still in it." For effect, without moving a finger, I crush the soda can in the holder. Both men flinch, and then look up at my smiling face. "Try to keep up. Don't want to keep his Lordship waiting." As I walk back to my car with a spring in my step, I key their car. Childish, but effective.

Hope they don't tattle on me.

EIGHT

GASLIGHT

Even on a Sunday night parking in downtown San Diego is a trial. I'm stuck parking five blocks away in a poorly lit lot with rats scurrying between cars. And I get to pay twelve bucks for the privilege. At least my two new best friends are in the same pickle. Merry and Pippin stalk fifteen feet behind me all the way to the club. I'm strangely calm as the club comes into view. It's nestled in the middle of the Gaslamp District. Tiny flames flicker in place of electric street lights with trendy boutiques, restaurants, and art galleries lining the red brick street. Gaslight stands right in the heart of the district. It's three stories of red brick with the name *Gaslight* illuminated by the same flames as the street lights.

I've actually been to this club before. Five times. Three with April, once with some friends from college, and once with Steven. Clubbing was never my thing. Too many people. Too loud. Too expensive. Never in a million years would I have suspected that some of the people I was grooving with were the living dead. Sure there were a few pale and black-clad people, but I never gave them much thought. It makes me wonder where else I've encountered vamps. The movies at night? The bookstore? It's frightening, like finding out your next door neighbor is a serial killer.

The dark brown wood door is closed, and the place the bouncer usually sits is empty. They must not be open yet. Which means no civilians. Which means no pretending to be human, because no witnesses. That calm I had before? Just vanished. Raised pulse and shaking hands are back.

My escorts flank me on either side before the driver knocks. A moment later the heavy door opens. A skinny African-American vamp in black jeans and shirt lets us in. Like all clubs, Gaslight is dark even with the house lights up. The majority of the red brick walls are unadorned save for glasses of gaslamps, speakers, and strobe lights. It's one of the classier clubs I've been to. There's ample seating along the walls with huge dark brown leather couches and chairs. The empty dance floor is the same color with a wooden railing along it, the same kind that's on the second level. It's like an old fashioned bar or hunting lodge. And I do love the chandelier with the gaslights dancing like the people below it. Exactly as I remember it.

As I anticipated it's empty except for the vamp staff. Off in the corner is a thickly muscled Native American man dressed in a black suit reading a newspaper. I recognize him from the last time I was here. He almost didn't let us in until Steven "accidently" flashed his badge. Three stunning women in black skirts and red corsets wipe down the tables and seats. In the DJ booth another black-clad vamp leafs through his records. Behind the bar are a man and woman. Like the rest, they're dazzling. The woman is petite and doesn't fill out the uniform as well as the other waitresses. She cuts something, I guess the garnishments, with vamp speed.

Working beside her is a smiling wet dream come alive, relatively speaking. Wiry, lean body adorned in a plain white V-neck T-shirt, light blue jeans, and platinum onyx necklace. His wavy auburn hair frames a peaches and cream complexion on his feline face with a straight nose and rectangular jaw. Super yummy. He lifts three crates of alcohol onto the bar as if it was nothing. So it's nine against one. Oy.

"Did you check her for weapons?" the vamp who answered the door asks with a Cockney accent.

"No," my escort Merry responds.

"I'm not armed," I say, as if the mere thought annoys me.

"Just in case, luv," the doorman says as he snatches my purse from me. "Pat her down."

Great. Getting felt up twice in two days. A new record. Rolling my eyes and sighing, I lift up my arms and spread my legs. As Pippin pats me down, and Cockney rifles through my bag, the yummy bartender watches with a smirk and raised eyebrow. The others could care less.

"Nothing," Pippin says.

"Not here either," Cockney says.

"Why would I bring weapons to a friendly sit-down?" I get my purse back. "Besides, I'm on holiday. I don't usually pack my Uzi. So if you could get your boss, please? I'm missing *It's a Wonderful Life*."

The bartender full on smiles, his blue eyes crinkling. I am a sucker for crinkly eyes. Footsteps above draw my attention away from the eye candy. A red-headed man with short hair, goatee, charcoal gray slacks, white dress shirt, and gray vest steps into view.

"Matilda, can you bring me up last night's receipts?" he asks with a clipped British accent.

That must be him. He merely glances at me as the female bartender stops chopping.

"They should be in the safe," Yummy says with an Irish accent. I almost melt inside. Irish accents are my Kryptonite. I've watched all of Colin Farrell's movies and interviews a dozen times just to hear him talk. Liam Neeson's too. And I wore out my copy of *Once*. I really hope I don't have to kill him now.

"Everything fine down here?" Connor asks the Irishman.

"Yes," he says with that voice. I really must be hard up if my G-spot is tingling *now*. I'll be rubbing up against trees in the middle of gun-fights pretty soon. "We shall be up in a minute."

Matilda the bartender locates the receipts and walks upstairs behind the departing Connor. He doesn't look like much. The three bodyguards will be the hardest, especially the vamp one.

"Care to sit?" Irish suggests, motioning to the bar. I glance around the room, but nobody seems to care about me except my escorts, so I sit. As I get closer, I notice I was wrong about his eyes. They're violet like Liz Taylor's. I've never actually met anyone with real violet eyes. He smiles again reassuringly. "May I pour you a drink?"

"No, thank you. I'm fine."

He tsks. "You obviously have no Irish in you."

Is he flirting with me? "Why is that?"

"We Irish will accept a drink even from our worst enemies."

"Are you guys my worst enemies?"

He puts both hands on the bar and leans in toward me. "If we are, Special Agent Alexander, then you must not be doing your job well." His eyes meet mine, and he smiles. Flirtatiously. And yes, a sliver of lust rushes through me.

I mask it by looking away. "Are you trying to capture my mind, Danny Boy?"

"I would never presume to do that, Special Agent. Why mar per-fection?"

I swear this guy and Oliver must have studied under the same seduction teacher, Mr. Casanova de Cheesy. "Rein it in, Danny Boy," I warn. "I'm here to meet your boss, not participate in Flirting 101." Heck yeah! Go, tough Bea!

The vamp frowns. "I apologize if I offended. It is not every day I can enjoy a conversation with a woman of your caliber and beauty, and I mean that with sincerity. I simply could not help myself."

Okay, maybe I could stand to hear a little more, but I don't let him know that. "It's okay, I'm used to it. I live with a vamp. I know if your mouth is moving, you're flirting."

He cocks one of those violet eyes. "You live with a vampire? Who is this fortunate man?"

"Special Agent Oliver Montrose. My partner." Not technically true partners but close enough.

"And you live together?"

"Not like that," I say. "We live in the same house. Separate bedrooms, though."

"But it is true you walked unarmed into a room of twelve vampires to save him from true death?"

"I wasn't unarmed, and it wasn't twelve. More like eight."

"But you were almost directly responsible for the death of the Lord of Dallas."

"*I* didn't kill him," I say quickly.

"You may as well have wielded the sword yourself," Irish says. "And is it true you dispatched, in a single twenty-four hour period, fifteen vampires, including two of whom were over three hundred years old?"

My spidey sense is tingling. "You know, for a lowly bartender, you seem to know a lot about me."

"It is my job to know these things, Agent Alexander."

Ugh. I'm an idiot. I fell for a classic bad guy move that anyone who's watched a Bond flick should have seen a mile away. Now I'm really glad I kept the drooling to a minimum. I lean back in my chair with a crooked smile. "Lord Connor, I presume." He bows his head and all the other vamps in the room chuckle at my stupidity. There goes my credibility. I am so going to die. "Nice one."

"I am afraid you caught me on my night off," Connor says, "otherwise I would have greeted you in proper attire."

"What? A tuxedo and cape?"

"I was thinking more along the lines of body armor and shotgun."

"You're cuter this way," I say with a sly smile. "Shotguns don't really do it for me."

"And what does, pray tell?"

I lean in a little. "Irish accents and crinkly eyes."

He grins back. "In that case, we should continue our conversation upstairs? With a bit more privacy?"

I lean in more so we're close enough to kiss while meeting his eyes. "Thought you'd never ask, your Lordship." And the Golden Globe for acting cool while really wanting to run screaming from the building goes to … the corpse of Bea Alexander.

I take the lead up the stairs, not the best defensive position, but there's not much choice since Connor gestures for me to go first. He stays a step behind me, making his presence known but not crowding me, though his hand on the railing is millimeters from mine.

Inside the small office, the fake Connor sits at the desk punching numbers into a calculator. There's nothing here but a safe, file cabinet, fax machine, desk, chair, and black leather love seat. Just from the décor I can tell Connor doesn't spend much time here. It's too drab for a vampire. They enjoy the finer things, and this place doesn't even have a window. The fact he didn't bring me to his base of operations tells me he's cautious. That he's afraid something might go wrong. Not good.

"I am almost finished here, sir," the fake Connor says. He bundles the receipts with a rubber band then jumps out of the seat like a scared mouse as Connor approaches.

"Please sit, Agent Alexander," Connor says as he takes his seat behind the desk. I take the plastic chair across from him. The other vamp lowers himself onto the loveseat so I can only see him out of the corner of my eye. "Will your police friend be joining us?" Connor asks. "I believe I requested both of you."

"Requested?"

"You are not here by force, therefore you are here by your own accord."

"You threatened my family."

"I did nothing of the sort," he counters, "and if you accuse me further, I wish to view proof."

"What do you call those two men parked outside my house? Or reciting my address?"

"Perhaps I sent those men to escort you in case you were unable to locate the club? Or merely out of courtesy? Gas is *quite* expensive these days."

This guy is good. "What? Were you a lawyer in your past life?"

He smiles. "No. This one. The Fifties were dull. I am a member of the bar and all."

"Then you know the law, human or otherwise. I have committed no offense to warrant your threats, overt or not. I am a sworn officer of the law, and I responded to a possible crime scene. There was no excessive force used or harm done."

"And your police friend?"

"He's a civilian and therefore out of bounds. I did call him and told him to be here, but I have no control over him."

"So you were not responsible for his actions today? He was not acting at your behest?"

"Huh?"

Connor glances at the other vamp. "Neil?"

"At one o'clock this afternoon, the emergency hotline received a call from one Mariah Turner, who identified herself as the consort of registered vampire Moon Lipmann. Two Chula Vista police officers, Weir and Rupp, arrived to her door and demanded entry. When it was denied, Rupp pushed his way in, and Weir followed. A litany of questions regarding both the incident the previous night and your involvement with both Turner and Lipmann followed. When she refused to answer, Weir threatened to arrest her. He punched a hole in the wall when she did not answer. The two officers then left, promising to return until their questions were answered."

"Oh crap," I mutter.

"You can see our concern," Connor says.

"Look, I had no idea he did that. *None.* The only reason he was there last night was we were together when I got the call. He followed me without my knowledge."

"Who is he?" Connor asks.

"My ex-boyfriend."

"Does he know about us?" Connor asks.

"Not at all," I say.

"Will he let this go or do *I* need to speak to him?"

Meaning get inside his head and erase everything. Sadly this is the best option, but I can't bring myself to serve up my ex to this monster. "He'll let it go. I can get him to back off. If I can't, then you can try."

"That seems fair," Neil says. "Better we have no exposure on this situation at all. It *is* the police."

Connor mulls over this for a second. "Agreed. This is your mess, you clean it up."

"Then I'll be going," I say with a smile. That was easy. I stand up. "It was very nice meeting you."

"Agent Alexander, please return to your seat," Connor says. "That was only the first issue in need of discussion."

"I'm sorry?"

"Sit, please," Connor says with an undercurrent of menace.

Neil stands up, folding his arms across his chest.

"O … kay," I say as I sit. "Next topic?"

"Oliver Smythe, now Montrose."

I roll my eyes. "Of course," I say. "What about him? He owe you money? Sleep with your sister? Or brother?"

"Agent Alexander, I have held this territory for over one hundred and fifty years, longer than almost anyone in North America, save the King. Do you know how I managed this?"

"With a smile?" I ask. "Or torture. I'm gonna go with torture."

"By perceiving potential threats and neutralizing them," Connor says.

"How proactive of you. What does this have to do with me?"

"Your mere presence in my territory could be construed as one of those threats."

"What?" I laugh. "I've lived here for years."

"That was before you became the known consort of an elder vampire who, with your assistance, helped to slay a Lord. You have already made overt threats and bodily harm to one of my subjects. For all I know you are here doing reconnaissance in an attempt to usurp my position for him."

"Um, *or* I'm here on friggin' vacation to visit my family for Christmas! And for the record, and I feel like I need to make an announcement on CNN or something, I am not 'consorting,'" I say, doing finger quotes, "with Oliver!"

"You registered as his consort on legally binding papers in Dallas under Oliver's human last name." *Huh*? "He has fed on you on multiple occasions, even marking you. And you admitted to residing in the same house as him. Therefore, you are his legal consort and are thereby an extension of him. He can be held legally responsible for your actions and vice versa. It is vampiric law. Did he never explain this to you?"

I am going to ... KILL HIM!

"No," I say, trying to remain calm. Dead. He is so dead.

"Therefore, your presence in my territory, coupled with the fact you did not make said presence known as you are required to do by law, and your own known lethality at least warrants a conversation between us."

Those violet eyes catch mine. There's no malice or fear, just amusement. "I'll bet you were top of your class in law school," I say.

"Second," he says with a smile.

"Well, I'm sorry for not registering with you. I didn't know I had to."

"Ignorance of the law is not a defense," Connor says.

"Then I don't have one," I say, shrugging my shoulders. "Look, I'm not here to do anything but shop, go to the beach, and celebrate Christmas. *Nothing else*. I swear on my grandmother's life. I don't want to usurp anything. I am in no way a threat to you."

"I wish I could take you at your word, but I cannot. I am sorry."

"So there's nothing I can say? You've just made up your mind?"

The telephone rings and Connor picks it up. "Yes?" He listens. "Provide him a drink on the house. We shall be down shortly." Connor hangs up. "Officer Weir is here. Right on time." My stomach tightens. It's one thing for me to possibly be at death's door, but the fact I dragged Steven here is ratcheting up my fear.

"Don't hurt him," I say.

"I have no intention of harming him," Connor says.

"And me?" I shake my head. "Look, I've lived here for almost twenty years without incident. I'm a Federal Agent, and so is Oliver. We don't want your territory, okay? The only way we're a threat is if you do something stupid here. You want to talk law? Then let's talk law. If you hurt me or mine without cause, the F.R.E.A.K.S. will descend upon you like a tidal wave and remove you by any means necessary. And I guarantee you, it will not be pretty. Just ask Freddy St. Clair. Bottom line: you stay out of my way, and I'll stay out of yours."

He doesn't even take time to think before saying, "I am afraid that is not good enough."

I cross my arms and scoff. "Then what do you suggest we do, Captain Paranoid?"

"As I see it, we have three options. One is that you leave town and never return."

"Not happening. Next?"

"You stay, I keep both you and your family under close surveillance until I find cause to kill you. Exposure of the vampire world to non-essentials, including your family, would be enough."

Oh fudge. "I can keep a secret," I lie.

"That is just one example. There are at least a dozen laws where death or imprisonment are the punishment."

"Such as?"

Connor smirks and his eyes crinkle. If he wasn't threatening to kill me, I'd be turned on. "I want you gone, Agent Alexander. If you do not know, why would I tell you?"

"Fine. And option three?"

He leans back in the chair, lacing his fingers behind his head. "You renounce all ties to Oliver Smythe and become *my* consort."

My mouth drops open. "Huh?" Okay, not expecting that. I was sure option three was a dual to the death, not what amounts to the vampire form of a marriage proposal.

"This would, of course, mean cutting off any and all communication with him," Connor continues. "You would have to vacate your current residence and spend at least six months of the year with me at my home. There would be some feeding involved, along with sexual relations at least once, but judging from the high level of lust I feel from you, I believe that would not be an issue."

I sit, dumbfounded for a moment, then say, "*Huh*?"

"Your pupils dilated and your respiration rate changed when you saw me."

"Oh."

"And I do find you incredibly attractive as well," he says. "More than I believed I would, which is a pleasant surprise."

"I'm glad?" I say awkwardly.

"I am very particular about choosing my official consorts," he says. "In the last hundred years, I have had only three."

Three ex-wives. Not a glowing endorsement. "What happened to them?"

"We grew tired of one another. I provided for them afterwards, even the ones I turned." He sits upright again. "I would give you almost complete autonomy and the freedom to take lovers if you so wish."

"Wow," I say sarcastically, "a relationship of convenience. How romantic. Every girl's dream."

"It could quickly grow to be more. You intrigue me, Agent Alexander. Not an easy feat. And I am excellent at reading people. I believe we could easily fall in love with one another," he says with certainty. "If you desire fidelity, I could promise that, as long as I receive it in return. And you and your family would want for nothing until the end of your days."

"And all I have to do in return is quit my job, never see my friend again, and be your concubine?"

"That or you are banished," he says. "Here or there. The choice is yours."

My mouth opens to retort, but nothing comes to mind. Here or there. Him or me. Us or them. Why does this keep happening to me? I'm getting fed up with people forcing me to make life-altering choices to suit them. On my friggin' holiday no less. "You do realize you're forcing me to choose between my job and my family?"

"Yes, I know," he says, sounding genuinely upset. "But if you look at it logically, the choice is clear. I am familiar with the exploits of the F.R.E.A.K.S. It is harrowing, disgusting work where violent death is a true possibility. But here, you will have not only your family but wealth. And power." He smirks again. "Not to mention a skilled and devoted lover who would do all in his considerable power to make you happy until your dying day. This I can promise you. Simply say yes."

Okay, is it bad that there's a tiny part of me that is considering this? Very tiny, but it's still there. He is hot, rich, and powerful. And … no. *No. Get a grip, Bea.* Don't let the accent or animal magnetism win. "You've thought about this a lot, I can tell," I say. And as the words flow I realize he *has* put a lot of thought into this. More than he's letting on. This was his endgame the whole time. This proposal is why I'm here. But why?

Before I can turn this over in my head, the telephone rings. Connor answers it. "Yes?" He listens for a moment. "Fine. We shall be right down." He hangs up. "Officer Weir is demanding to see you. He is quite belligerent. We will have to continue this conversation later."

I swear after the past few days I'm thinking that joining an all-female convent is the smartest thing to do. Neil opens the door for me, and the two vamps follow me out, Connor keeping only a few inches between us down the hall and to the stairs. Not big on personal space, I guess.

Everyone, including Steven—who must be on his lunch break as he's in his uniform complete with gun and handcuffs—gazes up as we descend the stairs. Steven is fuming. He breathes so hard he could blow down a little pig's house.

"Bea, what the hell is going on?" he asks as I walk toward him.

"Sorry," I say. "Sorry. My meeting ran late."

"Your *meeting*?" he asks, eyeing Connor and Neil.

I reach him at the bar and touch his arm. "Yeah. Sorry. Let's go outside and—"

"It is cold out there," Connor says, his eyes narrowing a little. "And we have not finished our meeting."

Steven steps away from me toward Connor. "And who the hell are you?"

"Steven!" I admonish.

"Connor McInnis," he says, not missing a beat.

"He's Moon Lipmann's lawyer," I say.

"Who?" Steven asks.

"He represents the man you harassed today," I say.

Steven glares at the unemotional vamp, sizing him up. "And why are *you* meeting him here?"

"I own this establishment," Connor says, "among others."

They are not making this easy for me. "Mariah," I jump in, "called him after you threatened her. And then she called me. I came here to smooth things over so he wouldn't report you. What the heck were you thinking going back there?"

His fury at these words almost knocks me down. "*Me*? What was *I* thinking? You of all people have the fucking nerve to ask me that?"

"Please calm down, Officer," Connor says. "There is no need for that tone."

"This has nothing to do with you," Steven says.

"Miss Alexander is a guest in my club, therefore it is my business."

Steven's attention whips toward me, flabbergasted and about ready to punch someone. "Are you kidding me with this bullshit?"

"Calm down," I say, "and let me explain everything."

Still on the verge of violence, he crosses his arms. "Fine. Talk."

"Everything I told you last night was true. I used to baby-sit Mariah, her boyfriend scared her, I went to get her. It was stupid. I should have asked for your help, but after what almost happened last night I didn't think I had the right and, quite frankly, I just wanted to get as far away from you as possible. I shouldn't have led you on like that, and I'm sorry. And that's it. That's all. I *swear*." Please, for the love of God and all that is holy, believe me.

Steven studies my face, that stony gargoyle expression not wavering. "This has to do with drugs, doesn't it? This man is your supplier, isn't he?"

Oh for God's sake. I glance at the amused Connor, who shrugs. My mess. Right. "Fine. Yes. Drugs. I'm into drugs. Lots of drugs. Millions of drugs. I'm a donkey or whatever they call it. I confess."

"I knew it." Without missing a beat, Steven takes off his cuffs and grabs my wrist. I'm too shocked to say anything. "Beatrice Alexander, I am placing you under arrest for drug trafficking and distribution." The good news is that I get to leave this club with all my limbs and not married to a scary vamp. The bad, jail sucks.

But before he can slap the metal on, Connor magically appears beside Steven, grabbing his hand. "I am afraid I cannot allow you to do this."

Steven jerks his hand away as if death himself was touching him. "What the fuck?" Steven shouts, stumbling back a step.

"Great," I mutter. "Smart. What happened to not revealing your true self?"

"Your approach was failing," Connor says. "Memory wipe is the only viable option."

Steven glances at me, then Connor, then back to me, breath ragged. I used to do the same thing when Oliver did his super-speed thing, but I'm used to it now. "Bea, what the fuck is going on?"

"Steven, calm down," I say.

He looks at Connor. "What the fuck are you?"

"Nothing you will remember." Connor steps toward him, trying to meet his eyes.

Steven doesn't give him a chance. He reaches down and grabs his gun, pointing it at Connor's head. All the vamps that were pretending not to watch the ensuing drama all tense and stop what they're doing. "Don't move another step."

My stomach lurches. We're dead. "Steven, put the gun down," I say.

He doesn't take his eyes off Connor. "No way."

"Steven, you have no idea what you're doing," I say with the hysteria breaking through the calm. "Put the gun down!"

"Listen to your friend," Connor says.

"Shut the fuck up!"

"You can't hurt him with that," I practically scream. "Put the gun—"

The doorman vanishes and reappears next to Steven, snarling to expose his sharp fangs. At the same time, he grabs at Steven's gun. The jerking motion causes him to fire. A burst of blood explodes on Connor's chest before he falls to the ground. I'm not sure which happens next, but my instincts take over. The doorman flies across the room into the bouncer, knocking them both down. Neil kneels beside the bleeding but conscious Connor.

Steven whips his gun around toward the two oncoming waitresses and fires. The one he hits falls, but the one he misses vanishes a millisecond later, grabbing him by the neck when she reappears. His cop instincts take over. The moment she makes contact, he karate chops the butt of his gun onto her nose. I hear a sickening crack and blood gushes from her face. She releases him, and he punches her in the face again. She glides across the room from the force. I don't think I was responsible for that. He must spend hours every day at the gym to get that strong.

Before she lands, the DJ leaps over his turntables toward Steven. One of the chairs I toss across the room connects with him before he lands, knocking him into a heap on the dance floor. Not that it matters. The doorman and bouncer have recovered and appear in front of Steven. And that's when I hear the cocking of a shotgun. Out of the corner of my eye, I see Matilda pointing its long barrel at my ex.

It's as if someone puts everything on pause and only I know it. They're going to kill him. They're going to rip his throat out and lap up his blood as if he's a human drinking fountain. And it's all my fault. Like it or not I brought him into this, and now he's going to die because of it. He never would have touched this world if not for caring about me. I can't let that happen.

The world goes from stopped to slow. The two vamps inch closer toward Steven, who positions his gun at the bouncer, oblivious to the real danger behind him. Lucky for him, I'm not. As the two vamps grab Steven's arms, I whip my head to the right. The shotgun lifts out of Matilda's hands and sails into mine. I point the barrel down at the still prostrate Connor's head. Neil raises his arms instinctively, but fear must not be in Connor's repertoire because instead of scared he appears gratified.

"Nobody move!" I roar.

All eyes fall to me. The two vamps holding Steven tighten their grip. Steven groans and bucks against them. "Put that down, or we'll kill him," the doorman says.

"No, you won't," I say. "Because if you do, first I'll blow off your bosses' head, then yours. Then, just by flicking my pinky, I will rip your spines out. Each and every one of yours. And since I'm sure you all know about the bloodbath in Dallas, you'll know I'm capable of it. Right, Connor?"

They glance at the now smiling and fully healed vamp. "Without a doubt."

"Good. Let Steven go. *Now.*"

They glance at Connor, who nods. They release Steven and he jumps away. He picks up his gun and trains it on the men, his hands shaking. "Fuckers."

"Good minions." I stare back down at Connor, meeting his eyes. "Now, I want *you* to listen to me and listen good, Danny Boy. I want safe passage for me and Officer Weir. There will be no reprisals for this incident. Both sides are at fault, so we'll call it a wash. Agreed?"

"Agreed," Connor says.

"Fuck that!" Steven shouts. "These assholes attacked me!"

"After you shot an unarmed man!" I shout back.

Steven walks backwards toward me, keeping his gun on the other two. "These are fucking vampires! We can't let them live!"

"Steven, shut up!"

"Bea, we need to—"

"Memory wipe," Connor cuts in. "I must insist now."

Crap. He's right. He'll never let this go now. He could bring the entire force here with torches, pitchforks, and stakes. "Fine. But I want to hear what you're putting in there."

"That is fair. Neil?"

"What the hell is a wipe?" Steven asks me. I hate to do this, but I knock his gun out of his hands with my mind. Simultaneously Neil is suddenly standing behind Steven, grabbing him from behind and putting him into a headlock. A stunned Steven struggles and gasps for air, but the vamp brings them both to their knees beside Connor. Neil forces Steven's red face right into Connor's. Eye contact is un-avoidable.

"You will remember nothing about the past two days. You will not remember following Beatrice to the Lipmann residence. You will not remember Moon, Mariah, or coming to the club tonight. You will leave here and never return." He breaks eye contact to look up at me. "What shall I replace the memories with?"

"He met friends for bowling, took me out to dinner, dropped me off at home, went to work the next day, and was coming to meet me here for drinks."

Connor turns back to Steven and repeats my words verbatim. "And now you will wait outside for Beatrice." He breaks the gaze. "Re-lease him."

Neil releases the catatonic Steven, who stands up like a good puppet and walks past the seething vamps. The bleeding waitress snarls at him, but Steven doesn't register her presence. He should come out of it when I meet him outside. Until then, he'll be trapped inside his own head. I loathe taking his memories and free will, but he'll be safer this way. The front door slams shut.

"First that mongoloid, then Oliver," Connor says. "You have abysmal taste in men."

"Oh shut up," I say.

"*You* are holding the gun," Connor says. "But now that the not so good Samaritan has departed safely, what comes next? Do you prove my suspicions correct by firing? Or may we continue our conversation in more comfortable surroundings and with less firepower?"

"You know, for a man with a shotgun to his head, you sure are calm, especially considering you're so convinced I'm here to usurp your throne."

"I am over six hundred years old, this is not the first and will certainly not be the last time I find myself in this predicament."

"Still. We both know I'm not going to pull this trigger, so listen closely, Danny Boy." I look into those violet eyes. "I want you to remember this moment. *This* is the moment I *could* have killed you. This is the moment when I probably should kill you for even thinking of threatening my family. But I won't. I'm letting you live. I'm not even going to report this to the F.R.E.A.K.S. And the reason I'm doing this is to prove you have nothing to fear from me. I am not a threat to you. And I never was. So I'm going to walk out of here, and you're going to leave me alone. If you see me on the street, you walk to the other side. If I even get a whiff of you anywhere near me or mine, I'll be back. And *then* you should be afraid of me. Do we understand each other?"

He smirks. "Oh yes."

"Groovy." I cock the shotgun, expelling all the cartridges to the floor and tossing the gun across the room. I pick up Steven's pistol and cuffs, sticking them in my pants. "And just a little friendly advice? Next time you want to make an indecent proposal, send candy not goons."

"I shall remember that for next time, Agent Alexander."

"Good. Happy Holidays."

It takes all my willpower not to run like the Flash out of that club, but since it was bravado that's more or less kept me alive in the past few minutes, I must keep up appearances. Instead I saunter out, narrowing my eyes at the bouncer and doorman who part to let me pass. I half expect an attack but make it to the door without incident.

When I step out into the cold night air, the thin fibers holding me together give way. My breath comes out in ragged spurts, and my knees almost give out. My appearance has snapped Steven out of his spell, and he rushes over to me.

"Oh my God, Bea! Are you okay?" he asks, putting his arm around my waist.

"Can you please just drive me to my car?"

His patrol car is only a few feet away, but I need to lean on him a little to make those steps. He opens the door and plops me in the front. I jerk when the door slams shut. I should be fine in a few minutes. The adrenaline will disappear, and I'll regain motor control.

Steven follows my instructions to the car, glancing at me on the way.

"Maybe you shouldn't drive," he says when we pull up to the lot.

"I'll be okay," I say. "I just felt nauseous for a moment."

"You're not drunk, are you?" he asks. "I can't remember. What did you order?"

"A Coke. We both had Cokes. Are you sure *you're* okay? You've been kind of a space cadet for the past two days."

"I have?" he asks, confusion all over his face. He thinks for a moment. "I guess."

"Have you been getting enough sleep?"

"I think so. Huh."

I open the car door. "Get some sleep." I'm about to step out but remember his gun. "Oh. Here." I hand him his service weapon and cuffs. "You forgot to get them back from the bouncer."

"I gave him my gun?" he asks, surprised at his faux pas.

"They wouldn't let us in otherwise. Remember?"

He puts it back in its holster. "Oh."

I smile sympathetically. "Steven, seriously. Get some sleep. I'll call you later." I get out of the car and shut the door.

I know I'm the world's worst ex-girlfriend. Lying, having someone mind rape him, confusing the heck out of him. I've lost at least a thousand karma points, but at least he's alive. That's what I hate about this job. The ends barely justify the means.

I start up my rental car and pull out of the lot.

Time to go home and face the music. At least it's not a funeral dirge.

"I would have preferred that you *were* into drugs," Nana says, extremely calm for the information overload I've just given her.

"You raised me better than that," I say with a weak smile.

"And that's where you were tonight? With … vampires?"

"Yeah."

I let this sink in. We sit on the couch in the living room facing each other. She's wringing her hands in her lap through our entire conversation. All in all she's handling it well, better than I would. I really didn't want to tell her, especially after all of Connor's threats, but I had to. My new life is affecting my family. They have a right to know. And it feels good to tell. Freeing.

"Did they hurt you?" she asks.

"No."

"Did you hurt them?"

"Not a lot."

She's silent for a moment, trying to form the correct words. "Why—How—Why . . ." She sighs. "I have no idea what to say in this situation."

"'I'm proud of you'?" I offer.

"I was thinking more along the lines of 'You're grounded.'" She shakes her head. "This is because of what happened to Brian, isn't it? I should have been more forceful with him growing up. I should have tanned his hide the first time he was cruel to you."

"Nana, stop it. This was all me. My decision."

But she's not listening to me. She stares at the coffee table. "And you lied to me. All these months?"

"I didn't want you to worry. That's all."

I try to touch her hand, but she pulls it away. "That's my job, Beatrice. And you didn't trust me to do it." She stands up. "I'm tired. I'm going to bed. We'll talk more about this in the morning."

She walks into the hallway, and a moment later her bedroom door shuts. I fall back into the couch and hug a pillow. That could have gone better. I wasn't expecting a parade or anything but some acknowledgement about my good deeds would be nice. I sigh. What a couple of days. Tomorrow I am so not leaving my bedroom. Not if there's a fire, an earthquake, or if Chris Evans shows up on my doorstep begging me to run off to Hawaii with him. With my luck a huge lava monster would chose *right then* to wake up and attack the tourists.

I lock my bedroom door and change into my pajamas. It's only 8:30, but I shut everything off and climb into bed. The problem with adrenaline is that when it wears off, you feel a hundred years old. Muscles hurt, your thinking is sluggish, and sleep is the only cure. I close my eyes and within minutes this horrid day fades away. Some holiday I'm having.

———

Pounding. On my door. Crap.

My eyes open as fist meets door again. It takes a second but the cobwebs vanish, and I can think again. There's another succession of pounds.

"Bea, wake up!" Nana says, her voice peppered with fear.

I jump out of bed, totally awake now. I open the door to find a wide-eyed Nana clutching onto her robe and a metal baseball bat.

"What? What is it?"

"I think they followed you home. The vampires."

Instinct takes over. I snatch the bat out of her hands and run to the front door just as the doorbell chimes.

"There's two of them!" Nana calls.

They can't get inside without being invited, but their human goons can. I raise the bat as I peek through the peephole. Of course. Because this day couldn't get any worse. I lower the bat, not because I don't want to hit the people outside, but because I do.

"Oh hell," I mutter.

"Who is it?" Nana asks.

With a groan, I unlock the door and open it. I can never get a freaking break.

"Hello, Trixie. Care to invite us in?"

I slam the door in his face.

NINE

UNWELCOME GUESTS

"I'm afraid I don't have, um, anything to offer you Mr. . . . " Nana says to Oliver as she hands Will a cup of coffee.

"Montrose, Mrs. Alexander," Oliver says with a gracious smile. "But I insist you call me Oliver."

They're in my living room. On my couch and chair. Making small talk with my grandmother. Who is acting like Emily frigging Post to a werewolf and vampire. Really wish I still had that bat in my hands.

"Yeah, we could have run to the butcher shop *had we known you were coming*," I say through gritted teeth as if the folded arms and dagger eyes aren't enough of a signal of my displeasure.

"Beatrice," Nana warns, "be nice. Your friends flew all the way from Kansas because they were worried about you."

"*Right*," I say sarcastically.

Nana shoots me a "behave" look before smiling back down at Will. "Are you sure I can't offer you something to eat? I'm not sure what your kind enjoy, but I'm sure we can find something."

Will glances at me, no doubt surprised to be outed, but I keep my eyes on the ceiling. "Um, no thank you, Mrs. Alexander, but I'm much obliged for the offer."

Nana smiles. "What lovely manners you have, Agent Price." She glances at me. "It's so rare in the young."

Oh barf.

"Thank you, ma'am," Will says, blushing.

Not to be upstaged, Oliver says, "You have a beautiful home, Mrs. Alexander. Not just the decor, which reminds me of my year in Arizona at the turn of the century, but I can feel the glow of happiness radiating from the walls. It is no wonder your granddaughter is such a well-adjusted, thoughtful woman. She obviously had a spectacular role model in you."

Oh projectile barf.

"Thank you, Oliver," a beaming Nana says. She lowers herself onto the couch next to Will. "Call me Liz. Both of you."

Oliver glances at me with triumph blasting from his smile. I narrow my eyes at him. "And we do apologize for our unexpected intrusion," Oliver says, turning his attention back to Nana, "and for frightening you."

"Oh, that's all right," she says, patting Will's hand. "I'm just so glad that there's someone out there looking out for my Honey Bea."

"Your Honey Bea can look out for herself," I say.

"Still. She just told me tonight what you all do. Needless to say, I'm very worried."

"Naturally," Oliver says. "But your granddaughter is one of our greatest assets. There is not a soul alive today I would rather have at my side when danger strikes. She is resourceful, level headed, and creative when most would crumble. She has saved my life on more than one occasion. You should be very proud."

Nana squeezes Oliver's hand. "Thank you."

Will's gaze drops to the floor as he sips his coffee. The look of defeat. He should know by now not to attempt a battle of charm against Oliver. It's like a toddler challenging a kung fu master to a fight. I'd feel rotten for him if I wasn't so darn angry right now.

Nana releases Oliver's hand. "Now, where are you two staying while you're in town? I can make up the spare room, but we only have the one I'm afraid. We might be able to squeeze your coffin in there as well but … you do sleep in a coffin, right?"

"On occasion."

"Well then—"

"They. Are. Not. Staying. Here," I say.

"Beatrice, they're our guests."

"I don't care!" I shout. "They're leaving tonight."

"But if you're in danger—"

"I'm not in danger! I took care of it!"

Will clears his throat. "It is very nice of you to offer, Liz, but we've already reserved some rooms at the Marriott. We'll be staying there. We don't want to impose."

"Too late," I mutter.

Nana shoots me another glare. "Well, if you change your minds, the offer is open."

"Thank you," Will says.

"Well then," Nana says as she stands, "I'll let you have some privacy to talk shop."

Both men stand as she does. "Thank you," Will says.

Oliver takes her hand and kisses it. "It was an honor to finally meet you."

Nana's face flushes red. "You as well."

I push myself off the wall I've been leaning against and pull Nana away. "Okay, Don Juan," I say, rolling my eyes. I usher my grandmother out of the room.

"Pleasant dreams, Liz," Oliver calls.

Nana and I walk to her bedroom. "You know, for monsters, they are very nice. Handsome too. I never would have guessed about their afflictions." She steps into her bedroom but turns back around. "And I'm sorry. For earlier tonight. It was … all just a shock."

"I know. There's nothing to forgive."

"I still want to have a long talk about this."

"I know. Tomorrow, okay?"

She kisses my cheek. "Good night. And be nice. They're here because they care about you. Quite a bit from what I can tell."

"I'll try to keep that in mind." Between their mental torture sessions. I kiss her cheek. "Night."

When I return to the living room, Oliver is pacing around the room, looking at pictures on the mantle, and Will is still on the couch with his leg twitching. He reminds me of a child waiting in the principal's office. Oliver picks up a picture. "Is this you? Pink is not your color."

I snatch the photo of me at homecoming in an ugly pink dress from his hand. "Give me that! Don't touch my stuff." I put the photo back. "What the hell are you two doing here? I told you not to come. I distinctly remember the words *do not come* leaving my mouth. And yet, here you are. In my house. On my vacation. Flirting with my grandmother. What the eff?"

"You called in a potential threat," Will says. "You were alone. Policy dictates—"

"Oh, shut up, Will! God! You know, *him*," I say, gesturing to Oliver, "I can almost understand showing up as this was *all his fault*, but why on God's"—Oliver flinches again, as I wanted him to—"green earth are you here? I didn't call you! I don't need or want you here!"

"That is precisely what I told him," Oliver says.

"Zip it, Oliver! You're lucky I didn't Mace you at the door!"

Will rises, the twitch in his leg spreading all over his body. I can feel his anger and frustration on my skin. "I will not apologize for following protocol."

"Cease with your idiotic protocol," Oliver snaps. "We all know why you are really here. Be a man and just bloody admit it!"

Like a wild animal, Will lunges at Oliver and I barely have enough time to push the men apart with my mind before the fists, fangs, and claws start flying. Obviously my absence has done nothing to improve relations between them. "Stop it!" I scream. "This is my grandmother's house, not a wrestling arena!"

"But—" Will says.

"But nothing! Will, go wait outside and cool off! I'm separating you two. Go! Now!"

Will glares at me but does as I say, stalking out of the room. When I look back at Oliver, he's smiling in triumph again. I literally slap the smile off his face. Shocked, he touches his stinging cheek. "You—"

"Shut up," I say. "I swear to the man above, you say another cutesy word, I will shove a chair leg into your chest."

Any hint of enjoyment vanishes. "I am sorry."

I scoff. "Which part are you sorry about? The part where you don't listen to me? The part where you show up on my doorstep without warning when I specifically asked you to stay in Kansas?" I shove him. "Or how about the part where you neglect to inform me we're friggin' married in your messed-up, violent vampire world?"

"What are you talking about?"

"Apparently I'm your consort. And I was almost killed tonight because of it."

"But you are not."

"Um, we live together. You've fed off me. And that's how you registered me in Dallas."

"We were undercover," he points out.

"You registered us under your real name, douche bag! Why the hell did you do that?"

"It was the name Marianna knew me under," he says.

I shove him again. "How could you not know this stuff?"

"We have not slept together, therefore all requirements have not been met."

"Um, idiot, in case you haven't noticed, *nobody believes that!* And there's no way to prove it! And since you neglected to fill me in on this consort thing, I didn't register and Connor dragged me in and called me on it."

"What did he do to you?" he asks, concerned for the first time.

"You know, the usual. Threat of torture. Gun fight. Mind raping my ex-boyfriend. An offer to become his mistress of the underworld."

"He propositioned you?"

"Yeah. Something along the lines of 'Dump him, marry me, or I'll find a reason to kill you.' It was all very romantic."

"So that is why they are parked across the street."

I do a double take. "What?"

"Across the street. Black sedan. Two men."

Fudge. I move to the window to peek out. Sure enough the same sedan, complete with key mark, sits directly across the street. "Bastard." I close the drapes. "Guess he decided on option two."

"What?"

"Nothing. I'm just an *idiot* for trusting the word of a vamp. And a lawyer one to boot. Now the goon squad has probably called Connor and told him you're here when I told him *specifically* you wouldn't be. You might as well just burn down my house now and save them the trouble!"

"My dear, I only understand half of what you say. Tell me everything that transpired between the two of you."

I do, only leaving out the Steven make-out session.

"So?" I ask.

"He wants you," Oliver says more to himself than to me.

"Duh. But why go to all this trouble?"

"Strategically, it's brilliant. It is like a marriage of convenience, the joining of two dynasties."

"I'm exhausted. English please."

"Who would dare challenge Connor with you by his side? A powerful psychokinetic with not only ties to the F.R.E.A.K.S., but who slayed fifteen vampires in one day?"

"He threatened me. Why would I lift a finger to help him?"

"Your family. Your life. If you are, by law, my consort you *are* bound by vampiric law whether you wish to be or not. He could leverage your law-breaking into a death sentence." He shakes his head, smiling to himself. "He is a sly fox. Never trust an Irishman."

"So what do we do to stop me from becoming the Bride of Frankenstein? Can we threaten him? Kill him?"

"We have no cause. He has acted within his rights."

"So *what*?"

"To be honest, at this moment, I have not a clue."

"Great. *Great*. Thank you," I spit out. "Thank you for dragging me into this mess. I am so glad you're here. Appreciate it."

I take a step, and he grabs my arm. "Trixie—"

I jerk my arm away. "Don't touch me. Don't you ever touch me again! You have caused me *nothing* but misery since I first set eyes on you. You attacked me. You literally scarred me. You almost got me killed half a dozen times. And now this." I stick my finger into his beautiful face. "Everyone hates me because I'm friends with you. My family is in danger because I gave a damn about you. And for what? A better wardrobe and a few laughs?"

"Trixie—"

"No! Shut up! I'm done. I'm done with all of this. I can't take it anymore." I bite my lip to stop the tears. "We fix this, we make sure my family is safe, and that's it. I quit."

"You do not mean that."

"The hell I don't."

I storm out into the back yard before he can see me cry. Or I kill him. It's about fifty/fifty at this point. Will is smart enough to not rush over to me but not smart enough to run back inside. "And as for you," I say to him, "how dare you attack someone in my grandmother's home? And how *dare* you speak to me the way you did earlier on the phone? Not only was it unprofessional, but it was hurtful. And mean. I thought after everything we talked about, you'd learned something!"

"I was just—"

"You were just what? Showing me how much you care about me? Let me give you a lesson about girls. *Yelling*, not a big turn on. I know what I did was stupid, but you know what? I'd do it again. An innocent girl needed help. I couldn't wait for you. So I did what I had to do. Just like tonight. Just like Dallas. And I don't want any crap for it. You got me, boss?"

"I—"

"And another thing! I *distinctly* remember telling both of you I didn't want to see you again until you'd settled things! And since you tried to tear his throat out in there, I'm thinking you haven't. So why are you here? Because I have enough on my plate without having to rip you two apart every five minutes!" I pause. "Well? Speak!"

Will just stands there looking at me, his mouth opening and closing slightly. "I don't—"

"You don't what?"

"Will you please let me talk?" he shouts. His eyes, hair, everything is wild now. "Jesus Christ! You drive me fucking crazy sometimes!"

"*I* drive *you* crazy? Are you on crack?"

"Just shut up for three seconds! Lord!" He throws his hands up in frustration. "I've just spent two and a half hours on a small plane with two men who despise me after a really bad day because I was scared to fucking death something happened to you, only to get attacked right off the bat! And now you won't even let me talk! So yeah, you drive me nuts! But here I am! So you will let me fucking explain! Okay?" He almost pants in anger.

I open my mouth for a snappy comeback, but it won't come out. "Okay."

He runs both his hands though his floppy hair and starts pacing. "This is not me, you know. I am not a yeller. I don't attack people, even when they deserve it." He looks back into the house then back to me. "But for some reason, when I'm around you, I just ... I lose it. I lose my fucking mind. My judgment gets clouded, and I don't mean what I say or do. But the thought of you getting hurt or ... " He stops pacing and looks at me. Really looks at me. "I don't like this person." He shakes his head. "You asked me why I'm here? Because I couldn't *not* be. I know you can handle yourself. I do. I've seen it. I'm breathing because of it. But the thought of you walking into a cabal alone with those bottom feeders drove reason clear out of my brain. And that pisses me off because I *pride* myself on being clearheaded and reasonable. And a part of me hates you for making me this person. That's why I yell. That's why I act like an asshole. Because I don't know whether to kill you or…" He finally takes a deep breath. "And I know it's not your fault. I *know* that. But it's not rational, it's just how it is. And I don't know how to stop it. So here I am. Yelling at you again and hating myself for it. And having *you* hate me for it. And that kills me. I don't want to be like this. I can't stand it, but I can't stop it. And I don't know if you're worth all this." He shrugs. "You can't be worth my sanity, right? So. Here we are. Yeah."

I'm shocked. Totally and utterly shocked. Him too, because his wild expression matches my own. I think this is the first time he's admitted these things to anyone, including himself. Part of me wants to smack him. The other … well, I guess we have that in common. "Um," I say, trying to keep my voice from breaking, "thank you. For your honesty. I appreciate it." Then the words hit my brain, and my stomach drops right down there with my heart. Those tears I've been holding back since yesterday can no longer be contained. "I've been, um," I sniffle, "thinking about this for the last few days. And I said it in there, but … I mean it out here. I make everything too hard. No matter what, I make things worse for everyone around me. So after this Connor thing is taken care of, I'm gonna quit."

"What? No, I didn't mean—"

I hold up my hand. "No. Just stop talking, okay? Just shut up. You've said *more* than enough."

I turn away from him, swallowing my tears. I refuse to let him see one more drop. Oliver stands from the couch as I enter, staring at me with anticipation. I know he heard everything, but I don't care. I don't care about anything except what I have to do next. Will takes a step inside, but just the one. "How do we get Connor off my back?"

Will glances at Oliver who hangs his head. "I do not know."

"The consort thing is key," I say. "Without it he has nothing. So how do we divorce?"

"We are not married," he says. "Vampire marriage can only occur between—"

"Don't care," I say. "How do we nullify the contract?"

He pauses, then says, "We cannot."

"Why the hell not?" Will asks.

"It is a lifetime contract put in place for the protection of the human. It makes it a crime to feed on or hurt the human, which is why I claimed you as mine in Dallas."

"Bullshit," Will says.

"I did not think it would be considered a true consortship once the real nature of our relationship was revealed," he says to me. "That and all the conditions have not been met."

"Which one hasn't?" Will asks.

"We haven't had sex," I say sternly. "Not that *anyone* believes that. And we can't prove it."

"Yes," Oliver says, casting his eyes down to the floor.

"So, if I'm your consort until I die, then how can I be Connor's too? Bigamy?"

"No, you can be *a* consort for life. You or the vampire you are tied to can transfer ownership to another vampire."

"Like a slave," says Will. "Nice."

"At least we do not kill our deformed young like your brethren."

"I would never—"

"Not helping," I cut in. The men sneer at each other then look away. "So I'm your consort. No way I can see around that."

"It would appear so."

"Then he'll follow me until he finds a reason to kill me or force me into his bed."

"Most likely."

"Then I see no other option," I say. "We take a chapter from his playbook. We go in there, and we scare the hell out of him until he does what we want. If that doesn't work ... we kill him," I say, my voice hard. "Who else did you bring?"

"Wolfe," Oliver says. "He insisted. The others are on standby."

"Bea, we can't—" Will says.

"Weapons?"

"Enough," Oliver says.

"Guys, this is not happening. We're officers of the law."

"Um, I'm pretty sure I just quit," I say.

"And I must protect my consort," Oliver says. "I shall call Wolfe. He should be done checking us into the hotel." Oliver flips open his cell phone, walking into the back.

"I'll put on some clothes," I say as I step toward my room.

Will grabs my arm, pulling me toward him. "You cannot seriously be considering this."

"Damn straight."

"It's suicide," he says, taking my arm. "We'll figure out a better way than going in there guns blazing."

"I'm all ears," I say, looking into his green eyes, challenging him. His mouth twitches but he doesn't speak. "Didn't think so." I pull my arm away. "We're going. Come, don't come, it's up to you."

I start toward my bedroom when he speaks. "You don't know what you're asking of me."

I spin around. "I'm asking you to help save my life. My family's lives."

"No, you're asking me to potentially break the law. Possibly get killed in the process."

"I know. It's a lot." I nod. "But I guess you have to ask yourself a question then."

"What?"

"Is she worth it?"

"It's not that simple."

"Yeah. It is. So ... am I?"

Oliver's intrusion back in the room stops Will dead. "Wolfe is on his way. I told him to meet us outside the cemetery. He is also phoning the police to report gunshots. They should be on their way. The gentlemen across the street would not dare leave their car to cause harm with the police there. Your grandmother will be safe."

"Good thinking. Thank you."

"Do you know a way to exit without arousing suspicion?" Oliver asks.

"We can hop the fence and cut through the neighbor's back yards. It's only two houses."

"Good." Oliver turns to Will, who hasn't taken his eyes off me this entire exchange. "And you, William? Will you be storming the castle, risking life and limb to save the fair maiden from the evil Lord who wishes to steal her away from us?"

His eyes bore into mine, all doubt and sadness vanishing. My whole exhausted body suddenly springs to life in tension and anticipation. A peaceful smile I never thought him capable of forms on his face. He says one word. Just one word and everything crappy in my life, all the pain, degradation, and doubt melts away. One word changes everything.

"Absolutely."

After I instruct Nana not to go outside for anything, we wait until we hear the police sirens out front before escaping over the back fence. My neighbors must be preoccupied with the three squad cars because they don't even check to see why their animals are going nuts as we run though. Two back yards later we're across Hilltop Street standing outside the huge gates of the cemetery.

From here I can still see the commotion on my street. Three police cruisers and six officers move around the house across the street while others try to answer my curious neighbors' questions. Merry and Pippin are being questioned by an officer, neither too thrilled. Ha ha.

"Why does it not surprise me that you live beside a cemetery?" Oliver asks, staring inside at the gravestones.

"Shut up," I say.

A minute later an SUV pulls up to us. Will climbs into the very back with me and Oliver in the middle. Agent Wolfe quickly drives down the street past the circus.

"Worked like a charm, huh?" Agent Wolfe says.

"Let's hope the cops keep them busy for the next ten minutes so they can't call Connor," I say.

"Shouldn't be a problem," Agent Wolfe says. "I said I was positive the shots came from inside the car. They'll search it, which should take awhile." He turns onto Market Street. "Are we sure this guy will still be at the club?"

"No, but if he isn't one of the other vamps should know where he is."

"We shall just have to pull it out of them," Oliver says, tone so cold I get a shiver.

"Are you cold?" Will asks.

"Um, a little," I say, not wanting to admit the real reason. I have to be tough and unemotional from here on.

Will takes off his brown suede jacket, passing it up to me. "Here."

Smiling, I take it and slip it on. It's huge on me but really warm. From his body. "Thank you." He smiles back, and the temp rises, not from the coat. He hasn't smiled at me in months and now twice in minutes. A familiar girly gooey feeling returns.

"What a gentleman you are, William," Oliver says.

Both our smiles drop. "Shut up, Oliver," I say.

Agent Wolfe clears his throat. "So, um, is there a plan or are we just going in guns blazing?"

"There's bound to be people in the club now," I say.

"How many vamps were there before?" Will asks, all business now. I fill them in on the players and layout of the club.

"They won't want to attack us in front of civilians," Will says.

"Violence should be a last resort anyway," I say.

"But we should be prepared for it," Oliver adds. "Only if reason and persuasion fail." He turns around to Will, challenging him with his narrowed eyes. "And they must believe we are capable of it."

Will's expression matches Oliver's. "I'm willing to do whatever it takes."

"Good." Oliver turns back around.

"Thank you," I say. "All of you."

"You'd do it for us," Agent Wolfe says.

"Still. Thank you."

"You're welcome," Will says with another delicious smile.

Agent Wolfe cruises past the club, and sure enough there's a line of scantily clad girls and coiffed men waiting to get in. The bouncer seems fully recovered from earlier. Agent Wolfe rounds the corner, parking on the side of the street. "So. Plan?" he asks.

I shrug. "Wing it."

We pile out of the car to congregate at the back. Inside is a black duffel with an arsenal inside. Pistols, sawed-off shotguns, knives, pepper spray, and my Bette. We load up. I hand Will his coat so I can have easier access to my 9mm with silver bullets. Bette and her black leather holder attach on the opposite side. Covered by my long sleeve is a silver dagger velcroed to my forearm. Will chooses a two-sided shoulder holster with a gun on either side, Bowie knife, and silver-plated baton. The coat covers them all. Agent Wolfe selects a Kevlar vest with hidden vial of Holy water, two guns, baton, and silver cross with spring-loaded blade inside. Oliver just watches us prepare for battle.

"Why aren't you getting ready?" I ask as I secure my belt.

"It would be unwise for me to confront Connor armed," he says. "It could aggravate the situation."

"He's right," Will says, placing his gold badge visibly on the outside of his coat.

"I trust you will protect me if need be," he says. Agent Wolfe tosses Oliver his gold shield and hands me mine. I set it next to the gun. Oliver sticks his in his pocket as Agent Wolfe closes the trunk. "Are we ready?"

"Let's have some fun," Agent Wolfe says with a grin.

I lead the way around the corner with the men a foot behind. People stop and stare at us with a mix of concern and awe. One girl's mouth literally drops when she sees the gun. I wink at her. The others whisper to each other and a few actually leave. Smart of them.

The bouncer went on high alert the moment he saw me, his bulky body visibly tensing. He folds his arms across his chest. I give him my sweetest smile and bat my eyelashes. "Hello, sweetie."

"You are not welcome here," he says.

"That has never stopped us before," says Oliver.

Will steps forward. "I'm Special Agent William Price with the FBI," he says, holding out his badge. "We have business with Connor McInnis."

"He's not here."

"Then where is he?" Agent Wolfe asks.

"Not here," the man says, close to gnarling.

"I grow bored with this conversation," Oliver says. "Elder Oliver Montrose and representatives from the legal body, the F.R.E.A.K.S., demands an audience with Lord Connor. If our request is not met, then in accordance with bylaw 57.8 we can bring him before a tribunal of his peers, including the ruler of Los Angeles. Tony would adore that."

The bouncer's lip twitches. Got him. "No weapons are allowed."

"Don't think so, cupcake," I say.

"We are members of law enforcement," Will says, "we're required to carry at all times."

"Yeah. Sorry," I say with another smile. "Though no shotgun this time. Promise."

He's trapped, and he knows it. "Go in."

"Thank you," I say cheerfully as I pass.

"Bitch," he mutters.

The club is packed, dark, and loud. House music blasts from the speakers with the people and lightshow moving to the beat. I liked it better before. Through the crowd I spot the bartender, Matilda, and two men I think are humans serving drinks. Like the bouncer, Matilda is nowhere near happy to see me. She even reaches under the bar for the gun, but I shake my head and she scowls, moving her hand away. The horde clamors for their drinks, but she ignores them as my posse saddles up to the bar. "What are you doing back here?"

"Guess," I shout over the music.

"He's not—"

"Yes, he is," Oliver says.

"We've been through this with the man outside," I say. "Call Connor. Now!"

She flinches with my last word. Still afraid of me, I see. This pleases me to no end. She picks up the phone and dials. "Sir? She's back." She listens. "No. Three others. One's a vampire." Pause. "Yes. Yes, sir." She hangs up. "He'll see you and the vampire alone. No weapons."

"We're all going up," Will says. "If you have a problem with that, miss, then I suggest *you* stop us."

Nobody does. I lead my posse through the dancers, up the stairs past the skinny doorman who almost drops his clipboard when he lays eyes on me, and through the velvet curtain that hides the office. Neil stands guard directly in front of the door. "I cannot allow you to enter with weapons."

"That's nice," I say before pushing him aside with my mind and throwing the door open. Connor sits behind the desk with a phone pressed against his ear as I storm in. "You bastard."

He holds up a finger. "Lawrence, I am going to have to call you back." He hangs up.

"I am sorry sir, they simply walked in," Neil says.

"We will discuss it later, Neil," Connor says. "Please wait outside."

"Sir, are you sure—"

"If I need you, I shall call for you."

"Agent Wolfe, keep him company?" Will orders, not taking his eyes off the strangely impassive Connor. I was expecting quaking boots, not amusement. Neil and Agent Wolfe eye each other before walking out.

183

Connor gazes up at me, that gorgeous face lit up with a smile. "Well, Miss Alexander. Twice in one night. If you continue to show up like this, people shall think we are in love."

"Not in this or any other lifetime, pal."

"We shall see."

"You shut your fucking mouth," Will says.

Connor ignores him, shifting his attention to Oliver. "And Oliver," he says. "This is unexpected. It has been what? Two hundred years since Venice?"

"Three," Oliver says with a matching smile.

"And how is Alain?"

"I do not know. We have not spoken for over a century."

The smile drops. "A pity." Now he acknowledges Will with a glance. "And who is your friend?"

"Special Agent William Price, F.R.E.A.K.S.," Will says, voice sharp enough to cut glass.

"Oh, I believe I have heard of you. Were you the wolf who assisted in the massacre in Dallas?"

"Yep," he says with a hard scowl.

"And now you are all here. I suppose I should be frightened," he says, anything but.

"Oh yeah," I say.

A small smile crosses his face as he surveys us and sits back in his chair. "And yet, I am not. I have done nothing to warrant this visit. I have not threatened, I have not harmed. You have no reason for further recourse."

Will rips off his badge, tossing it on Connor's desk. "What makes you think we're here in an official capacity?" Will, nostrils flaring, stares down the not-as-confident-as-he-was-a-second-ago vamp.

Their eyes remain locked in battle for a few seconds until Connor looks away first. I do believe we have just obtained the upper hand.

"You should have stuck to our deal," I say, crossing my arms. "I let you live, you leave me alone. Simple, easy, fair. I'm not *that* irresistible, Danny Boy."

Connor's eyes pass over us again, settling on Oliver. A smirk forms. "I believe every man in this room would beg to differ, Miss Alexander. Is that not right, Oliver? You take a consort, what? Once every two centuries? Mind you, I only made her acquaintance this evening, but I can see why you chose her." He eyes me up and down, savoring me. Will's breath quickens, and his hands ball into fists. If Connor notices, he doesn't let on. "Brains. Beauty. Power." Now he meets my eyes. "And I imagine she tastes of ripe cherries. Her blood, her lips, her tongue … everywhere. I wanted to rut her the moment I laid eyes on her." I try to stop the oncoming lust, but those words coming from that mouth with that accent, my nethers go as warm as the rest of me. Damn vampires. "To taste her. Explore her. With my tongue. With my cock. To slide inside her. In and out. In and out as she screams in ecstasy. Pure heaven." He licks his lips. "And she feels the same about me. I can smell it on her. She wants me. Inside she is begging for me. And it will be my name she calls out as I ride her. A—"

The blur of a man snaps me out of my lust bubble. "You motherfucker!" Will flips over the desk, the only thing is his way. Connor leaps out of the way in time to avoid being crushed, but he's not fast enough to avoid being grabbed by a two-hundred-twenty-pound pissed-off werewolf. Will's fingers wrap around Connor's throat, his wolf growling through his humanity.

"William, no!" Oliver shouts, leaping toward the fray. I'm too shocked to do anything but stare.

"You will not talk about her that way! *Ever*!" Will shouts with savage intensity, throttling the passive vamp by the throat. Oliver attempts to pull them apart, but apparently vamp strength is trumped by crazy werewolf power.

Neil and Agent Wolfe race in, but when they see the scene, they stop for a moment, unsure what to do. Join the club. Then I notice Connor hold up his hand, and Neil's tension wanes. That's when it hits me. The sneaky bastard. "Will! Stop it!" I dash over to them. "He wanted this! You're playing into his hands!" I meet Will square in the eyes. "Will, let him go! *Please*! He's not worth it."

"He threatened you! Your family!" There's a sickening crack from Connor's throat.

"I know. But you were right. This isn't the way to do this. Let. Him. Go."

Those green eyes glide from me, to the pained Connor, then return to mine. Humanity wins this round. He releases the vamp. Connor slumps to the floor in a heap. Neil and Oliver tend to him, examining this throat. Will is still vibrating with anger and adrenaline as he glares down at Connor, but I touch his cheek, moving his face toward me. Shame and fear now fill those eyes. "It's okay," I whisper. "It's okay."

He shakes his head and grasps my upper arms for an anchor. "I'm sorry."

"It's okay. You're okay," I whisper.

"Let me alone," Connor croaks from the floor. He finds his legs, holding out his hands to stop the fussing Neil. The man just had his larynx crushed and can still talk. Vamp healing is a wonderful thing. "I am fine!" He adjusts his white shirt to regain some dignity.

Every one of my limbs is shaking as I pull Will away from the now uncool Connor. My dazed defender doesn't put up much resistance as

I place him on the couch. Like a worried mother, Neil checks Connor's throat but is slapped away for his efforts. "Get away! Do not touch me! Get out. Now!"

Without protest, Neil scurries out the door. Oliver nods at Agent Wolfe, who nods back and follows Neil. The four of us remaining stay silent, except for Will's heavy breathing. Connor yanks his shirt down once more, takes a moment to regain his composure, then rights his desk. I alternate between watching him pick up the fallen papers and gazing at Will. His breathing slows then quiets as he twines his fingers together and rests his head on them. Oliver stands unmoving in the back corner, his eyes never leaving Connor. As the time passes, all of ten seconds, my adrenaline levels and I stop shaking. Connor finishes restoring order, sits behind his desk, and folds his arms on it as if the past few minutes didn't occur. "Shall we continue our conversation now?" he asks, his voice fully restored.

I blink. "Are you serious?"

"Nothing has been resolved."

"Oh my God,"—the vampires flinch—"are you insane? Haven't you figured out that there is no way I am *ever* going to go along with what you want? And is all of this ridiculous maneuvering really worth all this?"

"She is correct, Connor," Oliver says. "You have lost."

"The *law* is on my side," Connor says.

"Why do you even want me? I am *not* worth all this trouble."

"To me, you are," Connor says. "I want you. Now more than ever. And I will do anything, within the law, to obtain you."

"But the law is not on your side in this instance," Oliver says, rounding Connor's desk to stand by me. "She is not my consort. I swear to it."

"The conditions were met. I have a copy of the document you both signed while in Dallas."

"And if it's the document I think it is, I signed it Beatrice Smythe. *Not* my name."

"You signed it, that is enough."

"She is not my consort," Oliver says again. "The third condition has not been met."

Connor appraises me, then Oliver. "You have not made love?"

"I swear on my life," Oliver says.

Connor smiles and scoffs. "The great Oliver unable to bed a beautiful woman? I would sooner believe the sky is green."

"It's true," I say. "He's tried, but I've turned him down. Every time."

"And can you prove this allegation?"

"I can."

Our gazes find Will. All shame has vanished, replaced with sheer determination. His face, his body, everything is set for battle. He stands up tall, tossing those broad shoulders back, and scowling at his foe.

Connor tilts his head. "What is your proof, wolf?"

"The fact that he still has all his limbs," Will says, serious as cancer. Will steps toward Connor's desk. "If he so much as *touched* her in that way, I wouldn't hesitate. I'd stake him in half a heartbeat."

"She bears his mark," Connor says, glancing at my neck.

"That happened in the line of duty. And the only reason I didn't kill him on the spot was she stopped me. Knocked me unconscious. I'll show you the case file if you want. It's all in there."

"They reside in the same house."

"And she resides in my room," Will says, not missing a beat. "If they slept together I'd smell it on her. And then I'd kill him."

I can see a tiny crack in Connor's confidence. He's actually buying this. Heck, *I'm* buying it. Oliver remains inexpressive. "Is she your mate, wolf?" Connor asks. "Because I hate to be the bearer of bad news. Your mate spent the previous night with her ex-boyfriend, the volatile Officer Weir. If she cuckolded on you once, then perhaps it has happened before."

"I didn't sleep with Steven," I say.

"We've been fighting," Will says, ignoring me. "Actually, the fight was about her friendship with this asshole." Will gestures to Oliver. "But what happened last night has no bearing on the fact I know with one hundred percent certainty she has never had sex with Oliver. She cannot be his consort. I swear on my life, my badge, and God." The vamps flinch again. Will puts his hands on the desk, leaning forward and looking Connor square in the eyes. "And therefore you have no claim on her. *None.* She is mine: mind, body, and soul. Has been since the first moment I saw her. And you are *damn* lucky I didn't kill you the minute I walked through the door. The only thing stopping me from doing it right now is I don't want to start a war. Because not only do I have the full force of the United States government on my side, but with three phone calls—to pack leaders Jason Dahl, Tim Merrill, and Jefferson Monroe, all of whom are close, personal friends—every werewolf in the country will descend upon you and yours. And it will not be pretty. We don't like your kind to begin with, and we are *itching* for a fight. So if you even think of intimidating my mate, or threatening her family, nothing will stop me. I *will* kill you. I will rip you limb from fucking limb before eating your heart while you watch. I *swear* it. Are you hearing me, your Lordship? This ends. Now."

The men remain locked in a battle of wills for a few fraught seconds. It can go either way. But Connor glances away first, and all that tension vanishes.

That's it. It's over. We won.

"Is what he claims true?" Connor asks Oliver.

"Yes," Oliver lies. "Her heart and body have belonged to another the entire time I have known her. I freely admit to making countless romantic overtures, but all were rebuked. We are friends. That is all. I have no claim to her and therefore neither do you."

"But you do have feelings for her," Connor says, getting in all the jabs he can.

"My feelings are irrelevant," Oliver states plainly. "I have not slept with her, therefore she is not my consort. Our laws do not apply to her." Oliver pauses. "You lost, Connor. Accept defeat gracefully and let us all be."

Connor doesn't utter a syllable for a moment, no doubt trying to figure out all the angles. He rocks in his chair, still thinking, and then stops. He sighs. "Fine."

I let out the breath I didn't know I was holding.

"Smart choice," Will says.

"I will trouble you no more, Agent Alexander. Happy Christmas."

I feel like doing a victory jig but refrain. I just cordially nod. "Thank you."

Giving Connor one last sneer, Will grabs his badge, spins around, takes my hand, and yanks me toward the door. Oliver grins at Connor saying, "Always a pleasure," before leaving as well.

We move past Neil, adding Agent Wolfe to our little train. Us scary agents rush out of the club with Will pulling me through the crowd. The vamps on the floor stop working to watch us pass. We ignore them, including the bouncer outside, power walking without looking back until we get safely inside our SUV. Agent Wolfe, who climbs in beside me in the backseat, seems bewildered. He breathes fast enough for me to hear. I'm too shocked to do anything but stare at the front headrest. Will grasps the steering wheel tight enough to make it creak but doesn't turn on the car. Oliver gazes out the front, still on guard. Nobody talks for a minute. For once the silence is welcome.

Agent Wolfe breaks the quiet. "What happened in there?"

Too much. Too damn much. "We realized something," I say.

"What?"

"Will *really* needs to work on his impulse-control issues," I say with a chuckle. All three men glance at me, and when they see my smile, they're infected. And when I full on laugh, they join in. "You were like the Hulk or something with that desk! 'Will mad!'" I growl like the Hulk through the laughs. "Will, I'm surprised you fell for that!"

"Not as surprised as Connor," Oliver chuckles. "At least we turned it to our advantage."

"What are you talking about?" Agent Wolfe asks.

"Connor wanted Oliver to attack him," I say, "but he got more than he bargained for." I pat Will's shoulder. "You know, thanks for defending my honor and all but, dude, I have two words for you: *anger management*."

"Yeah, yeah," Will chuckles, starting the car.

"So it worked?" Agent Wolfe asks.

"Connor will not be bothering our fair Beatrice from here on," Oliver says.

"*And* I'll probably get a lifetime of free drinks at the club. I am *so* inviting everyone I know for a party there. Cristal all around. Least the bastard can do after this."

"But how?" Agent Wolfe asks.

The laughter subsides, and the smiles gradually fall as we drive away. Agent Wolfe never gets his answer. We ride in silence for a few minutes as Will maneuvers down Market Street. "Okay," Wolfe says to himself.

The remainder of the ride home, the quiet inside is anything but comfortable, the equivalent of a pair of stilettos jammed into your eyes. We all gaze out our respective windows, deep in thought. Well, not me. If I have to think about anything that happened tonight, I'll have a full mental breakdown. Out of the corner of my eye, I catch Will glancing at me in the rearview mirror but pretend not to notice. The street lights sure are pretty.

As we're about to turn down my street, Oliver breaks the hush of the car. "William," he says, "I believe you should stay with Beatrice tonight. In her home."

"What? Why?" I ask.

"It would look . . . odd if he did not. Considering the nature of your alleged relationship."

"You think Connor will still be watching her?" Will asks.

"It is entirely possible, yes." Oliver turns around to face me. "If you do not object."

"I—I mean we have a spare room," I stammer. "It—it would be the smart thing to do, I guess."

Oliver turns around. "Very well then."

Gulp.

The police cars are gone now, as are Merry and Pippin, and all my neighbors are back inside when we pull up. It's as if nothing happened. Back to normal. Everyone but Oliver gets out of the car. Will awkwardly smiles at me as I do the same to him. If he's happy about this situation, it doesn't show. Agent Wolfe rounds the car, and Will hands him the car keys.

"I'll bring your bag by later," Agent Wolfe says to Will.

"Thank you," Will says.

Agent Wolfe then smiles at me. "Thank you so much for everything," I say.

"You're welcome."

"And if you get bored or whatever tomorrow come on over. The door's always open."

"Are you kidding? The beach beckons. You think I came here only for you?" He smiles again and squeezes my shoulder. "Get some sleep."

"We'll talk later," Will says as Agent Wolfe gets in the car.

I look through the car window at the oddly quiet Oliver. He's deep in his own head, gazing out the opposite side of the car, face serious as if he's working out a math equation. "Night, Oliver."

"Good night, Beatrice," he says, not looking my way.

I don't know why, but the word "Beatrice" feels like an icicle to my heart.

Will takes my hand before I can say anything. "Come on." I open my mouth but have no idea what else to say. I allow Will to gently pull me toward the house. The SUV drives off.

The chain is on the door, so I ring the doorbell with a sigh. Will releases my hand and runs his fingers through his hair, his nervous tell. Nana must be waiting by the door because a second later she opens it, wide-eyed but relieved. "Oh thank goodness," she says, wrapping her arms around me and squeezing tight. "I was so scared."

"It's okay," I say. "It's all been fixed now."

She pulls away and smiles at Will. "Come in."

"Thank you," he says, stepping inside.

"Nana, is it okay if Will sleeps in the spare room tonight?"

"Of course. There are fresh sheets and everything."

"Thank you very much, Mrs. Alexander. I hate to impose, but—"

"It's not an imposition. You can stay as long as you like. And call me *Liz*."

"Liz. Sorry. It'll just be for one night. We're leaving tomorrow."

"So soon?"

"Yeah."

"That's a shame," Nana says. Then we three stand quietly for another awkward second. I keep my eyes on the carpet, and Will's hands haven't left his pockets. Nana gets a clue. "Well. Then. If the excitement's over, I'll just be heading back to bed. Bea?"

I jerk my head up. "Yes, ma'am?" *Ma'am*? I haven't called her that since she caught me sneaking out ten years ago.

"Can you show your friend where the fresh towels are?"

"Yep. Uh huh," I say, nodding my head.

Her eyes narrow in confusion. "Good. Pleasant dreams."

"You too, Mrs. Al—um, Liz."

She eyes us, then smiles. "Good night, you two." Still grinning, she walks to her bedroom, leaving us alone feeling like guilty teenagers.

"She's nice," Will says.

"Yeah. Um, let me show you to your room." Eager to flee, I lead Will down the hall to Brian's old room. Like mine it's suspended in time with baseball pendants, trophies, and AC/DC posters. I flip the light on and Will steps in, surveying the place. "Hope it's okay."

"It's fine."

"Good. So the bathroom is right across the hall, towels are under the sink. You can help yourself to anything in the fridge," I say as fast as an auctioneer, "Internet, cable, anything you like. I'm just next door if you want me." I mentally slap my head. "*Need me*. I mean need me."

"Thank you."

"'Kay. Night." I say, shutting the door.

"Bea?"

I open the door all the way. "No. Not tonight. I have had the day from hell. I'm exhausted in every conceivable way, and I don't have enough energy for the insanely long, awkward conversation we need to have, okay? I need to process, and think, and—"

"I just wanted to know if I could use the phone to call George. It's long distance and my cell's about to die." He holds up the phone. "The charger's back at the hotel."

And now I want to die. "Oh, um, of course. No problem."

"Thank you. Good night."

"Night." I shut the door, cursing my mouth to heck.

I trek back to my sanctuary, flip on the light, close the door, and promptly fall against it, sliding down it onto the floor like a lump. I'm amazed I stayed upright as long as I did. I just rest on my carpet staring into space in total and utter shock.

Not because of what he said.

Not because of what he did.

Because it hit me. Something I must have known for months but just couldn't admit. Something scarier than armies of vampires, zombies, and basilisks combined.

I am truly, madly, deeply, completely in love with William Price.

In spite of his temper, in spite of what he says, in spite of what he does, in spite of a million reasons why I shouldn't be, I am. I am in love for the first time in my life.

And I am so screwed.

TEN

I COULD NEVER BE YOUR WOMAN

Reasons why I absolutely, positively *cannot* be in love with Will Price: He's a werewolf. He has serious anger issues, though I know he'd never raise a hand to anyone he loves. He's moody. He's mucho possessive. He's over twenty years older than me, though he doesn't look it. He's probably still in love with his dead wife. He's my boss. But wait, I pretty much quit my job. Okay, so I'll probably never see him again. Nice save, Bea. Okay, the biggie. We've never kissed. How can I possibly be in love with someone I've never even kissed? It's unthinkable.

As I climb out of bed, I have more or less convinced myself that there is no chance I'm in love with him. It's only taken two hours of staring at the wall, but I've come to my senses. I walk out of my bedroom ready to face the day and—

Oh. My. God.

Nope. I was wrong. Head over heels in love.

Will stands shirtless and sweating in my kitchen, drinking milk with a little dribbling down his chin. His everything is perfect. Flat stomach, well-defined muscles all glistening, and rugged face turned up in ecstasy. I blush from tip to toes. My little whimper draws his attention. The glass drops from his mouth as he sheepishly smiles. "Morning," he says putting the milk on the counter and grabbing his shirt from beside it.

"Hi," I all but sigh and wave. Wave!

He pulls on his shirt. "Sorry. I was thirsty after my run."

"You ran? You went for a run? That's nice. Running's nice." Shut the heck up, you crazy person.

"Yeah. I, uh, ran around the cemetery."

"Cemetery. Good place to run, a cemetery. They're nice." I need to staple my mouth shut right this instant.

"Peaceful," he says, shaking his head vigorously. "Peaceful ... run. Refreshing," he says as an afterthought. And then a full ten seconds of brutal, uncomfortable silence where we look at everything but each other.

My brain reboots and the social-niceties link opens. "Did you sleep well?" I ask. "Was the bed comfortable? The sheets? The pillows?"

"Yes. Thank you," he says, relieved. "And your grandmother is just wonderful. She made me breakfast before she left."

"She did?"

"Um, yeah," he says, grabbing two coffee cups from the hooks on the cabinet. He turns around and I sit on the stool at the bar that faces the kitchen. "She's great." He pours the coffee and milk. "She's really proud of you."

"She's not angry that I lied?"

"I explained the situation to her." He spins back around and hands me a cup of coffee. Milk and sugar, the way I like it.

"Thank you." He remembered. I coo inside but outside my poker face remains for all of three seconds until I glance at the dining room table and notice the photo albums piled on it. Oh no. She didn't!

Will's gaze follows mine. "So, yeah. She wanted to show me a few photos."

I know what she showed him. Me and Brian as kids naked in a bathtub. Fat ten-year-old me squeezed into a pink tutu surrounded by munchkin six-year-olds. Me at thirteen with zits, braces, and a horrible haircut that made my head look so big people thought I had the mumps. Sixteen-year-old me in blue, yellow, and white polyester shorts, shirt, and go-go hat during my tenure at Hot Dog on a Stick. She did the same thing with Steven.

"Of course she did," I mutter. Black hole in the ground, take me now.

"You were cute. I mean, you are cute. Now," he stumbles. "But you were cute then too. You, you know what I mean."

"I can figure it out," I say. And awkward silence time. "So, um, do you have plans for the day? Are you guys leaving right away?"

"Um, no. We're gonna stick around until tonight just to, um, keep up appearances. Just in case."

"Oh. Good. Appearances and all. Very important." All day. Alone. Just him, me, and my mouth. I give it an hour before I blurt out my ridiculous feelings.

"Your grandmother asked me to help with the tree and decorations. For Christmas."

"I totally forgot about that," I say. I'd feel like such a sucky granddaughter if she hadn't shown the man I love a picture of me in a bathing suit. "You don't have to if you don't want to."

"No, I'd love to. Haven't really celebrated Christmas in years."

"Really? What do you guys do?" I ask, stunned. Not celebrating the holidays is a crime against nature, completely inconceivable, and just plain wrong.

"Well, Chandler and Rush usually fly home unless something comes up. The rest of us just give gifts on the day."

"No tree? Carols?" Even Brian managed to suppress his rage long enough for us to get through "Silent Night." "What about Nancy? She's only seventeen. She deserves a Christmas."

"We have a massive tree, we just don't put it up ourselves. George hires people to come in and decorate."

"Then I am sure glad I came home," I say, mortified. "No Christmas," I huff. "Barbarians."

His eyes crinkle as he smiles. Oh, I hope our kids inherit that. And his eyes. And his devotion. And—

"I've missed it," he says, just realizing it. "Mary always made such a huge deal about Christmas," he says, referring to his dead wife. All thoughts of hypothetical children vanish.

"Really?"

He starts playing with his ring finger as he does when he thinks about her. Makes my stomach hurt every time. "Yeah. We'd go out to this Christmas tree farm every year and dig one up. Then we'd go home, put on her favorite movie, *The Sound of Music,* and decorate. It took hours just to do the popcorn garland. Then at the stroke of midnight, we'd open presents."

"We open one on Christmas Eve," I say, "but I'd usually stay awake and sneak another after Nana went to bed."

"I used to do that too. As a kid." He stops playing with his finger. "I always loved Christmas."

"Then you are more than welcome to help with ours."

"Thank you." He takes a last swig of his coffee and smiles shyly. "Guess I should hit the shower then." He puts the coffee cup and milk glass into the dishwasher. *And* he's a respectful house guest. I bite my lower lip to stop the longing sigh from escaping. I don't move until I hear the water turn on in the bathroom.

I grab the portable phone, running out back to the side of the house while punching in April's number. Someone picks up on the third ring. "Diego residence," Javi says.

"Javi, it's Bea. Is April there?" I ask, not hiding the desperation in my voice.

"Yeah. Are you okay?"

"Relatively."

"Give me that," April says. The phone exchanges hands. "Bea? Are you okay? We've been worried to death!"

"You didn't get my message?"

"Not until this morning! I called and Nana Liz said you were safe, but … you scared the hell out of us!"

"We're all safe. I promise."

"Then why do you sound like hell?"

"Because something horrible has happened," I say, near tears. "And I have no frigging clue what to do about it."

"What?" she asks. I open my mouth, but the words won't come out. If I say it then it becomes real, and I don't know if I'm ready for that. "Bea?"

I open again, and the words geyser out. "Will is naked in my shower right now and I need you to talk me out of going in there, ripping off all my clothes, and screwing him twelve ways from Saturday because I'm totally, completely, crazily in love with him. I am! I love him so much I can't think straight. I think I have been for months, and now that I know it, I'm scared I'll blurt it out and he'll freak or something even though I'm pretty sure he feels the same way, but he could have been lying to Connor to save me, but I don't think so because he choked him for talking dirty to me. And he threatened a vampire/werewolf war if Connor tried anything, but he also said I literally drive him crazy and then there's the werewolf thing and the Oliver thing and the dead wife thing but right now I don't care because I love him and he didn't have a shirt on this morning and I almost died on the spot and now I have to spend the day with him pretending to be a couple in case Connor is watching so there's going to be touching and I don't know if I can control myself. And I have no idea what to do. Help me." I take a deep breath to make up for the fact I haven't had one in thirty seconds.

"Okay," April says, "I didn't understand a word you said except *naked in shower, I love him, choked,* and *no shirt.* Start from the beginning." I rehash the whole night. Everything. Connor, Steven, the whole shebang. She doesn't say a word until I'm done. "Holy shit."

"I know! Right? What the heck am I going to do?"

"Are you nuts? Follow your instincts. Go in there and stuff your tongue down his throat. I can't believe—"

The shower shuts off, and I turn into a living statue. "Shut up," I whisper.

"Why?"

"I gotta go," I whisper. "He's out of the shower. He might be able to hear us. Call you later."

I shut off the phone and quietly tip-toe back to my room. I close the door as the bathroom door opens. Yes, I know I'm acting like a paranoid dork, but I don't even blink until I hear Brian's door shut. I flip on the radio and carefully choose my outfit for the day. Dark blue jeans, dark purple long-sleeved undershirt, and black Blue Oyster Cult girl-cut T-shirt. Casual, warm, and covers as much as is possible without wearing a burka. As I'm putting my hair into a high ponytail, there's a knock on the front door.

Will and I both step out of our rooms in unison. His hair is wet from the shower but sadly he's dressed. Gray cargo pants and loose green sweater. "You expecting someone?" he asks, all business.

I shrug and walk to the door with him just a few paces behind, my ever-present shadow. I peek out the hole. It's not an assassin. It's someone worse. "April," I mutter. This is going to suck so bad.

She stands on the porch all smiles, as if she's not here to make my life a living heck. "Hi! How are you? I was worried!"

Worried she wouldn't get to meet Will. "I'll bet you were."

Ignoring my snideness, she pecks my cheek and steps in. Her smile reaches both the east and west coasts when her eyes lock on Will. "Well, hello," she purrs.

"Will, April; April, Will."

She holds out her hand, which he shakes. "Nice to finally meet you," he says. "I've heard a lot about you."

"Ditto. I feel like we're practically family. Though the pictures she sent don't do you justice. Are all werewolves as gorgeous as you, because if they are . . . " She clicks her tongue. "I might just start howling at the moon."

"You're married," I remind her.

"I'm not *that* married."

Will's face becomes as red as a Santa suit.

"You'll have to forgive my ex best friend. She forgets herself sometimes."

"It must be your animal magnetism," she says to Will.

I have to get her the heck out of here before I die of embarrassment. "Okay, so you see I'm fine. All limbs in place. Time to go. I'm

sure you have loads to do today what with the pageant tonight, so…"
I gesture to the door.

"Pageant?" Will asks.

"My son's playing a snowflake in his school's holiday pageant tonight. You should come. It's at seven."

"We'll probably be gone by then," Will says.

"But Bea said you have a private jet. You can leave when you want. You're coming. There. Settled. You can leave afterwards. Or not, right?"

"We'll play it by ear," Will says.

"Oh goody," she says clapping and squealing like a child. "I have the utmost faith in you." Her head whips around to me. "Bea, walk me to my car?"

"You're kidding, right?"

She laces her arm around mine, locking them together, then practically drags me to the door. "It was nice to finally meet you, Will. I am *more* than sure we'll be seeing a lot more of each other. See you tonight!"

She yanks me out the door and shuts it. We walk to her car. "I am so going to kill you!" I say.

"Oh my flipping God! He looks like the Marlboro Man!"

I shush her. "He can hear you," I whisper. "Shut up! Get in the car!"

We both climb into her minivan and shut the doors. I doubt he can hear but turn on the radio just in case. "Bea, you have to be out of your mind not to be riding that man like a bull every chance you get!"

"Eww! Graphic!"

"I am so jealous," she screeches. "And he totally declared his undying love for you last night!"

"Yeah, after I stopped him from killing someone!"

"He was defending your honor!"

"He could have been acting. Or lying. And let's not forget he's been tres jerky to me for a long time."

"And yet you are, and I quote, 'totally, completely, crazily in love' with him."

"You know, the more I think about it, the more I realize it's not love. It's just, you know, infatuation and hormones."

"Yeah, and I'm still a virgin," she chuckles. "I called it months ago. You love him. I can see it clear as day. You're practically glowing."

"It's just my new moisturizer."

"Oh my God, you are hopeless!"

I rest my head on the dashboard. "I know. I suck at this stuff. And now I have to spend the whole day with him. Alone. Doing couple things like buying a Christmas tree and going to a school pageant." I sit up. "Which I cannot believe you brought up."

"I am including your future husband in our lives. Better he get used to us now so he knows what he's getting into."

"Don't call him that. *Please.*" I groan and wince. "I should get back in there."

"You can't even be away from him for five minutes," she teases. "It's *so* love."

I roll my eyes. "I'll see you tonight." I peck her cheek and climb out. She blows me a kiss before driving off.

"*… and I wanted to say what a nice time I've had with you the past few nights,*" is what I hear when I come back inside. Steven's voice emanates from the answering machine while Will stares at it with a blank face. "*The bowling, the club last night. I forgot how much fun you can be.*" Will's eyes leave the machine to appraise me.

I lunge for the phone. "Hello? Steven?"

"Hey."

"Sorry. I was outside talking to April. What's up?" I put my back to Will.

"Nothing. Just wanted to make sure you got home okay."

"Oh yeah. It must have been something I ate for dinner. I all but passed out when I got home." Should I go to my bedroom? No, that's rude and makes it seem like I have something to hide.

"Yeah, I felt out of it too," he says. "Better now. So what are you up to today? I'm not on until late tonight. Maybe we can go to a movie or something."

I swear I can fell Will's eyes burrowing onto my back like a mole in the dirt. I'm sure he can hear Steven's side of the conversation from here. I don't dare look back. "Actually, I can't. I have Christmas duty all day. We're gonna hang some decorations, make cookies, the tree, usual stuff."

"And tonight?"

"Manny's pageant."

"Right. Forgot about that. Nana Liz going with you?"

"No, she's got her knitting club tonight."

"Right. Well, maybe some other day. Before you go back."

I wince. Oh, why the heck did he have to say that? "Yeah. Great. I'll call you."

"Okay. Talk to you soon. Bye." He hangs up, and I do the same.

I turn around but Will's gone. Vanished. Once again my mind goes to that annoying, girlie place where I have to overanalyze. Did he leave because he wanted to give me privacy? Or because he couldn't stand me talking to the man I made out with? Okay, I so need to stop this. He left the room, and I need to interpret every step. I've never been this bad, not even in high school. I hate people like this. Okay, I'm done. I won't make it through the day if I keep this up. My head will explode.

I finish getting ready, barely putting on makeup just because. I'd wire my jaw shut if I could, but instead toss a pack of gum in my purse. I'll chew all day. If my mouth is preoccupied, I might be able to stop it from forming words. Worth a shot.

Will's on the couch fiddling with his cell phone when I walk out. He glances at me as I move into the kitchen, but listens to his messages. I fix myself a bowl of Count Chocula and examine the back of his neck. "Wolfe, it's Will. Please call me when you get this." He slaps the phone shut.

"He's probably at the beach," I say, "or asleep. It's a nice day out."

"I need his report," Will says, "and yours too."

"Do we have to do it today? We can have *one* day off, right?"

"I suppose."

"So, is there anything you want to see? To do?" Activities are good. If we're busy with activities, there's less talking involved.

"I have no idea," he says, finally turning around. "Do you have anything planned?"

"Just getting the tree."

"Oh." From the quick smile I can tell he's relieved. "The beach maybe?"

"Okay, so the beach, tree, decorate. Sounds good."

"What about the pageant?" he asks.

"You really don't have to go if you don't want to."

"I don't mind. We weren't planning on leaving until the night anyway."

"Oh. Great." I put the half-eaten bowl in the sink. "I'll get my purse, and we can get going."

Compared to yesterday, today is beautiful. It's in the low sixties with puffy clouds against the blue sky. There are no strange cars on the street either. I climb into the driver's seat of my rental with the silent Will beside me. Off we go.

We're both quiet at first with him watching the scenery and me furiously chewing gum. I turn on the radio. "Can't Fight This Feeling" by REO Speedwagon starts. I switch it but it's Etta James's "At Last." Will and I glance quickly at each other then look away in sync. I find a Christmas station before the car explodes from our nervous energy. "Blue Christmas," no subtext there.

"You know, on second thought," he says, "I'm not really in the mood for the beach. I think we should just get the tree."

"Really?"

"Yeah."

"Well, is there anything else you want to see? The Maritime Museum? Midway? I know you're into naval history."

"How did you know that?" he asks, surprised.

"We've lived in the same house for months. That's all you read." I pause. Silence is bad. Keep talking. "My grandfather was in the Navy."

"He was?"

"Yeah. He served in the Korean war on a carrier."

"I almost joined the Navy."

"Why didn't you?"

"Um, my father," he says. "He developed lung cancer when I was seventeen. Mom was a mess. I just couldn't leave them then. So police officer was my second choice."

If I wasn't already in love with him, this would be when I fell. "Did he recover?"

"He hung tough for two years, but by then I had already joined the force."

"I'm so sorry."

"It was a mercy at the end. He was in so much pain," he says trying to remain strong but a little haunted too. "He was a good guy. The best. He was an airline pilot so he was gone a lot, but he never missed a baseball game or crew tournament he promised he'd make." He shakes his head. "Anyway, that's why I never joined."

"He sounds wonderful. You were very lucky to have him."

"Both of them," he says sadly. "She was one of those moms who just instinctively knew what you needed. I'd get home from school some days in a real bad mood, and she'd turn on the Beatles and make me sing and dance with her. She was sort of the neighborhood mom. All my friends loved her. Especially her brownies. Damn, I miss those things."

"Has your Mom passed too?"

"About a year after Mary. She had, um, dementia." He pauses. "She didn't even know who I was in the end, which is kind of funny." He runs his hand through his hair, another nervous tic. He does it a lot around me. "I had her transferred to a care facility near the mansion, so I could go visit her."

"No brothers or sisters?"

"No. Come from a long line of only children. I have some cousins on my dad's side, but we were never close."

"Same here. An island unto ourselves." We ride for a few quiet seconds again, but there's no way I'm letting this conversation go. I've found out more about him in the last minute than in all the previous months. "What's crew?"

"I'm sorry?"

"Crew. You said your Dad never missed a crew tournament. I don't know what this is."

"Oh. Rowing."

"Like in a rowboat? They have contests for that?"

"No," he chuckles, "we use a flat skiff with arms and legs moving in unison to power it."

"Like our rowing machine," I say.

"Yeah. I joined crew in high school and just kept up with it." He smiles at the memory. "Three times a week I'd wake up around five and go for a run. The sun would just be rising over the Potomac, and there'd be nothing but me, the water, and the rhythm."

"You miss it."

"I do. I love the water."

"Me too. I used to fantasize about buying a boat someday, just sailing around the world. No people, no responsibilities."

"Sounds like heaven."

I cock an eyebrow. "Well, I'm game if you are. We could go. Right now. There's plenty of boats for sale. I'm sure if we pool our money, we could afford one."

"Just run off? Not tell anyone?" he asks with a sly smile.

"We'll call them from Hawaii."

He thinks I'm kidding. I'm not. Not in the least. There is nothing I've wanted more in my life. Him and me all alone in the middle of the vast ocean. Stopping in exciting ports like Fiji and New Zealand. Spending our days sunbathing, reading, making love on the deck for hours on end. Just the two of us. If that's not heaven, I don't know what is.

The man I love stares at me. Maybe he does know I'm serious. As our eyes briefly meet, I can tell he's more than tempted judging from the way his mouth's twitching. We could do it. He just has to say the word. *Say the word*! But I don't get my wish. He looks away while chuckling nervously. "Yeah, and on the first full moon I'll rip a hole in the boat. Or you. Or both. No, I think I'll stick to dry land." He rolls down his window and shifts in his seat, once again all the joy and playfulness sucked from him.

He might have actually done it. He wanted to as much as I did. But that jerk reality snatched him away from me. I *so* can't stand him. For a brief moment I feel like crying but bite the inside of my lip to stop myself.

I drive with nothing but the holiday music between us for a minute. Then, out of the blue, he says, "Do you think because of what we are we don't deserve happiness?"

My head snaps in his direction. His gaze doesn't leave the window. "What?"

"Because I don't know. We're human but … not. We're killers. We've killed and let people die. Do you think that God made us this way for a reason? As punishment?"

"I was born this way. I didn't do anything to deserve it."

"There wasn't a reason for what happened to me either," he says. "Not really. Just a … casualty in a war I had no place in. One minute I was normal. In love. Happy. And then … a force of nature swept in and ruined everything. My wife, gone. My job, gone. My sense of the world, just gone. Nothing but blood and pain left in its place. But you get used to it. It becomes comforting. You're at the bottom. You know it can't get worse. Nothing and no one can hurt you as badly ever again."

"But that's not life. That's just existing."

"Maybe that's all I deserve now."

I shake my head. "Not you, Will." I pause. "You're not a monster." He finally looks at me; if I couldn't already feel his despair, I'd read it like a book on his face. "You're a strong, handsome, *decent* man who deserves every happiness in the world. Every. Single. One. But you have to reach for it. Rise from that bottom. And yeah, it's scary. And

210

hard. And there's no guarantee you won't end up exactly where you were. But at least you can say you tried. That is for just one day, one *moment,* you lived. That life was full of possibility and happiness. That's all any of us can hope for. You just have to take the first step. Come what may."

He turns away from me. "I wish it was that easy."

Me too. But the best things in life rarely are.

———

We barely talk at the tree lot or on the drive back. We get the tree inside the still empty house, leaning it against the wall. It's perfect, tall and full. "Where's your Christmas stuff?" Will asks.

"Crawlspace above the hall. I'll get the ladder."

When I return from the side of the house with the rickety ladder, Will's already got the crawlspace open. He climbs up and sneezes. I've never heard him do that before. "It's really dark. I can't read the writing."

"Just bring them all down." He begins handing me box after box of stuff: mine, Brian's, one marked "Stella," and three Christmas boxes. I hand him back Brian's but keep the others. When that's done, we get the tree on the stand and start unpacking the lights and ornaments. "Look," I say, holding up a ceramic pink snowman missing one of her arms. "I made this when I was nine. Her name is Princess Icicle."

"Cute," Will says as he starts untangling the lights. I then pull out a miniature Scarlett O'Hara in her drape dress. This is my favorite. I caress her with a smile. "Is that from *Gone with the Wind*?"

"Yeah. My mom gave me this one our last Christmas together." With a sigh, I put her next to Princess. "She came home Christmas Eve from a late night at the bar thinking I was asleep. She kissed my forehead and left Scarlett and this tiny box beside my head. Inside was this gold-plated charm bracelet with shoes and sunglasses and animals on it. I loved it. I took it to show and tell. Even wore it every day until I lost it in college. Looked everywhere. Put up fliers around campus. I swore if anyone ever found it I'd marry him or her in an instant. Like Cinderella and her shoe or something."

He looks away from me. "What was she like? Your mom?"

"What?"

"I told you about my parents," he says. "What were yours like?"

"Afraid my childhood wasn't as Norman Rockwell as yours," I chuckle nervously. I start unwrapping more ornaments. "I have no idea who my father is. She never got his name or anything, and I was too young to ask many questions before she died. I just knew other kids had dads, but since Brian didn't have one either, I never thought it was a huge deal. Then when I got older and I realized it was, there was nobody to ask."

"What about your Mom?"

"A free spirit. She hated being tied down to one job, one place, one man. But she loved us. No question. When she could, she'd read us bedtime stories and sing to us. She loved to bake too. Once a week the three of us would crank up the tunes and sing and hop around while making cookies or cupcakes or spaghetti." I shake my head. "But she wasn't perfect. Brian likes to pretend she was some saint, expanding our horizons with adventure and freedom. But we were poor. Really poor. She couldn't or wouldn't keep a job. And more often than not she'd get involved with some loser and move us in with him until he got sick of us. We ended up living out of the car at least half a dozen times that I can remember. She called those the Gypsy Days. We'd just keep driving until the gas money ran out, and the cycle would begin anew. Until Leonard." I haven't looked at Will until now. He's grave and has stopped working on the lights. "But you've read my file. You know all about that." I avert my gaze and resume unwrapping the ornaments from the paper towels.

"I'm sorry," he says. "I'm *so* sorry that happened to you."

"Yeah," I say softly. "But it all worked out in the end. We came to live with Nana, and the rest was pretty dull. Went to school, got a job, had a boyfriend. Almost normal."

He nods and starts with the lights again. "I miss normal."

"What about it do you miss?"

"Stupid stuff. Going out for drinks after work with friends. Mowing the lawn. Trips to the grocery store. Cleaning the gutters." He scoffs. "Privacy. Not knowing by smell when people are afraid or angry. Not having to keep track of the moon. Untangling Christmas lights," he says with a small smile. "Like I said, stupid stuff."

"That's not stupid, Will. That's life. It's all in the details, right? And you can still do those things. Heck, you can go clean out our gutters and mow the lawn right now. I won't stop you. Hey, do Mrs. Ramirez's too."

"You know what I mean."

I do. I want the same things. And I want them with him.

"You know, you have the right idea," he continues, "about quitting. I've considered it about a thousand times. I'm sick of the pain. Of the suffering we see." He starts violently pulling at the lights. "I'm sick of hotel rooms and greasy food and that ridiculous plane. I'm sick of dead bodies and guns and everyone dying on me. I'm sick of seeing my friends' throats ripped out and withering away and me not being able to do a fucking thing to stop it. I'm sick and tired of failing everyone. Of being so goddamn angry and taking it out on people I care about. Wounding people I'd rather die than hurt for no reason except..." He must realize who he's talking to and stops, shocked by his outburst.

"Except…" I say breathlessly.

He shakes his head, throwing the lights down. "Nothing."

I bridge the gap between us. "No. Say it. Please."

"I can't," he says as he steps away from me, embarrassed and pained by himself.

He turns his back to me, but I spin him around by the bicep. I don't release him and he doesn't pull away. "Yes. You can. Just say the words."

"I can't," he whispers. "I just can't. I'm sorry." He brushes my hand off.

"Will."

"What do you want me to say, Bea?" he blows up. "That I care about you? That I might even be—" He stops himself, shaking his head. "Even if I did. Even if I was, it wouldn't matter. It wouldn't. I'm still a monster. I smell blood, and I get excited. Someone challenges me and it takes all my willpower not to go for the jugular. Literally. I turn into a deadly, vicious, wild animal. An *animal.* It never leaves me. I don't get a normal life. I don't get happily ever after."

"You think I do?" I ask. "Will, I kill people with a thought. If you're a monster then so am I."

"It's not the same, and you know it. I'm not human, Bea."

"Will, I don't care that you're a werewolf. It doesn't define you unless you let it. When I see you it's not as a monster. I know monsters, met my first at age eight, and you sure as hell aren't one of them." Nothing can stop me from touching him now. I grasp his arm again, but this time he doesn't move away. "When I see you, all I see a good, strong man who would do anything for others. Who cares with all his heart about people, even total strangers. Making their lives better. I see a teacher. A protector. A leader. Someone who I care about. *Very* deeply. Who I want more than anything, and who I think feels the same way about me."

Hesitantly he caresses my head, then my cheek. "Of course I do," he whispers. "You're beautiful, and sexy, and smart, and you have the best heart of anyone I know. You drive me crazy. But that's the problem: *you drive me crazy*. You have since the moment I saw you. And since then…" He runs his thumb down my sensitive lips, and I shiver. His eyes are as lustful as mine. But then he pulls away, lust replaced with sadness. "But it doesn't matter. Can't you see that? Can't you understand that? There's no future for us. Despite what you think, we cannot have what we want."

"Why not?"

"What are we going to do? Move to the suburbs? Lock me in the basement once a month?" he asks wildly. "One time, that's all it takes. One forgotten lock, one false move, and I get out and I kill you. Or some man makes a rude comment, and I see red like last night. Or someone tries to kill you…and I can't…" He's angry now. At himself, at me, at whatever hypothetical situation he's concocted inside his head. His hands ball into fists. "Staying in control is the only way I can get through the day. It's the only way I can keep even a sliver of my humanity. But around you…you're chaos incarnate. You cloud everything, and that scares the shit out of me. You make me want things I can't have. And being around you makes me think those things are possible. But I *know* they're not, and trying to pretend they are…that's not fair to either one of us." His fingers relax. "I'm sorry." With those final words, he walks out of the room into the back yard, leaving me alone with this new reality.

And that's it. I've lost him before I ever had him. I have no idea what to say or do. I could go out there, I *should* go out there. Fight for him. Scream, or cry, or plead, I don't know. But I can't. I don't have it in me anymore. Because deep down, maybe I know he's right.

The monster never gets a happily ever after.

ELEVEN

LOST AND FOUND

HE LEFT.

He took the keys to my rental car and left.

Thank God.

I've never had my heart pulverized before. I'd rather have any supernatural creature kick my butt than go through this. I used to scoff when I heard people died of broken hearts. That they threw themselves off bridges or ended up in the madhouse when the one they loved rejected them. Now I get it. I've had chunks of my flesh ripped from me and suffered blinding headaches where I prayed for death, but this … this is proof that the soul is infinitely more powerful than the body. It's as if every bit of joy has faded, never to return. It's hard to breathe even. Everything is oppressive as if the air is crushing me like Giles Corey being stoned to death.

I wish I could get angry. Lash out. I wish I could curse him or shoot him and make him hurt as badly as I do. But I can't. Because it's not his fault. He has to do what's right for him, and being around me isn't that. And he's correct on a lot of points. Normal isn't in the cards for us, no matter how much we want it. Pretending it's possible can't be good for either of us in the long run. Would have been nice to have had the chance though.

Nana knocks on my bedroom door after sunset and enters a second later with a cup of tea and ice cream sundae on a tray. I almost smile as I push myself into the sitting position.

"Here you go, Honey Bea," she says as she sets down the tray.

"Thanks," I whisper.

She lowers herself onto the bed as I take a spoonful. It tastes like nothing. Like eating air. I put the spoon down. Nana smoothes my hair. "It'll be alright. Just give it some time."

"Yeah."

She ceases stroking. "You know, when I was seventeen, there was this ranch hand named Jack who worked for my father." She closes her eyes and smiles. "He was the most handsome man I had ever seen. Tall, lean, blonde, tan from all his time out in the sun. And he had this scar that cut through his left eyebrow. It was so sexy." She opens her eyes. "We snuck around for six months. Meeting at his trailer or out on the arroyo under the stars."

"Nana!"

"What? I was in love. And he returned that love. To this day I'm convinced he did. He even asked me to marry him, and boy was I all set to do it, elope with him in the dead of night. But apparently one night when we had a fight, he cheated on me and had gotten a girl pregnant."

"Oh God."

"He said it was a onetime mistake, but I didn't care. It killed me, but I told him he had to do the right thing and marry her. And he did. He left with her, and I never saw him again. It wasn't meant to be." She takes my hand. "Take it from one heartbroken woman to another; the pain fades. Not completely, but I do believe it makes your heart stronger. Once open it'll be ready for when the right one comes along. Love, no matter what, is a glorious thing. It is never wrong. It teaches us. It makes us grow. And I have no doubt you will get through this that much wiser and with a fuller heart." She leans down, kissing my forehead. "Now, I can skip my knitting club if—"

"No," I say. "You go. Have fun. I just want to be alone."

"Okay." She kisses my cheek. "I love you."

"Love you, too."

She walks out, and I set the tray on the floor before resuming my corpse interpretation. I close my eyes, and visions of my young, beautiful grandmother and her Jack lying under the stars with her head on his chest come to me. I wonder what her life—

There's a light knock on the door. Nana pokes her head in again. "Bea? Someone's here to see you."

Oliver steps in, and the strange thing is I am *so* glad to see him. That heavy oppression Will dumped earlier is sliced in half. Just him being in the same room as me can make me feel better. In spite of last night, and all the hate I spewed, here he is. One of my best friends who always knows the perfect thing to make me feel better. I need him now. Not that I'd ever let him know that. "Thank you, Liz," he says.

As she closes the door, I push myself into the sitting position. "Hi."

"I am sorry to intrude." He pulls a set of keys out of his black slacks. "I believe these belong to you."

"Yeah. Thanks."

He sets them on my desk before pulling the desk chair up to the bed. "I shall assume, judging from your melancholy demeanor and the two empty bottles of bourbon next to the passed-out werewolf on my hotel room floor, something wretched occurred between you and William this day."

"Do you really what to talk about this with me?"

"Not particularly, no," he says, "but you do. And I wish to show I am better for more than wardrobe tips and a few laughs."

Great, now I can add guilt to my burden. "I'm sorry I said that to you. I didn't mean it."

"You were angry, and rightly so. Last night was my fault and my fault alone. So allow me to make up for it. I am here for you in your time of need. Always."

I didn't think it possible, but I manage a small smile for my friend. "Thank you."

He nods. "So, do you wish me to kill him quickly or slowly?"

"Neither. We just talked things out and decided . . . " I shake my head to stop the tears, "it wouldn't work out. No one's fault."

"This was a mutual decision?"

I open my mouth to lie but "No" pops out, along with another fresh set of tears. I've cried enough. I push the sadness down where I keep my stockpile. "He said I drive him crazy. That if he's with me, he'll lose control and turn into a monster." I wipe my tears away. My cheeks are so raw from all the wiping. "I mean, come on! What can I say to that?"

"My dear, I have known William far longer than you. His response does not surprise me in the slightest. I have no doubt about his deep feelings for you, none whatsoever, but William's watchword is restraint. It is the only way he knows how to survive. You challenge that on its basest level. You touch and frighten him to the core."

"So you agree with him?" I ask, flabbergasted.

"My darling, if I had the providence to be desired and loved by a woman such as yourself, there is not a force in existence that would keep me from her. Not heaven, not hell, and most assuredly not myself." He pauses. "But William is not me."

A different form of sadness overwhelms me, this one tinged with regret, but I push it down. One emotional upheaval at a time. "Yeah."

"He is a fool. And a coward. Not fit to shine your shoes. I have been telling you this for months."

"I know."

"And besides, all is pointless. You have decided to leave us freaks. You shall never see or hear from him again. He will fade from memory, as shall the rest of us. You are still quitting us, are you not? Or was that just another threat as the previous hundred other times?"

In all the hullabaloo I'd forgotten about that. "I don't know. My mind has been on other things. But now ... I mean I have to quit, right? I can't live across the hall from him now that we ... it would just be unbearable. Right?"

"I cannot give an opinion on this. I am far too biased."

"Then I guess I'm quitting." Relief. I should be feeling relief right now, right? Then why do I feel nothing but another desolate pang? "For the best, right?"

"Hardly."

"I thought you weren't giving an opinion."

"You know my position," he says, looking away from me for the first time. "I would miss you."

"I'd miss you too." More than I'd ever admit to him. "But I can't face him."

"I would like to murder him," Oliver mutters.

"It's not his fault. He's right, I'm chaos incarnate. You'll all be well rid of me."

"That is the most foolish statement to ever escape those beautiful lips. I have been with the F.R.E.A.K.S. for decades, and I have never seen a soul take to the job as quickly as you. I meant what I said to your grandmother. There is not another living person I would want beside me in battle. You are meant to be with us, my dear. Of that I have no doubt. And to let some frightened dog not worthy of your affection derail you from reaching your full potential is lunacy and quite frankly downright sickens me."

"You're giving me too much credit."

"And you are not giving yourself enough. But this is a pointless conversation. You are also obstinate, so once your mind is set, there is no changing it. I am wasting words."

"But they're lovely words." I touch his hand. "And I appreciate them. And you."

The ringing of his cell phone, which I programmed to play "The Stripper," stops our love fest. "Hello?" He listens for a moment, glances at me, and stands up. "Pardon me, Trixie." He walks out, shutting the door behind himself.

Like I'm going to let him get away with that. For the first time in hours, I get out of bed. Oliver stands by the still bare Christmas tree, phone pressed to his ear. "Then order steaks from room service. It will help." He listens, rolling his eyes. "All you can do is toss him in the shower and ply him with water and food. With his metabolism, it should take an hour or so." He pauses. "No, you do not want me there." A pause. "Because the way I feel towards him at this moment would certainly lead to a physical altercation of epic proportions. I am sorry. You must handle this on your own, Kevin. Call me when he is fit to fly." He slaps the phone shut.

"How bad is he?"

"Drunken rambling and a broken coffee table. Wolfe will be fine. We just have to postpone our departure until he is sober." He smiles at me. "You certainly have a way with men, Trixie."

"So I've been told. Maybe I should join a convent. Get the habit and everything."

"My dear, it is as if you are reading one of my letters to *Penthouse*."

My mouth gapes opens, and I chuckle. "Pervert! I so didn't need to know that!"

"It garnered a smile, did it not?"

I snap my mouth shut. "No." But the edges of my mouth creep up a little. "So, I guess you're stuck here awhile?"

He raises an eyebrow. "Yes. In your empty house. With your empty bed. With *hours* to kill. Whatever shall we do with ourselves?"

I smile seductively while I lean down over the back of the couch, shifting my hip to arch my back and butt. Grin Number One with full fang fills his face, but disappears when I toss a bag of ornaments at him. "You can start with the lights by your feet." I jump off the couch. "I'll get the tinsel."

———

"There."

I place the star on top of the tree and leap off the chair next to Oliver. He studies the tree as if it were painted by Monet. All in all I think we did an excellent job. The colored lights work, the ornaments are evenly distributed, and the star is level.

"Very nice," he says. "Per usual we make an excellent team."

"Maybe you should quit too. We can become professional tree decorators. Alexander and Montrose."

"Montrose and Alexander," he corrects. "I *am* the one who hung the lights and tinsel."

"Fine. Have it your way," I say as I put the chair back at the dining room table.

He starts picking up the discarded baggies and paper towels everything was in. "What shall I do with this mess?"

"Stick everything back in the boxes. They're in the corner."

As I wash the sap off my hands, he locates the boxes. But after stuffing everything in an empty one, he smiles and lifts up another that reads "Beatrice." "Well, now. What do we have here?"

"Leave those alone," I say, drying my hands.

He collects all of them, setting them on the coffee table. "I think not." He opens the top one before sitting on the couch.

I'd fight but it wouldn't do any good, so I join him on the couch. He pulls out some badly drawn pictures of mermaids. "Oh wow," I say.

"An artist you are not, Trixie." He hands me the drawings.

"I liked mermaids."

"They are quite beautiful in real life."

"Have you met some?"

"Once or twice." Next he pulls out some My Little Ponies, raising an eyebrow.

"What? I'm a girl."

He sets those on the floor and brings out some collages April and I made. Just the heads of Jonathan Taylor Thomas, Mark Paul Gosselaar, and Brad Pitt. He points at Mark. "Who is this?"

"Don't you know anything? That's Zack Morris! *Saved by the Bell*?"

"I missed that one."

"I was twelve. Everyone loved them."

The rest inside are just dolls, some homemade jewelry, an old music box, and ceramic unicorns. The second box is nothing but stuffed animals and toys. But when he opens the third, my chest tightens a little. Mom's box. There are high school pendants, a pair of silver platform shoes, a roach clip, some cassette tapes by Devo and Michael

Jackson, and a few loose photos. One of Mom in a bikini and huge sunglasses at the beach with a group of friends. Another is of her smoking a joint while a man I recognize as Brian's father plays the guitar. She ran away with him when she was seventeen, and Brian came a year later. I think his name was Hank. He was long gone by the time I came onto the scene. In the third picture, Mom stands on a stage dressed in a top hat and tails as part of a chorus line. She took dance lessons for years, ballet and tap, and later used those skills to work a pole at multiple clubs along the Southwest.

"Your mother was quite beautiful," Oliver says. I toss the pictures back in the box along with all her other stuff. "Do you miss her?"

"Not really," I admit, throwing in the last thing. "Is that wrong?"

"Absolutely not. She let you down. She committed a purely selfish act when you needed her most. The best thing she did for you was leaving you to your grandmother. It is only natural you would have mixed feelings."

"Only you would give me that answer."

"I shall always tell you the truth, Trixie."

I squeeze his hand. "I know, and I appreciate it." The telephone rings, and I get up. Now leaving Memory Lane. "Hello?"

"Where the hell are you?" April asks on the phone. "The pageant starts in ten minutes."

I groan. "Oh heck. I'm sorry. I forgot."

"You forgot?"

"I'm on my way. I promise. Bye." I hang up.

Oliver gazes up at me with the opened music box in his hand. "What did you forget?"

"Manny's winter pageant. Crud." I run into the bedroom and toss on my clothes from earlier not bothering with makeup or hair. When

I return all of a minute later, everything is cleaned up and Oliver is putting on his jacket. Super-speed has its uses.

"Are you ready?" Oliver asks.

"You want to come with me? To a children's pageant? Wouldn't you rather stay here and rifle through my things?"

"Tempting, but no. I would much rather meet the famous April and her brood."

Disaster waiting to happen, but there isn't time to argue. I toss on my leather jacket. "Fine. But no...being yourself."

"I would never." He vanished before my eyes and reappears by the front door as it swings open. "Must not keep them waiting. After you, my darling."

Well, this should be interesting.

———

Walter J. Porter North Elementary School is one of the newer schools in San Diego. The small front parking lot is full so we have to park down the street and walk. The problem is that Mt. Erie Church, with its huge cross hanging outside, overlooks the school. If the huge number of parents milling around the lot notice me leading a vampire with his eyes closed through the gate, they don't let on. Though all the mothers do check him out. Ugh.

The auditorium is toward the back of the outdoor campus. Some of the smaller children sprint around on the playground while their parents catch up with each other, but when they spot my companion all conversation stops. He winks as he passes. This used to bother me, but since it happens *every time* we go out, I've gotten used to it. Something about vamp pheromones or glamour magic that makes women and men become willing porn stars. Doesn't work well on me, though.

Our best guess is Mom was bitten when I was in the womb and the enzymes used to close the wound made me immune. That or I'm a freak among freaks.

I spot April and Javi just outside the auditorium with Carlos and Flora. April scans the crowd, spotting me. We each wave before she thrusts Flora into Javi's arms and rushes over. I glance at the grinning Oliver. "Best behavior," I warn him.

"Of course, my darling." He so doesn't mean it.

April gets within a few feet of us and slows down, her eyes popping out of her head. In a second her tongue will be on the grass with the rest of the mothers. "Um, hi!" she shouts, not taking her eyes off Oliver. "Oh my God!" Oliver flinches. "I can't believe you're here. This is him, right? The you-know-what?"

"This is Oliver."

He takes her hand, pressing his lips against it. "*Enchanté*."

She chortles like a mentally deranged person. "Oh wow." He releases her hand. "You are … wow!"

"Thank you," he says graciously. "As are you. Your pictures did not do you justice."

"Uh huh" is all she can manage.

Javi, no doubt worried that his wife is acting like a drugged-out groupie, strolls over with the kids. April's eyes never leave Oliver. "Hello, Bea. Who's your … friend?"

"Oliver, this is Javier. April's husband."

They shake hands. "You are a lucky man," Oliver says.

"Thanks." They break apart. "This thing's about to begin. We better get seats."

"You go right in," April says. "We'll be there in a second."

"Yes," Oliver says, "we must give them time to discuss me." He nods at me with Grin Number Three, no fang but nice, and walks toward the auditorium with Javi and the kids.

April grabs my arm, pulling me to a slightly secluded spot. "Oh my God! That man is walking sex! And I never would have guessed he was a you-know-what. How have you not jumped his bones yet? He's even more gorgeous than Will! And where is Will? Did you dump him for Oliver?"

"April, calm down!"

"We're about to begin," someone shouts. "Please come inside!"

"Shit! Stupid children," April says. We power walk with the rest of the stragglers. "Okay, quickly, is Will coming?"

"No."

"Did something happen? Something bad?"

"Yes, but I don't want to talk about this right now."

"Fine."

We get inside the stuffy, crowded auditorium and spot our guys in the middle. Javi and Oliver are chatting like old friends, and Javi even laughs. I sit between Oliver and April, who pulls Flora onto her lap. "So, Oliver," April says, "what did that rat bastard do to my best friend now?"

"April!"

"Rats are yucky," Flora says.

"Yes, they are," April says. "Especially big, jerky ones who look like the Marlboro Man. So are you going to have to kick his booty or should I?"

"Can we please not talk about this now?" I ask.

Mercifully, the lights dim and the principal walks on stage before further embarrassment ensues. The pageant is cute with some of the older kids singing non-denominational holiday songs, and then the younger ones doing a little play about a snowman trying to get home. Manny doesn't have any lines and just stands off to the side, occasionally running around with the other snowflakes. Javi and April seem so proud, and every time I glance at Oliver, he's smiling. I lean over and whisper, "I'll bet in five hundred years you've never seen one of these before."

Still smiling, he whispers back, "No."

"Glad I help you expand your horizons."

"Perhaps later we can return to your bedroom and I can expand yours."

I laugh and smack his arm. "There are children present!"

"They are not invited."

I smack him again and chuckle, but someone behind shushes us. We bite our lips to stop the laughs. April's grinning from cheek to cheek. I scowl at her, and she stops.

About ten happy, peppy minutes later the snowman is reunited with his snow wife and the audience applauds. All the children line up and take a bow before jumping off the stage in search of their parents. Short, just the way I like these things. Oliver and I take the restless Carlos and Flora outside while Javi and April find their snowflake. Flora grips Oliver's hand and refuses to let go even when we stop walking.

"Your brother was quite good," Oliver says to Carlos.

"He didn't do nothin'."

"Just stepping on that stage is a triumph. I could not do it."

"You talk funny."

"Carlos!" I say.

"It is alright, Trixie. I do. I am from England, and this is how we speak."

"Oh," The boy shifts on his feet. "Are you Aunt Bea's boyfriend?"

"No," he answers without hesitation.

"Carlos, stop being rude," I say. "Go take your sister to the playground. Now." Carlos has to pry his sister from Oliver, but they obey. "That kid is going to be heck on wheels when he's a teenager."

"He is just jealous of the attention his brother is receiving," Oliver says. "I remember when I brought Catherine a kitten from the O'Mara farm. Samuel cried for an hour then smashed his dinner bowl. I had to tan his hide."

My mouth hangs open a little, but I have no idea what to say. "You're talking about your children, aren't you?" finally comes out.

He doesn't take his eyes off the playground but nods. "Yes."

"What were they like?"

"Mischievous. Loving. Beautiful. The loves of my life."

"Did you ever see them after you were turned?"

"No. I had no desire for this life to touch theirs. I simply sent funds as often as I could."

"What happened to them?"

"My wife, Sarah, returned to her family's farm. She and Samuel died five years later of the Black Death. Catherine married her cousin and shortly died in childbirth."

"Do you still miss them?" I ask, studying him.

Those gray eyes turn my way, deep never-ending melancholy radiating from them. "Oh yes. Every single day."

We stare at one another, the pain so deep it crushes me again. I reach up to touch his cheek. "I—"

"There you are!" April calls from behind us. The spell's broken. I quickly lower my hand and both plaster smiles on as we turn around. April, Javi, and snowflake Manny walk up. "Please tell me you sold my other children."

"Nobody would take them," I say. I look down at Manny. "You were so good. Best snowflake ever!"

"Thank you," the boy says.

"Well, Mr. Snowflake here wants to go to Johnny Rockets for milkshakes. You guys in?"

I'm about to reply, but Oliver beats me to it. "I am afraid I cannot. I really must be returning to my hotel to pack. Our flight is scheduled to leave in an hour."

"Really?" April asks, disappointed.

"I am afraid so, but it was very kind of you to include me in the festivities."

"Of course," Javi says.

Oliver touches my back. "Trixie, I shall meet you at the car." He looks at the Diego family. "It was lovely to finally meet you all." He shakes Javi's hand and kisses a surprised April's cheek before walking off.

"Was it something—" April says.

"No. Look, I have to drop him at the hotel, but I'm gonna swing by your house later, okay? I have *so* much to tell you."

"I'll bet. Is this a wine or tequila conversation?"

"Tequila with a side of moonshine." I hug her. "See you in an hour."

I run off after Oliver, catching up with him at the gate. The huge cross still looms. Without a word I take his arm and lead him up the street to the car. To anyone we'd look like a couple strolling arm in arm.

"I was rude," he says.

"It's okay."

"I simply … "

I squeeze his arm and rest my chin on his shoulder. "I know."

The ten-minute drive to the hotel is made in silence as we both think about those fatherless children dead for five hundred years. I imagine the girl, Catherine, petite with her father's brown hair, pale skin, and wicked sense of humor. Samuel was probably a carbon copy of his father complete with mischievous smile and charm. I have a million questions but don't dare ask. Some things are better left unexplained and in the past. Oliver just stares expressionless out the window.

I park the car at the hotel's curb, but he doesn't get out. We just sit for a minute, neither of us ready to break the invisible tethers entwining us to the other. I have the strongest urge to touch his exquisite alabaster face one more time. "This may be the last I see of you," he finally says.

"I'll fly back to pack up my things."

He turns and looks at me with beautiful, aching eyes. "Perhaps."

He's right. This is it. I'll never see him again. We can swear to call, e-mail, or visit, but we both know we won't. All or nothing, that's who we are. Bond forged in blood and tears, the strongest kind there is. I try to hold back the tears but can't. I shake my head. "I am going to miss you. *So much.*"

Hesitantly he raises his hand. He touches my wet cheek, wiping a tear away with his cold thumb. I press his hand in mine. "Do not cry, my darling," he whispers. "I cannot bear to see you cry."

"I always seem to be doing it in front of you," I say with a chuckle. "And you're the only one. You ... " I can't say it. It'll make it all too real. "Just ... " I lean in and embrace him, holding him tight and breathing him in for the last time. I think my heart is breaking for the second time today.

He hugs me back, holding me as tight as I am him. "Thank you, my goddess. Goodbye."

And then in a blink, he's gone.

The car door is open, and I'm hugging air. The only remainder is the gold bracelet sitting on the dashboard. I pick it up with a gasp. My charm bracelet. The one Mom gave me. He found it. He brought it back to me. My friend. My partner. My dark angel.

Goodbye.

I shouldn't be driving like this. I can barely see through my tears and my hands tremble, but I have to get home. I want Nana and April and my bed and a place to think.

But I'm not that lucky. Never ever. Halfway home a police cruiser begins flashing its lights, and I have to pull over. Crap. We end up at the corner of a residential street. I take deep breaths to calm myself down. It works. I'm only weeping as the officer shines his flashlight through the window. I roll it down. I sniffle and say, "Here's my license and—"

"Hey, Bea," a familiar voice says. I look up, and Steven smiles down at me. "You look like hell."

"Steven?"

"I would say I'm sorry about this, but I'm not."

"What?"

I see his hand move, but don't register what has actually happened until after the sharp stab of the needle in my neck. Then the world goes from fuzzy to black.

After this day, I welcome it.

TWELVE

DOWN THE RABBIT HOLE

I WAKE UP BUT ... don't. Everything seems far away from me. Unreal. Right as I open them, my eyes refuse to stay open. When they open again I have no idea how much time has passed. Seconds? Days? I feel squishy and gooey and sleepy. Very sleepy. This time I force my eyes to remain open for a few seconds.

I'm lying on a cot. The room is sparse, with a chemical toilet and two bottles of water next to it. That's it. Oh, and the heavy chain coming from the floor and ending at the handcuff on my ankle. This should be the part where I freak out, but instead I give my eyes what they want once again.

The next time they open about half the fuzzies have vanished and complex thought is possible. As is walking. Well, after the second attempt. I devour the unopened water of half its contents and use the toilet, but that's all I can manage right now. I flop back on the cot before my legs give out.

Okay, I've obviously been kidnapped. Again. This makes three after the necromancer and Freddy. They both ended bloody, but at least I knew what they wanted from me. I was a means to an end in both cases. Was this Connor? Likely suspect, but I doubt it. I'm not much use to him unless I'm willing. Who … Steven stopped me. He injected me with something. Steven. But why? I really don't want to consider the possibilities. I can't think of a single good one. Pure, unadulterated fear pushes through the drug haze, and I curl into the fetal position. I don't fight unconsciousness this time.

The sound of the door unlocking jolts me awake. But instead of my bastard ex-boyfriend, Kristen steps in with a grocery bag in one hand and pistol in the other. Per usual, she is not pleased to see me, pretty face ugly with a sneer, but for once the feeling is not mutual. The woman can't stand me, so it's doubtful she'll sexually assault me. I'm hanging onto any sliver of hope here.

"Oh God, you're awake," she says as if I've inconvenienced her. She grips the pistol tighter. "Move and I shoot you." I stay still as she approaches but try to take the gun out of her hand with my mind. It doesn't budge. Stupid drugs. She tosses the bag by the bed and a jar of peanut butter rolls out. "Your dinner, Countess."

"What the hell is going on?" I ask, my voice cracking. "Where am I?"

"My great-grandfather's cabin. The last place you'll ever be."

"What … " I can't think of the words. "Where's Steven?"

"Helping your FBI buddies search for you. Everyone's *so concerned*," she says in a baby voice.

"How long have I been here?"

"A day. Two more to go."

"Until?"

"I'll let your imagination run wild with that one." Keeping the gun on me, she pulls out a hypodermic needle. "Time for your medicine. I laced it with something fun this time. Move or try any of your magic mind shit, and I'll blow your fucking brains out."

She presses the barrel right into my temple, and as hard as she can, jabs the needle into my neck. I cry out in pain as the bitch just smiles.

"Pleasant nightmares," she says before fading to black.

———

When I open my eyes, heavy as boulders, there's someone standing in the corner of the almost black room. The only light emanates from the hanging bulb swinging left and right like a pendulum. As with everything else, the person is distorted, at a slight angle, and out of focus like watching a 3-D movie without the glasses. But when he steps into the light, I scream. Leonard Bentley, the man I killed as a child, remains motionless as worms crawl in and out of his flaky yellow skin. A zombie, he's a zombie. He studies me, his mouth contorting into a grotesque smile. Cockroaches climb out all over his face. He lunges at me, howling like a madman, and I flip on my side, pulling my knees to my chest. But he doesn't touch me. I lay there sobbing and rocking myself for a few minutes. "It's okay, it's okay" I say in a loop through the sobs. He's gone. He's not real. He's not real, and he's gone. He's gone. When I can breathe again, I quickly turn my head over my shoulder just to make sure he's not there.

"He went away," a woman's voice echoes though the silent room.

I know that voice. My boogeyman has changed form. I catch only a glimpse before I shriek again, close my eyes, and put my fingers in my ears. This doesn't stop my tormenter. My once beautiful mother, now bloated and red from the gas, rests on the bed next to me. I feel it move under her weight and can smell her White Diamonds perfume as she lowers her head to my ear. Though my ears are plugged, her voice is as clear as day. "You murdered him. The only man I ever loved. Then you killed me. I couldn't stand the fact you came out of me. I hated you. You killed the love of my life, you selfish bitch! I'm dead because of you! You're a freak! An aberration! A fucking monster! I should have killed you in the womb!"

"No!" I bellow.

I swat at her, but she's gone. Gone, gone, gone. I'm all alone. Alone, alone, alone. Forever alone. I close my eyes again, panting until I can't breathe. I don't know what's real and what's not. Is this bed real? Is the smell of urine real? This must be what it's like to be crazy. Trapped in your own mind, not trusting anything or anyone. Madness. A lunatic. It's finally happened.

"Oh God, help me," I cry into my hands. But am I really? Are these my real hands?

"What the fuck did she do to you?" a man asks.

Real fingers open my real eye, and I view Nick kneeling beside me. He seems concerned and shakes his head. When he pulls away my eye closes again. I struggle not to fall back into my hell for a few seconds. "Hey," Nick says, "Kristen did something to her." He pauses and I slip away. "I don't know..."

I open my eyes again, but my prison has changed. I'm back at the mansion in my own pink bed. Everything is so bright the light stings my eyes. I blink a few times to bring the figures in the room into focus. Bad idea. Oliver, dressed in a tuxedo complete with cape, sucks the blood from a woman in a red satin dress. I blink a few times to make sure what I'm seeing. She's me. Or was me. Her arm is limp and her head lolls to the side, blood dripping from the side of the other me's mouth. Oliver gazes up from her neck, giving me a bloody grin before sinking his fangs in again.

"He is such a pig," Will says. At least I think it's Will. A giant, furry wolf wearing tattered pants sits cross legged in the chair beside me. The green eyes are the only remnants of him.

"No, he's not," I say meekly.

"Look at him." I do. Oliver sinks has fangs into the other me's neck for the third time. "He doesn't know when to quit. He is a hedonist. Pure excess. And let's not forget he's dead. He's not human. He will never be able to give you what you need. Fidelity. Normalcy. *Home*." Oliver drops my corpse to the floor like a sack of garbage and wipes the stray blood from his chin. "He will tire of you. Leave you. And in the end, he will destroy you."

I close my eyes. "I know," I whisper. When I open them again Oliver is gone, but my corpse remains.

Werewolf Will's barely there lips are pulled back into a smile, his jagged teeth visible. "Thank you," he says.

"Why?"

"Now it's just the two of us. Just the way I want it."

"But you don't want me."

"I want you more than any man has ever wanted any woman in history. As Romeo wanted Juliet. As Paris wanted Helen of Troy."

"You rejected me."

"To save you." He gestures to himself. "From this."

"I don't mind you like that."

"*I* do," he says. "This and this alone is how I see myself now. As the beast. As that." We both turn our heads to the sight behind him. A second Will is on top of me, biting and clawing at me as I try to fight him off. The other me screams and cries, but the wolf's snout rips my throat out. "That is all I see when I think of you. I'm no better than him."

I blink. The wolf and corpse are gone. My Will has tears cascading down his furry cheeks. I reach across and wipe them away. His pelt is so soft, like feathers. He nuzzles my hand. "This is not the you I see." I push myself up and lean across, kissing his lips right under his nose. When I pull away, he's transformed back into human form. "*This* is the man I love."

"Then maybe it's time *you* tried to save *me* for once."

"Do you think you'll let me?"

This time he kisses me. It's deep, passionate, perfect. He moves his mouth to my ear, his hot breath against my neck, and whispers, "Only one way to find out."

Something wet splashes my face and my bedroom vanishes, replaced with my real dank, dark prison. Nick and Steven, who holds a water bottle over my head, stand beside the bed. Neither seems pleased. I thrash and wipe the liquid off my face.

"What..." I ask. That one word takes quite the effort.

"I'm gonna get her some new sheets and pants," Nick says. "You'll be okay?"

"Yeah. She's still drugged." Nick nods and walks out, locking the door behind himself. "Thirsty?" Steven asks. He tips the water bottle into my mouth, and I drink until it's all gone. Steven grabs the bag Kristen left then sits on the bed. I shrink away. Shaking his head, he pulls out a banana, peels it, and puts it against my mouth. Hunger replaces common sense, and I eat.

Nick returns with sweatpants and sheets, tossing them at Steven. "I'm gonna take off," Nick says. "If anyone asks about you?"

"Taken care of."

"Okay. Artie'll stop by tomorrow afternoon to check on her."

"Okay. Safe drive back," Steven says.

"You too." Nick barely glances at me before leaving.

A smiling Steven looks down at me. "Still hungry?"

"Fuck you," I slur.

He's taken aback. "You know, that's the first time I've ever heard you cuss. Doesn't sound right coming from you." He picks up the peanut butter and spoon from the bag, feeding it to me. I spit it out. "You know I'm trying to make this as painless for you as possible."

"Let me go."

He stuffs more peanut butter in my mouth instead. This reminds me of the time he had this horrible virus and was bedridden for a week. I came over and fed him soup, much like he's doing now. "Sorry. Not happening." This time I spit the food right into his face. He flinches then smacks me across the cheek, fresh pain blossoming through the haze. He raises his hand again but groans and hits his leg instead. "Jesus Christ, Bea! Why'd you make me do that?"

My cheek throbs so bad. I stifle a sob. "What are you going to do to me?"

"We're going to sacrifice you. To a troll."

Okay, not expecting that answer. "*What?*"

"Six months ago Kristen inherited this place. She was surveying it and found an old mine shaft. It led to a cave, and there he was. Best we can figure, her great-grandfather kept it as a pet. She found his journal, and apparently once every two months, it came out on the new moon. After he fed it, it passed out and he harvested some of its blood. Bea, the man died at age one hundred fifty! You have no idea what this shit does. I can bench press four hundred and run ten miles without stopping. It's fucking amazing!"

"You've done this before?" I ask, shocked. "You've killed people?"

"But I've saved more! I stopped a gangbanger with my bare hands. Jawan ran down a pedophile for three miles. We usually only take the homeless. Criminals. It's for the greater good."

"And doing this to me? Is that for the greater good?"

"I just figured your blood is special. It can only add to the potency of the troll's."

I feel sick to my stomach. Two years. I was with this man for two years. I let him into my life, into my *body,* and I never had even the slightest inkling he was capable of something like this. I choke back vomit. "Who *are* you?"

"I could ask you the same question," he says, visibly hurt. "You served me up to that vampire like a rib-eye."

"You remember that?"

"Troll blood," he says with a shrug. "You let that vampire attempt to mind fuck me without batting an eye. Not to mention the fact we were together two *fucking* years and never told me you could move shit with your mind. How could you do that to me?"

"I didn't trust you." I hold up the chain. "Gee, wonder why?"

He stands up, folding his arms across his chest. "I loved you. I wanted to marry you. Fuck, I wanted you to be the mother of my children! And you lied to me."

"At least I didn't kidnap you and feed you to a troll!"

His hands ball up into fists. "Shut up."

"You're pathetic. Any way you dress this up, it's murder. You're a monster."

"Well, you're the lifelong expert on monsters, right? Takes one to know one."

"You won't get away with this. Eventually, someone will figure out what you've done to me."

"I'm a better actor than you give me credit for. I've been playing the concerned friend to perfection. Not even your FBI pals have a clue. I am *that* good." He reaches in his back pocket, taking out a syringe. "If it makes you feel better, your death won't be in vain. I promise to use this gift for good. It's the least I can do for you." He moves too fast for me to stop him. The needle goes into my arm, and the void returns. Good. Rather have it than spend another millisecond with that man.

———

When I wake for the millionth time in the bomb shelter or whatever the heck it is, I find that someone has changed my urine-soaked pants, sheets, and underwear. Fear grips me again, but from what I can tell he didn't go any further. I still feel unclean.

I manage to stay awake through sheer force of will. Not easy. I do jumping jacks. I eat. I sing show tunes as I examine every inch of the room. There's no door handle, no windows, and my power is on the fritz from the drugs. Next I try to pull the chain out of the floor, but it's futile. Same with the shackle. It's just the standard opened with a handcuff key. Really wish Will had gotten around to teaching me to pick a lock. I could always break my ankle to wiggle out of it, but I'd still have the door to contend with and God knows how far away I am from civilization.

So I pace. And I plan.

An hour or twelve later, I can't tell in here, I hear footsteps descending the steps. Then the familiar unlocking of the door. Who steps in, I don't know. I lay on the bed with my eyes closed playing the part of drugged-out troll meat. Not hard as there are still drugs making me woozy. But I *can* do this. He or she sets a plastic bag by the bed before sitting down. A second later, the person opens one of my eyelids. Artie. I groan and "slowly" come back to consciousness.

"Let me go," I slur. With unsteady arms I weakly push him away, but he grabs my wrists. "Don't touch me."

"You know," he says, pinning my arms on either side of my head, "Steven said you were a shitty lay. But you look like a wildcat to me."

"Stop," I whimper.

"Make me." He bashes his lips against mine, but I move my head side to side and whimper.

"Please don't hurt me. Please," I cry.

He moves my wrists up above my head, holding them down with one hand while the other clumsily works his belt. His attention diverts down, his head swiveling so he can see the problem. The opening I need.

As hard and as deep as I can, I sink my teeth into his neck right at the jugular. The tangy taste of blood and flesh fill my mouth. I chomp down as Artie releases me and howls. Blood gushes down my chin as I rip his flesh out. I spit the quarter size hunk of meat on the floor. Yuck.

The shocked and screaming Artie presses his hand against the wound, more blood spilling between his fingers. He looks at me with revolt, and that's when I deliver the second blow. I toss my head back then forward, my forehead connecting with his nose. There's a sickening crack followed by more shrieks of pain. They make it look easy in the movies but in reality, head-butting hurts like a mother. I'm momentarily dazed but recover quicker than him. Artie falls to the ground, more blood billowing from his nose. I jump off the bed and deliver a nice kick to the crotch. Then another. "Bastard!" He sobs as I get in one more. For my final act, I lift the chemical toilet above my head and smash it into his. He stops sniveling. Is it wrong that that was sort of enjoyable?

No time for reflection. I rifle around his pants, finding the handcuff key that frees me. I also snatch his car keys before racing out of the unlocked door, up the wooden staircase, and into the cabin. Car keys in hand, I rush out into the extremely bright world. I'm temporarily blinded and miss the stairs. I lose my footing and tumble down them, landing on my left elbow and stomach. Intense, vomit-inducing pain radiates up my arm. I scream so loud birds fly away. I roll over onto my back, cradling my bad arm. Crap. Crap. Thirty seconds, that's all I give myself to sob and scream it out. To acknowledge the pain, the fact my ex kidnapped me, and that I just savagely beat another human being. And that's all. When I hit thirty, I take a few deep breaths, wipe my eyes, and find my feet.

Artie's restored Gran Torino is parked right out front. It's difficult but I manage to get it unlocked and climb in. It springs to life without issue, but I can't get it to move. My luck has never been good and now is no exception. Out of all my captor's cars, I make a break for it with the one who drives a stick. I keep pressing what I think is the clutch and move the gears, but the car keeps groaning and stalling. "Come on, you piece of crap!" I shriek as I switch gears. It stalls again.

On my fourth try my luck gets worse. A blood-soaked, pissed-off Artie stumbles out the front door, gun he must have gotten from the house pointed right at me. "Get the fuck out of my car!"

I have no choice. As fast as I can, I throw open the door and dash through the woods. Artie fires and misses, hitting the tree next to me as I pass it. He follows behind, how far I don't know as I don't dare look back. I just run. My legs hurt, I have a stitch in my side, and I can barely breathe, but I run. And how. I'd win the damn gold.

Artie shoots four or five times, missing me by inches. The chase lasts an eternity with the trees getting denser and my body growing more tired with each step. I just run, pushing branches and bramble out of my way with my one good arm. The terrain is uneven, but I'm in decent shape and not as injured as he is. My only hope is to lose him. He fires again, but this time hits me. The bullet goes through the edge of my bad arm, just a graze really, but I scream. I don't stop running.

Then the woods end. Just end. They just stop at a hill with dead dry-brush and the odd wildflower patch scattered around. There's no cover. Of course there isn't. I keep going but do see the boarded-up entrance to a mine next to a small creek. For a split second my heart soars. Protection. Then I remember what's in there. I stare at it for a few seconds to catch my breath but hear footsteps and sprint again. The hill makes it harder, as does my arm, but I don't stop. I leap over the creek and make it about two hundred yards before my body can take no more. It's as if someone impales a javelin into my right side. My feet trip each other, and down I go in the dirt. I can barely bring air into my lungs, let alone move. The deep breaths hurt my everything as does my arm.

Artie appears over the hill a few seconds later, panting as hard as I am. I should care but pain trumps all. He jumps over the creek and spots me. I know because he slows to smile. I'm still rubbing the stitch out as he saunters over with the gun raised. I manage to get to my feet, not that it matters. He has a straight shot, and we both know it.

"You are such a bitch, you know that, right?" he asks through his gasps.

"You need me alive," I say through my own.

"That's more of a guideline."

This is it. My death. With both a bang and a whimper. I think of all the people I love. They'll never find my body. This time tomorrow I'll be troll poo. I die alone in this field. So unfair. As he squeezes the trigger, I shut my eyes. I won't give him the satisfaction of seeing my fear.

There's a click. Not a bang, but a click. A beautiful, wondrous click. My eyes fly open. Artie yanks the trigger with the same result. I don't wait for the third time. I take off running. Artie's footsteps start a second later. But the chase, Part Two, is short lived. I run about another hundred feet when the ground literally collapses under me. One moment I'm on terra firma, the next I'm falling down a dark hole with clumps of dirt along for the ride. The ground swallows me up, my body weightless. I've never wanted to go skydiving, but this must be what it feels like. Scary as hell, yet freeing. I scream as long as I fall. As the ground gets closer I realize I should do something. My unconscious listens. When I'm about three feet from the bottom, I suddenly stop falling. I just stop. My stomach hits my spine, but I don't go splat. I hover, afraid to move. Some days I *love* psychokinesis.

Footsteps and shifting earth above break the spell. I descend the rest of the way onto my stomach, my bad elbow sending more white hot pain every which way. "Fuck," Artie mutters above me. His voice echoes through the chamber. "Bea? You alive down there?"

I don't dare move and even hold my breath as best I can. A second later a rock hits my upper back with the force of a bullet. It hurts, but I bite my lower lip to stop from crying out.

"Fuck," Artie says again. A few seconds later he starts talking again. "Hey, Steve, it's Artie. Something happened." He listens. "No actually, I think she's dead. She got out." He's quiet. "Calm the fuck down! I chased her toward the mine, and she fell into the caverns." He's quiet, then, "I mean I'm not going down there to check or

245

nothing but she fell a good three stories onto fucking rock, and she's not moving. Besides, even if she did, all her arms and legs and shit would be broken. There's only one way out. She's troll chow anyway you look at it." He listens again. "Bro, this is what you fucking wanted. The bitch is dead. No going back now." A beat. "Look, I'll keep watch at the entrance just in case." Silence. "No, it's close enough to night. We shouldn't need another sacrifice." A beat. "Ask Kristen then! Jesus Christ! I'll see you tonight." He slaps the phone shut. "Fucking pussy."

With that, I hear footsteps departing. I wait a minute or two before I open my eyes and roll onto my back, close to hyperventilating. I just lay there looking up at the hole above. It's smaller than I thought, maybe four feet wide and across. It provides the only light. The cavern is pretty big, nothing but rock and a few ancient gas lamps hanging on the walls. This must be part of the tunnel system. And per Artie, there's a way out.

A large part of me just wants to lie here for an hour or seven to let my body recover. And *boy* do I want to listen, but I don't. Haven't reached the finish line yet. *Get your butt up, Bea.* Okay. I stand on unsteady legs already sore from my marathon. My body is nothing but painful knots coupled with exhaustion. I can either go right or left. Both are just black tubes of nothing. I choose right. Within seconds I can't see a thing. I may as well be blind. I run my hand along the uneven wall, listening and letting the freezing wind lead me through. Minutes pass with nothing but the sound of the wind to tell me I'm alive and still on earth. Or in it, I guess. Then I smell something. Dead meat. Been smelling it far too often the past few months. My foot smashes into something smooshy. And fetid. For once I welcome the pitch black. I change course back the way I came as fast as possible. Left. Left is better.

When I see the first hint of light from the hole, I stop to catch my breath. It's freezing down here, maybe in the forties, and I use my good arm to rub myself. That's when I hear and feel it. *Boom. Boom.* Coming from the way I want to go. Of course.

Trolls. There are two varieties, the two-foot kind who live under bridges and holes, and the ten-foot ones that live in caves. Guess which is coming right for me? Like all predators, the trolls are attracted to blood, which I am covered in. He steps into the light. He's ugly. And huge, easily weighing a thousand pounds. All his limbs could double as tree trunks. And his teeth! Razor sharp. He has no shame, his genitals hanging loose. My eyes skitter away from that area as quickly as possible, but there's really no *good* place to look. It sniffs the air, then stares directly at me with milky white eyes rimmed with green mucous. Time to run again.

I spin around and high tail it down the black tube with Ugly right behind me. I have no idea what I'm doing, but as long as I can I'll run. Got me this far, though that's not saying much. I end up back in the death chamber, the smell rocking my already wobbly stomach. I brush up against what I assume are bones and flesh. Really glad I can't see. Then I hear something a little farther down. Running water. I make it through his pantry without tripping or gagging. *Winning.* Ugly gets closer, the footfalls actually making the tunnel vibrate, but I press on. All I care about is that water.

I don't have to wait long. There's a speck of light in the distance. When I reach it, the water is as loud as the troll. I turn left and there it is. A river. An underground river rushing as fast as traffic on a freeway. Without a moment's hesitation about where it goes, if it dead ends, or what's inside it, I run down the incline to the water. The shock of the frigid water fazes me and I cry out, but only for a moment. I think the troll pokes his head out and roars, but it's too late. I'm too far away for him to reach.

The river twists and turns around the rock like a water park ride. Within minutes my entire body is numb, and I'm fighting not only to stay afloat but to stay awake from the exhaustion. My teeth clatter and I shake violently, but at least the pain wanes. My luck changes. I'm in the water only a few minutes when I spot beautiful, brilliant sunlight. The cavern opens onto land. Stalactites with bats hanging from them are silhouetted against the daylight. It's almost pretty. It gives me a second wind. I swim for land with my one good arm, kissing the mud when I reach it then sobbing for joy as I gaze up at the sunshine. I did it. I made it.

I'm alive. And they're gonna be fucking dead.

THIRTEEN

MEN AND OTHER BEASTS

A WONDERFUL TRUCKER NAMED Dave picks up my broken, bloody, and mud-caked self from the side of the road and drives me straight to the hospital. He doesn't ask too many questions, for which I am grateful. He even lets me use his cell phone. Nana begins sobbing when she hears my voice; if I had any tears left I'd join the misery. She asks a million questions, but my teeth are chattering so much—despite Dave's jacket and the heater—that I just tell her to meet me at the hospital, and to call Will and have him only tell people in the F.R.E.A.K.S. about my resurfacing. No exceptions. I need to stay presumed dead as long as possible.

At the hospital I give the alias I was told to use for just such instances, and they take me right in. I'm X-rayed, poked with needles, stitched up, casted for my arm, and finally put to bed with electric warming blankets to treat my mild hypothermia. About three seconds after I get into bed, I receive visitors. Nana, April, and my teammate

Nancy rush in. I must look like I feel judging from the expressions on their faces.

"Oh my God," Nana says as she hugs me so hard I wince. "Oh. I'm sorry."

"It's okay. I just have a bruised rib."

April, who I've seen cry half a dozen times ever, brushes her tears away before gently embracing me. "Oh Bea."

"Don't cry," I say into her shoulder. "I'm okay now."

She releases me. "We were so scared! We thought you were dead!"

"I'm sorry." I kiss my friend's cheek and look over toward the door where an awkward Nancy stands. "Hi."

"Hi," she says with a smile.

"I know you told me not to tell anyone, but she was at the house when you called," Nana says.

"It's okay. She's a friend. I trust her." For some reason Nancy looks shamed.

"Are you badly hurt? Let me look at you," Nana says, cupping my cheeks in her hands and examining me.

"I'm okay. I just have a broken arm, a few cuts and bruises, and mild hypothermia."

"Just!" April says. "*Just*? They said you were shot!"

"Just a graze," I assure her. "I might have to have surgery for the elbow, but there shouldn't be permanent damage. I was really lucky."

"Honey Bea, what the heck happened to you?" Nana asks. "Three days. You've been missing three days! We thought you were dead!"

"When you didn't show at my house after the pageant, I called and called," April says. "Then I went to Nana's, and you weren't there."

"When you weren't home by midnight, I phoned your work," Nana adds. "I spoke to your boss, who called your friends."

"George called the plane," Nancy cuts in, "to see if you were with them or if they knew where you were. Will made them turn the plane right around."

"Then I called Steven," Nana says. The sound of his name makes me cringe inside. "He got the police out searching for your car right away. They found it a few hours later with your purse still inside. What happened?"

As much as is possible, I calmly and objectively tell them. To say they're shocked is an understatement.

"I don't believe it," April says. "No way. No way in hell! He wouldn't do that! It's nuts!"

"I know," I say.

"But he was so worried about you," Nana says. "He coordinated with the police. He put up fliers all over town. He held me when—" Nana look disgusted with herself. "He's a monster."

"So it *wasn't* Connor?" Nancy asks.

"No."

"Crap," she mutters.

"Why?"

"Um, nothing."

"Nancy?" I ask sternly. "What happened?"

Nancy moves over to my bed, excitement brimming from her body. "Okay. I only know some of this stuff secondhand, but apparently Will heard you were missing and, like, lost his shit. He ordered the pilot to totally turn the plane around *mid-air* under the threat of violence. So, like, an hour later, they landed and drove right over to that club you guys were at the other night. But the dude wasn't there! One of his flunkies was and tried to calm Will down, but Will, like, went ballistic! It took like five vamps, including Oliver, to bring him down. He was Hercules or something.

"So then Connor shows up and swears up, down, and center he totally had nothing to do with you being missing. And according to Wolfe he's like totally convincing. Something about how you're not worth a war, and what good would you be to him there against your will, and he doesn't break the law, and blah blah blah. Not that Will is all into reason at this point. He pulls out this huge knife and almost kills Connor, but Oliver stops him. *Then* Connor, like, threatens to have Will arrested, but I guess Oliver convinced him it was a bad idea or something, at least until we found you. And just to prove he had nothing to do with it, Connor offered his help."

"Did he help?"

"Oh yeah. I think he had, like, all these vamps out looking for you and called all sorts of contacts. But we didn't find anything."

"Is the whole team here?"

"Yeah. Mobile command's at the airport and everything. But it was like aliens abducted you or something. Everyone was going nuts. Will and Oliver actually got into a fist fight!"

"What?" I ask.

"It was bonkers," Nancy says. "They've totally gotten in each other's faces and stuff, but it never got physical like this. I was in the kitchenette making coffee when Will came in. You'd been missing, like, a day, and he was personally chasing down like every lead himself, so he was, like, exhausted and emotional and totally snippy. I think he asked Chandler for a status and I don't know what Chandler said, but Will just went off on him, calling him incompetent and all sorts of nasty stuff. Oliver was there too and sort of stepped in. He'd been, like, über-calm and quiet since you vanished, and he told Will to go outside and cool off. I couldn't hear what Will said, and Chandler couldn't either, but the next thing we know, *Oliver* grabs Will and super-speeds him outside. I watched the whole thing from the window.

"Oliver threw the first punch, and it totally knocked Will right on his butt. But he got up and *it was on*! Like Ultimate Fighting on steroids! They just kept punching each other, and pinning each other, until I swear, like, every bone in their faces and torso were broken. There was blood everywhere! Finally Will's had enough, he's, like, on the ground crawling away, but Oliver flips him over and pounds him in the face. A lot. And the entire time Oliver's saying something, but I don't know what. Then he raised his fist again, but Will said something back. Oliver just looked down at him, said a few words, and totally let Will go. Oliver flopped down on the pavement next to Will, and they just, like, talked for a couple of minutes. Then they walked back in as if nothing had happened. Ever since they've been totally cool. They even ran down some leads together. It's so weird." She shakes her head. "I just hope Connor doesn't have him arrested."

I'm stunned into silence. It happened. They actually did it. They're getting along. All it took was my probable death and a barroom brawl. Men are so strange.

My doctor walks in. "Hello, all."

"Hi," I say.

"Is my granddaughter going to be okay?" Nana asks.

"Your arm was fractured in two places and will most likely require surgery. I also got your toxicology report back and we found Thorazine and trace amounts of LSD in your system."

"LSD?" I ask.

"Yes. We want to keep you overnight for observation and raise your core temperature."

"You're the boss. Thank you," I say to the doctor as she leaves.

"They gave you acid?" Nancy asks. "What was it like?"

I think of the nightmares. "Horrible."

Nana's cell rings. "Oh. I forgot to turn it off." She looks at it. "It's your brother. Can I tell him? He's been so worried."

"Really?" I ask with a raised eyebrow. Damn, even that hurts.

"Of course. Should I let it go to voicemail?"

"No. You can tell him. But only him. This can't get back to the police."

Nana nods, stands, and opens the phone. "Brian?" She walks out. "Yes, there's news."

"Can I tell Javi and the kids?"

"No. Not yet."

"I am going to murder that cocksucker," April says. "I will fucking shoot his balls off! Never in a million years would I have thought..." She shakes her head.

"Neither did I. He—"

"Where is she?" a man's voice booms outside.

A second later he's there, his terror becoming relief and joy when we lock eyes. And love. No doubt about that. Nancy smartly steps out of the way as he rushes over to me, scooping me into his arms, pressing me against his racing heart. "Oh my God," he whispers. "Thank you. Thank you."

I clutch onto him as hard as I can with my one arm, each of us digging our nails into the other as if we're holding onto the edge of a cliff. He kisses my neck, quick chaste pecks moving from my neck up my jaw to my cheeks, forehead, and finally my mouth. Hypothermia is no longer a concern—the second our lips find each other, my body is on fire. Chaste quickly becomes deep. Consuming. Soft lips and savage tongue moving against mine with frenzy. Our first kiss. More than worth the wait. If I wasn't in bed, I'd swoon. It's that good. The kiss of a lifetime. Will breaks away first, resting his forehead on mine and breathing heavily. God, I love this man.

"Um," April whispers. I forgot she was here. Heck, I forgot my name. Will and I release each other. "We're just going to…" She points to the door.

Nancy nods and walks with April toward the door but turns back. "Bea? I'm glad you're okay. And I'm sorry for—"

"You're forgiven."

Nancy smiles to herself and closes the door. Alone at last. Will turns back to me, touching my cheek and rubbing his thumb along it. "You're really here," he whispers.

"Can't get rid of me that easily."

He hugs me again, softer this time. "I was so scared," he says softly. "I'm sorry. I'm so sorry."

"There's nothing to be sorry about."

"I should have been there. With you."

I pull away. "I don't think it would have mattered."

"Who did this to you? Connor? Did he—"

"No. It wasn't him."

His face goes scary, almost as if the wolf was trying to get out. "Who was it?"

I tell him. He takes it well.

"I am going to pull his spine out of his ass," he says and means it. "All of them. I'm going to—"

"Calm down," I say, touching his hand. "We need to go into this with a plan."

"Oh, I have a plan. It involves a shotgun to his fucking head!"

"Please calm down. Please." I entwine my fingers with his.

"You have no idea what I went through," he says, squeezing my hand. "I thought you were… and our last words…"

"I forgive you, and you'll have plenty of time to make it up to me." I lift up his hand and kiss it. "But now we have business to attend to.

We need to mobilize the team. The group's going to be at the cabin tonight, it's the best time to get them all. If I had to guess, I'd say there's seven of them, but they're all cops juiced up on troll blood, so it might not be easy to arrest them. And we need to keep them thinking I'm dead. Maybe you should call Steven and see if he's heard anything. I know the basic layout of the cabin, but if they're already at the mine, it'll be harder to find them. We should try to get them before they reach the troll. I don't know how—"

"*We* are not doing anything," Will insists. "*You* are staying in this hospital with an armed guard outside that door even if I have to tie you to this bed."

"You need me. You'll never find that mine without me."

He rises from my side. "End of discussion. We'll make due. You've done enough. Let us do our jobs. You quit, remember?"

"Fat lot of good it did me," I point out. "Me being kidnapped had nothing to do with the job. It had to do with my crappy taste in men."

The words visibly sting him, but he recovers. "You're staying here."

"But—"

"*No!*" he almost shouts. "No. You stay here, got me? *Please*? Let me take care of this. Of you. I'll come by and check on you when it's over." He walks toward the door, and I fall back into the bed defeated. I don't want to fight with him. Not now that I just got him back.

I sigh. "Will?"

He turns around. "What?"

"If you can avoid it … don't kill Steven."

"What?"

"Try to take him alive."

"Why?"

Good question. In spite of all this, we have history. He was the first guy to actually want me and see something in me worth loving. "He thinks he's doing this for a good cause," I settle on. "Helping people with his power. He's sacrificing undesirables for the greater good."

"And that's why he kidnapped and tortured you? For the greater good?"

"No. He did that because I broke his heart. I can sympathize."

Will looks away, knowing I'm talking about him. "I'll do my best." And he walks out.

I'm gonna need a black dress for the funeral.

———

Since I've been unconscious for three days, I can't fall asleep. And the TV only has five channels. Ugh. Despite this, I sent Nana and April out for dinner. Horrible as it is, I don't really want to be around people right now, with their pitiful looks and constant questions. So I just lay here trying not to think about what's playing out right now.

Steven. My Steven. A serial killer. This must be how the BTK killer's wife felt when she found out. Stunned. Hurt. Disgusted. There were no signs. None. Sure he liked guns and scary movies, but loads of people do and they don't serve up people tartare to a troll. What is it about me that attracts monsters? I'd blame the telekinesis but he didn't know about it. Or maybe it was me. Maybe I just infect normal people with evil. Maybe April drowns kittens in her free time, I don't know. What if no matter what I do, if I stay with the job or leave, crap like this will keep happening to me? At least with the F.R.E.A.K.S. I'm prepared for it. Fudge. Post-traumatic depression is a bitch.

The door opens, but instead of April and Nana coming through the door with candy, some eye candy walks in himself. Connor carries a vase of pink roses, looking very spiffy in designer jeans, maroon V-neck shirt, black suit jacket, and various platinum necklaces. Rock star chic and he pulls it off well. "Are you feeling well enough for a visitor?" he asks with that gooey accent. Yes, even love and kidnapping cannot keep my hormones from raging.

"Depends. Can what I say be used against me in a court of law?"

He sets the flowers on the dresser and sits in the chair to my left. "I hereby grant you immunity."

"How kind of you, Danny Boy." With some effort, I push myself into the sitting position. He moves to help me, but I hold out my hand to stop him. "I got it." I yank the covers up and sigh. That was harder than it should have been. "How did you get past the guard?"

"Flattery," he says with a mischievous smile.

"You didn't make him think he was a chicken or something, did you?"

"I shall if it would amuse you," he says.

"Give me half an hour. I'm going nuts here. I've traded one place I can't leave for another," I say. "And how'd you know I was here?"

"Oliver. He was at my office when we received the news. You gave us quite a fright."

"Well, I'm a frightening person."

"I see you made it through with your sense of humor intact."

"If you can't cry, laugh."

"Sensible," he says with a nod. He eyes me up and down and not in the good way. "So, in his haste to leave, Oliver was not forthcoming with details. What happened?"

"Kidnapping. LSD. Psycho ex-boyfriend sacrificing me to a troll so he can play Batman."

"You certainly lead an interesting life."

"Yeah," I say quietly. I push the bad feelings away. "So, I hear you and your minions helped search for me."

"Oh yes," he says with pride.

"And why would you do that?"

"I was protecting a valuable asset."

"And that's it? I'd think you have ulterior motives to your ulterior motives."

He grins, showing off those fangs. "We have only been acquainted a short time, and you already know me so well. My ulterior motive in this instance was the belief that your compatriots would think that if I was assisting in the search then I could not possibly be the culprit."

"Well, it worked for Steven."

"It did. Nary a person, the exception being yours truly, suspected him. I always had my doubts."

"Why?"

"I recalled his fury the night at the club. He was capable of cold-blooded murder, without a doubt. Though no one would listen to me. He played his part to perfection. And had an alibi."

"Which was one of his fellow crazies, I'm sure," I say. "Well, thank you. I guess I forgive you for trying to force me into marriage."

"I did have to take my chance," he says. "You have no idea how valuable you are."

"Yeah, next time just ask me to a movie or something. Make a mix tape."

"Agent Alexander, I am taking my life in my own hands simply visiting you," he chuckles. "Your wolf would rip my tongue out just for speaking with you. He has attempted that very thing twice already."

I frown. "Yeah. I heard about that. Sorry. He's just very … overprotective. You're not going to have him arrested or anything, are you?"

"I have been considering it. I am well within my rights. He nearly killed two of my men and myself."

"I'll owe you one," I say, knowing full well this is exactly what he wants.

He raises an eyebrow. "Anything?"

"Within reason."

Connor nods. "Then all is forgiven. I only hope that forgiveness goes both ways."

"Meaning?"

"Upon reflection, I have come to realize I have behaved abysmally toward you. When one has to rule with an iron fist, one forgets that honey draws more flies than napalm. I can only hope as we continue to associate, you do not judge me too harshly by my past transgressions."

"So you're apologizing for threatening to kill me if I didn't sleep with you?"

"In essence, yes," he says with a smile, those beautiful eyes crinkling. "From now on, I vow to be your ally, not your enemy. And perhaps later ... " His smile turns mischievous, "something more."

I lean in, once again so close we can kiss. "Prove it, Danny Boy," I say cocking an eyebrow.

As if reading my mind, his smile grows.

———

"If I do shoot, it'll have to be one handed. I need something with a little less kickback. Damn, I wish I had my machete."

I must still be high. I've checked myself out of the hospital against doctor's orders, left with a man who less than a week ago threatened my family, and am now on my way to confront a cult and their pet troll. At least I'm traveling in style. Nothing like riding shotgun in a Ferrari with one of the most powerful vamps around.

"Jim, did you hear her?" Connor asks his minion over the phone.

"Yes, sir," Jim says over the speaker. "I have a .38 that should suit."

"Bring what you have and meet us at the rendezvous. Neil?"

"Yes, sir?" Neil asks over the speaker. Yes, we're having a conference call in a Ferrari.

"What is your ETA?"

"Fifteen."

"How many are you?" I ask.

"Four."

"Should be enough," I tell Connor.

"Excellent. See you all at the rendezvous." He presses a button to hang up. "I just hope we do not miss all the fun."

Yeah, this is going to be a blast. Okay, why am I doing this again? A pound of flesh? In part. I want to see those bastards' faces when I come back from the dead with my vampire buddies. But it's not all blood lust. I'm worried. Worried my team will underestimate the bad guys. They're cops. They'll never give up without a fight. And I'll just be there as backup.

But mostly it's the revenge thing.

"I'll see what they're up to." I punch in Will's number on the console.

It rings twice. "Special Agent William Price."

"Will, it's Bea."

"Where the hell are you?" he asks frantically. "Your grandmother just called! She said you left a note and checked out. Are you okay?"

"I'm fine. I'm with Connor."

"Felicitations, Agent Price," Connor says.

"What? Connor? Why? Bea, what the hell—"

"We're on our way to meet you guys. I'm bringing six vamps with me."

"What? No. No! Absolutely not! You've been shot. You have a broken arm. You need to go back—"

"I'm fine. I have six bodyguards with very sharp teeth to protect me."

"*This!*" he shouts. "This is exactly what I'm talking about! You do … I … " He's so angry he can't talk.

"Give me the phone," I hear Oliver say over the speaker. "Trixie?"

I close my eyes to savor this moment. "Hi, Oliver."

"Trixie," he says it as if he never thought he'd say it again. "You have … no idea … " But he doesn't finish. Then he's quiet for a moment. "Are you well?"

"Yeah," I say, emotion quaking in my voice. "You?"

"Infinitely better now," he says. He clears his throat. "So, you are with Connor?"

"Yeah. We're about ten minutes from the cabin. Some of his vamps are meeting us there."

"There is no way I can talk you out of this, is there?"

"No. I need to do this."

He's silent again. "I know."

"See you a mile from the cabin?"

"I will attempt to hold off the siege until you arrive."

"Appreciate it."

"And Connor?" Oliver asks.

"Yes, Oliver?"

"If any harm comes to her tonight, and I mean *any*, I will kill you. And nothing will stop me. Do you understand me?"

The always composed vamp actually looks frightened for a second. "I understand."

"Good." The line goes dead.

Connor reaches across, shutting off the phone. "I must say, there is never a dull moment around you, is there Agent Alexander?"

"Still think I'm worth all this trouble?"

He switches gears, and we zoom down the freeway. "Oh yes," he says with a wink.

———

My vampire posse and I arrive too late. Jim, a burly, plaid-clad survivor-man vamp with an arsenal in the back of his jeep, was the first to arrive and scouted the cabin. He made it just in time to find the F.R.E.A.K.S. walking out. Connor and I blow in five minutes later, not bothering to hide our arrival. Nancy and Carl sit on the porch with Agent Chandler. Agents Wolfe and Rushmore come out with a bunch of rifles. Will and vampire Jim stand at the hood of a car examining a map. Everyone welcomes me back, Agent Wolfe actually hugging me, but Will makes it a point not to look up.

"I gather we missed them," Connor says.

"Their cars are still here," Carl says.

It does look like a car lot. Seven cars, including the Gran Torino and Steven's Jeep. All the tires are slashed, though. They're not getting far.

"Then they must be at the mine," I say.

"Wherever the hell that is," Agent Rushmore says with his Jersey accent. "It's not on any maps."

"We can wait for them to return," I offer.

"High on troll blood," Agent Wolfe says. "And there's no guarantee they'll all come back here at once."

"So we have to find the mine," I say.

"Yep," Nancy says.

"Wish I could help more," I say. "I just sort of ran. Wasn't paying attention to anything else."

"Did you bleed?" Connor asks.

"Only toward the middle when I got shot. But Artie did."

"Then that is how we locate them," Connor says. "Follow the blood trail. Jim!"

Jim gazes up from the map over to his Lord. "Yes, sir?"

"Find the blood trail into the forest."

"Yes, sir." The vamp starts sniffing the air in search of blood.

Will glances at me, then back at the map. Still mad I see. I clear my throat. "Where's Oliver?" I ask Carl.

"Inside."

"Thanks." I peer over at Will, who ignores me, before I enter the cabin. "Oliver?" I call out. He isn't in the living room, or the kitchen, or either of the two bedrooms all decorated in rustic décor. Which leaves only one place. I have no desire to go back down those steps and into that room, but the desire to lay eyes on my friend is greater. I find him sitting on my cot staring at the blood and blue chemical on the floor. I sure did make a mess. He gazes up, but instead of relief or happiness, he just seems sad. "Oliver?" I ask.

"This is not your blood," he says.

I sit next to him shoulder to shoulder. "Nope."

"You look terrible," he whispers.

"You should see the other guy."

My quip doesn't get a grin. We just sit in silence for a few seconds before I rest my head on his shoulder and stare at the ground too. His head lowers onto mine. "Never do that to me again," he whispers. "*Never.*" I wrap my good arm around his and settle in. Amazingly, I feel at peace in this room.

The footsteps on the stairs a few seconds later break the mood. Agent Rushmore pokes his head in and says, "That vamp found the trail."

I raise my head with a sigh as Rushmore leaves. "Oh goody."

264

"What trail?" Oliver asks.

"Artie left us a breadcrumb trail to the troll only a vamp could find."

"Blood?"

I smile. We stand up and start toward the stairs. "I was serious. *Wait* until you see the other guy."

"You do not know how much I live for the moment."

Everyone has amassed around Will including Neil, the bouncer from Gaslight, and two huge vamps I've never seen before. All humans hold automatic weapons or shotguns, standard in a raid of this kind. "About a mile through the forest and—" Will stops mid-sentence when he spots Oliver and me coming out, but he quickly recovers. We stand next to Connor. "And then there should be a field, a hill, and the entrance to the mine near a stream. There's just the one entrance, so I'll want Jim and Wolfe to wait out there in case any make it past us. And I want two people to stay here. Bea and Nancy."

"Trixie is coming with us," Oliver says before I can.

"No," Will states plainly.

"She is the only one of us with knowledge of the layout of the tunnels. You know this."

Will's mouth opens to protest, but he bites his tongue when every vamp straightens his back and glares at him. Connor smirks at me. "Fine. Oliver? I want you to go ahead of us as a scout. Follow the trail and wait. Jim will lead us non-corpses."

Oliver turns to me, and I smile. "I'll be fine," I say, squeezing his hand. "See you there."

"Do not worry, Oliver," Connor says. "I will not let anyone touch so much as a hair on her head."

"You had best not," Oliver says before vanishing into the woods.

Will rolls his eyes. "Nancy, you and Carl stay here."

"If they do come, do we shoot them?" Carl asks.

"No," I say before anyone else can. "Only if you have to. Stun them if possible."

"Sir?" Neil asks Connor.

"You heard the *lady*," he says, not so subtly emphasizing the last word. "Only kill if there is no other option."

"*All* of you," I say, my eyes burrowing into Will's.

Will sneers before looking away. "Let's go. I'll take point behind Jim." He raises his pistol to the ready, as does everyone else. Connor hands me a .38 special, which I take with a smile. Will's lips purse before he follows the vamp with everyone else carefully walking behind.

"He is in love with you, you know," Connor says as he pulls the slide back on his 9mm.

"You think so?" I ask, staring at Will.

Connor follows my gaze. "Oh. The wolf is as well." He mischievously grins and walks into the woods before I can even process those last words.

Neil and the bouncer flank me as we make our way through the trees and bramble that I was running through for dear life just hours ago. An owl hoots and twigs crackle, but otherwise there's no noise. Connor walks a few feet in front of us, and I have a million questions for him, but every time I move up to him and open my mouth, he presses his finger to his lips to shut me up. But when all of this is over ...

This trail seemed to take forever when Artie was after me, but it must have been just a few minutes because it takes only fifteen minutes walking. When we reach the hill, we crouch down and walk up it, stopping right at the crest. We all lay on our stomachs and peer over. The mine is lit up inside, I think from the gas lamps I saw on the wall, and Oliver hides off to the side, his back to the mine. Will waves his arms to signal, and Oliver vanishes, only to reappear with us on the hill. He lies between Will and Agent Chandler.

"They appear to be in the chamber Trixie discovered," he whispers. "The troll is unconscious, and there is a dead human next to it. I counted six people, including Officer Weir."

"Only six?" I ask.

"Four men and two women. All appear to be distracted."

"How?" I whisper.

"One is off to the side staring at nothing, one is unconscious, and the others are … enjoying one another." Oh. Eww. "I made it through the tunnels to the chamber undetected before you arrived. It is a straight walk down, and then a left turn at the fork. If we wish to capture them, now is the time to do it."

"Looks like we don't need you," Will whispers to me. "Oliver, lead the vamps in first and wait by the entrance to the chamber. Rush, Chandler, follow me in and then Oliver and his team. Understood?"

Everyone nods.

"What about me?" I ask.

"Cover us from above."

"Will…"

"I won't be able to concentrate with you in there. *Please*," he says through gritted teeth.

I sigh but say, "Okay."

"Thank you." He looks at Oliver. "Ready?"

Oliver turns to Connor, who nods. "See you inside," Oliver says before he and all the vamps but Jim stand up and vanish, becoming nothing but blurs in the field.

Will glances at the rest of us. "Let's go."

We all rise and run toward the mine, stopping at the entrance. Will listens for a second then points to Jim and Agent Wolfe, signaling them to stay put. The he points at me and signals toward the hole. I nod. Finally he signals Agents Chandler and Rushmore to go in. The three men take a step, but I hold up my finger at Will for him to wait. He looks confused and shrugs. But when I press my lips to his, kissing him as deeply as the hole he's about to go into, all his confusion vanishes. It's quick, seeing as we have, you know, bad guys to catch, but sweet. "For luck," I mouth. I give him a quick peck on the cheek before running off to my hole. When I look back, he's gone.

The hole is easy to find; it's lit up like a spotlight against the pitch-black night. I'm very careful with my footing in case there are more weak spots but make it without incident. As best I can with my arm in a sling, I rest on my stomach and peer in. The troll lies on his side in the corner fast asleep. Beside him is what was once a human. I can tell from the severed leg and exposed rib cage. That could have been me. I suppress a shudder.

The most fudged-up bowling team in history is entirely accounted for. Mel sits with his back against the wall examining his hands as if they have diamonds on them, he's fascinated. And stoned. Mostly stoned. The rest, well … Jawan's naked butt pumps up and down on an unconscious Leslie. Right next to him Kristen's mouth works on the blissed-out Steven with Nick behind her, doing something I think is illegal in some states. This makes me want to throw up more than the corpse. They're all covered in black liquid, which must be troll blood. Steven tosses his head back and groans three times. He's done. I recognize the sound. Kristen releases him, but Nick doesn't stop. Yuck. My groggy ex stands up, exposing his everything. I close my eyes. I never want to see that thing again. Too many boring memories. Someone else grunts, and I force my eyes back open. Steven is putting on his pants, but Nick finishes with Kristen. I'm going to be watching kitten videos non-stop for a week to cleanse my palate.

I hear the footsteps the same time as they do. All four tense and don't move until Will sprints in, shouting "FBI! Hands up!" In their fogged minds the group doesn't understand what's occurring as the good guys enter the chamber with their weapons pointed at the naked people. "Don't move! Don't you fucking move! Hands on your head!" Will says before grabbing Steven. "Give me a reason. Give me a fucking reason!"

Neil pulls the barely awake and naked Leslie up, and I scoot closer to the edge to get a better view. Bad move. I let lose a barrage of dirt and almost fall in again. Everyone below looks up.

Distractions are never a good thing in situations like this. The supercharged Steven grabs Will's gun and cold cocks him across the jaw. Another distraction. The rest of the bad guys seem to magically come out of their stupor and attack. Steven opens fire, shooting wildly at whatever moves. I barely have time to duck before he points the gun at me. The bullets hit where I was, and I cover my head. There are more screams and gunshots echoing below. The troll bellows and all the noise ceases but his cry. A second later the gunshots resume. Okay, coming here was a stupid, stupid, *stupid* thing to do.

By the entrance, Agent Wolfe shouts, "What's going on?"

"One of you, get in there now!" I scream as loud as I can.

Jim vanishes.

I wait five seconds before forcing myself to resume my post. Fudge. The troll has Mel in his arms and breaks the man's back over his knee before biting his head off. Below the troll's foot, the bouncer from Gaslight struggles to push the appendage off. Neil drags one of the vamps, who is missing an arm, out of the cave. A still naked

Kristen fires at Connor with a stolen shotgun, missing as he speeds around the room. He reappears behind her, teeth plunging into her neck. Leslie's bullet-riddled body lies on the ground with a vampire feeding off her. Agent Chandler takes one in the vest from Jawan, but Agent Rushmore returns fire. Oliver and Nick punch each other. It's bedlam. There is no sign of Steven or Will.

Time to earn my paycheck.

As Nick throws his fist back again, I lift him up and launch him across the cavern right into the troll. The force frees the bouncer, who rolls away. A bloody Oliver slumps against the wall. He looks up at me and shouts, "William!" He points to the right tunnel. I am so on it. I jump up and sprint toward the mine.

"What?" Agent Wolfe asks as I run past him.

"Stay here!" I shout as I run inside the tunnel. The shouts and gunshots are even louder in here, resonating so I can't pinpoint where they're coming from. The rock vibrates all around. Loose earth creates dust all through the tunnels, causing me to cough. Even the gas lamps on the walls flicker. I have no plan. I just know I have to save my past and my future from each other.

I find the fork Oliver mentioned but make a right instead of a left. The gunshots cease a few seconds later. I hear nothing. But I run. Soon I'm at the killing grounds. Thousands of bones of animals and humans along with rotting carcasses fill the place. Good lord. Wish it was still pitch black. I sprint though it as quickly as I can toward the water that saved me last time. One more corner, and I see them.

No. Oh God no.

Steven stands over Will's lifeless body by the edge of the river, pressing his face into the water. I react without thinking. I raise my gun but not in time. Steven must have heard me because he spins around, gun in his free hand, and fires at me before I can squeeze the trigger. I duck behind the stone just in time. After a second I peek around the corner, see him, and I shoot too. I hit the wall where Steven was. He fires twice more, and I do the same.

"Give up, Steven!" I shout. "You can't get away."

"Bea? Is that you?" He chuckles. "We thought you were dead."

"Nope." I peek again and fire, but he returns the gesture.

"No wonder the troll was so hungry. Poor Artie. He thought for sure you were dead."

"You killed him?"

"He failed. We did what we had to."

I peek again and he fires, the bullet hitting closer this time. "First your ex-girlfriend, then your best friend. You're gonna run out of people who care about you pretty soon."

"Fuck you, Bea. You never cared about me."

"Yeah, I did. I really did."

"Bullshit! You lied! You dumped me!" He shouts again, "I loved you. And you led me on! Tried to make me the butt buddy of a vampire. I was never enough for you! For any of you! I fucking hate you all!"

"I'm sorry, okay? I'm sorry. I'm sorry I lied. I'm sorry I made you think I had feelings for you when I didn't. *I'm sorry*. It was horrible of me, and I'm sorry. But please put the gun down and let me check on Will, okay? He's hurt. *Please.*"

He's silent for a second, then chuckles like a maniac. "*Him*? This asshole is the one you want? You're risking your life for him? I mean, what the fuck is he? I shot him through the eye, and he didn't die. He turned into some half human, half wolf thing. What? Humans not good enough for you? You want to fuck dogs?"

"Steven, please," I plead as I glance around the corner. He fires, and I fire back. One bullet left. Crap. "You can't make it out of here. It's

271

surrounded, and they all want to kill you. Will you please let me get you out of here? I can. I don't want you to die here, okay? Let me help you." He doesn't say anything. "Steven?" I inch around the rock, but a hand grabs my hair and someone knees the gun out of my hand. Ow.

Steven tosses me to the ground on my bad arm. I scream. Not missing a moment, he bends down, grabbing my hair and pressing the gun to my head. "I don't need jack shit from you, you bitch." He jabs the gun deeper into my temple, cocking it for effect. "If I shoot you in the head, will you live, you fucking freak?"

"No," I say, my voice quaking.

"God, I hope not," he says, shuddering with revulsion.

"Don't you fucking touch her."

We both glance back just in time to see a claw punch through the back of Steven's chest. Will, more wolf than man—with hair all over his body with viscous fluid matting it, half a snout, a bullet hole in his left eye—rips Steven's heart clean out the back of his chest. Blood geysers onto my face and body, pooling all over me. A shocked Steven slumps onto me a moment later. Dead. Um…

Will collapses to the floor, clutching his stomach in one hand and the heart in the other. Shuddering, I push Steven's body off me and back into the wall, too stunned to move any more. Will trembles a few feet away. For the first time, he looks like a monster to me.

As if reading my mind, the man I love looks up, snarling at me. "Don't look at me!"

I thrash my head to the side. "Okay."

"It's not silver. I'll be fine. But I can't hold off the transformation," he pants though the pain. "You need to go."

"You've been shot," I say lamely.

"I don't want you to see me like this. I can't … the blood … " He doubles over in pain, howling like a madman. He takes a deep breath and groans. "I want to eat you." He cries out again and whimpers as more fur grows like weeds. "Go."

"Will—"

"RUN!" he bellows though his expanding snout.

I leap up and back out of the tunnel, shaking violently. The sound of muscle and bone cracking and reforming hurts me almost as much as it does him. He howls and gazes up at me, baring his serrated teeth. Looking at me as if I'm dinner.

So I run.

FOURTEEN

AN ALEXANDER FAMILY CHRISTMAS

TRAGIC. SO TRAGIC. SEVEN officers of the law dying in a house fire so near Christmas. Apparently they were at a cabin in the woods celebrating the holidays when there was a gas leak. Kaboom. Horrible. Good thing I packed a black dress. And I've been practicing my bereaved ex-girlfriend expression for the funeral. It's pretty convincing. Steven would be proud; he did teach me a lot about hiding your true self. Or maybe it was the other way around.

I messed up my arm again going back to the caves, as it turns out. Surgery is scheduled for next week as soon as the swelling goes down, and I have weeks of physical therapy to look forward to before I'm cleared for duty. I might actually get some rest now, but not privacy anytime soon. I doubt Nana will let me leave the house without an escort ever again.

The good news is I didn't miss the holidays. Nana, using her preternatural powers of persuasion, managed to convince everyone to stay and celebrate with us. George even flew in. Right now he and

Nana are standing in the kitchen talking and giggling. I swear he's *flirting* with her. That'd be just what I need, my boss and my grand-mother an item. Ugh.

Nana's house has never been so full. I move around the festivities sipping eggnog. Renata and April chat outside about breastfeeding as Carl and Andrew entertain the kids with chalk and scary stories. Javi and Agents Rushmore, Chandler, and Wolfe rest in the corner talking guns and hunting. Apparently elk is harder to kill than deer. Who knew? Nancy is in my bedroom trying on the shirt I bought her. (Johnny Depp can do no wrong.) My brother sits in his old bedroom rifling through that box of Mom's examining the photos while trying to remain unemotional. And failing. He actually hugged me when he came in. Sure, it was awkward and stiff, but the man touched me. For-ward progress times ten. I walk past the room to leave him alone with what remains of our mother. As for Will...

We found Steven's corpse, or what was left of it. He...um...it was bad. I try not to think about it, but when the man you love rips the heart of your ex inches from your face and then eats him, it's quite difficult. Will hasn't left mobile command. We found him un-conscious in wolf form around the location I crawled out of the river. He must have thrown himself in. He was completely healed, thank-fully, but didn't wake up until yesterday. I tried to see him, but was informed I was *persona non grata*. I haven't tried again.

There's a knock on the front door, and I set down my eggnog. Oliver waits outside with a stack of presents, a Santa hat, and Grin Number One. "Happy Christmas, my darling. May I come in?"

"I don't know," I say playfully, "promise not to hit on my sister-in-law?"

"Yes, but your grandmother is fair game."

I smile back. "I think George beat you to it. Come on in."

He steps in, sets down the gifts, and hugs me. It's awkward because my left arm is in a festive sling, courtesy of Nancy and the kids, but I hug him back as best I can. "Thank you," he whispers.

"For what?"

We break apart. "Including me. Not dying. Being you."

"You're my friend, Oliver. You're always welcome here. No matter what. Especially when you come bearing gifts." I eye the boxes. "So, what did you get me?"

He plucks the top present off the pile, handing it to me. "I hope you enjoy it."

I can't wait. The man gives good present. I rip it open. Inside is a necklace, a small gold compass on a simple chain. Inscribed on the back is, *To always find your way back to me.* My heart actually warms. Oliver smiles as he fastens it around my neck. "I love it. Thank you. I'll never take it off."

"And … " he says, reaching into his pocket and pulling out my charm bracelet. "You keep losing this." He helps me put it on too.

My skin tingles where he's touched me. I have to look away. "So. How'd you get here?"

"Connor drove me. He is waiting for you outside. He wants to give you a gift as well."

"Oh," I say, disappointed. "So Will's not … "

"Still cataloguing evidence. I will send him your regards."

"Thank you," I say quietly. I sigh. "I better go talk to Connor. It might be a crime to keep a Lord waiting."

I open the door and step outside before Oliver says, "Trixie?"

"Yeah."

"He does not deserve you. Not one whit."

Once again he leaves me speechless. I have to walk away before I do something I may regret.

Connor waits inside his Ferrari while I get in. "Hello, Agent Alexander."

"Lord McInnis. You summoned?"

With a smirk, he reaches under my seat, lightly brushing my legs. He pulls out a small red package, handing it to me. "Happy Christmas."

Surprised but curious I unwrap it, finding a first edition of *Villette* by Charlotte Brontë. Signed. "Wow," is all I can say.

"Oliver informed me Miss Brontë was your favorite author. I have no use for it."

"It's signed!"

"Yes. I met her once. Shy creature but quite talented."

"I—I can't accept this. It's worth thousands of dollars."

"A peace offering."

"More like you're buttering me up," I say slyly. "I've got your number, Danny Boy. You want something. Out with it."

He clicks his tongue. "You see right through me, do you? Well, in that case, I was wondering if you would accompany me to dinner and the cinema. To begin with."

I smile but don't hesitate to answer. "No, thank you. I have enough man trouble without throwing a ruthless leader of vampires into the mix. Especially one who only wants me for my mind."

"That was before," he says. "Now I want your body as well."

I try to suppress the chuckles but a few escape. "It's closed for repairs at the moment."

"I am a patient man. I just ask that when you are weighing your options, you keep me in mind. I shall be waiting."

"You do remember that I have a boyfriend, right?"

"Yes, but that has never stopped me before."

He leans across and kisses me. I let him. It's nice, soft. For a second I kiss him back. But after the initial thrill, I feel nothing. A gorgeous man who, yes, I do lust after quite a bit, is kissing me and I'm not happy? It's good, no doubt, but not great. There is only one great.

I pull away and smile to myself. "Thank you. For everything." I take my book and climb out, hustling into the house for my purse and car keys. There's something I have to do. Before it's too late.

———

Will is in the conference room at mobile command cataloguing the evidence we collected from the scene—weapons, troll body parts, you name it—when I walk in.

"Hi," I say.

He stands from the table, startled to see me. Almost horrified. "H-Hello."

This would be the point for one of our awkward silences, but not this time. "Why haven't you stopped by? Everyone's at my house for Christmas. Why aren't you there?"

"I . . . I didn't mean . . . I just have a lot of work to do before we go back."

I move toward him, taking a bag of troll teeth from his hand. He tenses as I do. "Well, not tonight you don't. You're coming with me, and you're going to open presents and drink eggnog and—"

He takes a step away. "Bea, stop it! Just stop it! I don't want to go back and play nice with everyone and—and—" he stammers. "I just don't."

I step toward him, and he steps back. "So what? You want to spend Christmas alone with a bunch of troll parts? Is that what you want, Will? Really?"

"Yes."

I take another step forward, and he takes another step back. "Liar. Stop lying. Stop torturing yourself. So, you're a werewolf. A couple of times a month, you're a killing machine. At least I know you're part monster. I spent *two years* with one and didn't have a clue."

"And I *ate* him," Will says. He takes a menacing step toward me, and now it's my turn to take a step back. "And I would have eaten you too. That thing in the cave, *that* is me. That is what I am. You really want that thing?"

I meet his pained eyes, smiling cheek to cheek. "Yep. And it wants me."

He retreats from me and holds up his hands with a scoff. "No. I won't let you do that to yourself. You deserve *so* much more than what I can give you. No."

"Will, my last 'normal' boyfriend turned out to be a serial killer. I'm thinking I'm gonna have to change my definition of that word."

He holds up his hands again. "Well, it's a moot point anyway," he says. "You're quitting. I won't accept any calls from you. I'll—"

"I'm not quitting."

"What?"

"I'm not quitting."

He's speechless and shakes his head. "It's too dangerous. You said it yourself."

"So is crossing the street. So is *everything*. Will, *I'm* not normal. I never have been. There's always been something a little off about me. There always will be. And when things go south, I'd rather have people who have my back around."

Will simply looks at me, defeated. "Don't make this any harder. *Please*."

I take the final step. Our bodies almost touch as I gaze up at him. This particular dance is done; I'm taking the lead now. He refuses to look at me until I tilt his head down so our mouths are just inches apart.

"This is what's going to happen. I'm gonna take a month off to recover from my so-called holiday vacation. I'll have elbow surgery, do PT, go to the movies, but when I have the all clear, I'm flying back to Kansas. No matter what. I don't care if you've given my room away, I don't care if you move the mansion to Sweden. I'm coming back. Because for the first time in my life, I have a chance to get what I want. What I dream about. What *drives me crazy*, in the best ways. What I *know* wants me back. In spite of everything."

Will's eyes are locked on mine and his breath is coming faster now. Oh, this is *fun*.

"So I am going to make it my mission to save him from himself, whether he likes it or not. And I have no doubt I will succeed, because I have the most powerful thing in this universe on my side."

"W-What is that?" he whispers, face full of scared confusion and undeniable heat.

I press my lips against his softly, then harder. The kiss is so deep I can taste a part of his soul. Great. Toe-curling, choir-of-angels-in-the-background *great*. But just as he starts to kiss me back, I pull away, smiling mischievously. "You have a month to figure it out. I'll be waiting."

With that, I turn my back on him and begin to saunter out, the present I brought him on the counter flying back into his hands. I glance over my shoulder and put a saucy smile on my face.

"Merry Christmas, Will." I wink. "And a *very* happy New Year."

THE END

ACKNOWLEDGEMENTS

As always, I must first thank Sandy Lu at the L. Perkins Agency for sticking with me.

Thanks to the Midnight Ink gang, especially Terri Bischoff and Nicole Nugent for correcting my many, many mistakes.

Thanks to my beta readers Susan Dowis, Ginny Dowis, and Jill Kardell. I am honored to be descended from such kick-ass women who love to read.

Thanks to Newport Beach Library, Huntington Beach Library, the Fairfax County libraries, and Prince William Libraries for giving me a place to go and work that isn't my house.

Thanks to all the people who read my books and follow me on Twitter, Facebook, Pinterest, and read the Tales from the Darkside blog. You make this possible.

Finally, I thank my wonderful family. I love you all more than words can say.

© Bill Fitz-Patrick

ABOUT THE AUTHOR

Jennifer Harlow (Manassas, VA) earned a BA from the University of Virginia in Psychology. Her eclectic work experience ranges from government investigator to radio DJ to lab assistant. She is also a member of Sisters in Crime.

Visit her online at http://jenniferharlowbooks.com and http://blog.jenniferharlowbooks.com.

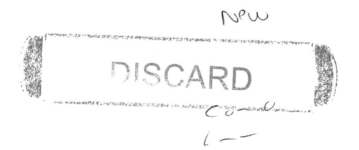